Boat Sailors
(Vietnam War Action by Fleet Submarines)

by
James W. Nelson

Back Cover Photograph
by
William (Rat Meat) Moore,
Electronics Technician Communications
Second Class Petty Officer (SS)

To the men and women of the United States Navy &
Marine Corps

Also to the memory of Evelyn Anderson and Beatrice
Kosin

# Introduction

### *This is true*

In the mid-nineteen-sixties some conventional fleet submarines were refitted to carry small teams of combat swimmers (Underwater Demolition Teams [UDT{also known as frogmen}] and Sea, Land and Air teams [SEALs]) for a variety of combat operations. Their primary mission was beach reconnaissance. Detachment Charlie operated from the USS Perch APSS 313 (USS Hagfish in the novel) later the USS Grayback LPSS 574, and USS Tunny LPSS 282.

These submarines were left over from World War II, but all were still plenty spirited.

\*\*\*\*

### *This is fiction*

This novel follows Brice Wesley Moser, a seventeen-year-old farm boy from Iowa from his induction at Des Moines, through bootcamp and Class A Weapons School at San Diego, to his first short duty at a guided missile unit at Pearl Harbor, to volunteering for submarine duty and landing on the USS Hagfish, a boat specially-fitted for hauling troops and dispersing special ops UDT and SEAL team members while submerged.

## Acknowledgements

Without the help of William (Rat Meat) Moore, Electronics Technician Communications, Second Class Petty Officer (SS)(qualified in submarines) of Wisconsin, who served as an Escape Trunk operator and Gerry (Beans) Darnell, Electronics Technician Radar, Third Class Petty officer (SS) of California (who led me to *find* Bill Moore) both of the USS Perch APSS 313, this novel would not have been possible.

The operations the Perch participated in during 1965-66 during the early years of the Vietnam War are used as a basis for this story.

This novel is pure fiction, and not meant as a history of the USS Perch, nor of her crew, and, except for what happened to the two young missionary women, any semblance of similarity to any living person is purely coincidental

This fictional novel is based upon operations of the USS Perch APSS 313 and her crew.

Her Vietnam War zone operations began March, 1965 and mainly ended in July, 1966, when she participated in operation Deckhouse II. Again in August she conducted several more independent beach surveys with UDT personnel along the coast of South Vietnam. For operation Deckhouse IV in September she landed UDT personnel on five successive nights for preinvasion beach reconnaissance.

Many of the USS Perch's operations consisted of Search and Rescue, training U.S. Marine's Amphibious Recon Battalion, Army Special Forces, Navy UDT and SEAL teams, also British commando forces and ROK Republic of Korea, Philippine, and Nationalist Chinese Special Forces. She participated in the operations Jungle Drum III, Dagger Thrust, Double Eagle, Deck House II, and Deck House IV.

By October, 1966 she had done her job and left for Pearl Harbor via Hong Kong, the Palau Islands, Guam, and Midway. She would operate in Hawaiian waters until 1967, then to San Diego to serve as a Naval reserve training vessel. In Vietnam waters she was replaced by another fleet-type submarine that had been refitted to haul troops, and several of the experienced men from the Perch would be transferred to their replacement. The Perch had experienced a long but productive war patrol.

The Grayback in June 1972, carried a team of SEALs into the coastal waters of North Vietnam, as part of Operation Thunderhead, the last attempt to rescue American POWs. (This according to Wikipedia)

The Tunny conducted reconnaissance in preparation for amphibious assault operations and gathered navigational and oceanographic information, and participated in Operation Deckhouse VI.

Contents

Part 1 In Training

1
Induction

Brice Wesley Moser pulled the handle for a pack of Oasis.
The green and white package clunked into the bottom tray.
Moser plucked it up, pulled the little red plastic thingamajig
and the top wrapping came off. He walked to a trash container
and deposited that item, then tore the foil covering one corner
of one end of the pack, then the other corner and exposed the
filtered cigarettes.

The aroma of fresh tobacco wafted up to him. It was the
very first package of cigarettes he had ever bought, or opened.
For one second longer he appreciated the smell, then, not
wanting to look like the rank amateur he was, he finished
tearing off the foil-covered wrap, deposited that in the trash,

then snapped the pack against his left index finger by the knuckle, as he had seen other more experienced smokers do it.

Five cigarettes came loose and extended from the package about three-quarters of an inch. They all were the same so he pulled one free, pushed the others back down into the pack, placed the pack in his shirt pocket, then pounded the filtered end on top of the cigarette dispensing machine…also how he had seen others do it.

No matches.

Then he noticed a second handle just for dispensing books of matches. He pulled it. A book clattered to the bottom tray. He plucked it, put the filtered end of the cigarette in his mouth, tore a match from the book, struck it with one try, watched the flash of sulfur, lit his cigarette, and took a strong drag…and felt like coughing—instead just swallowed a couple chokes— and did *not* like the taste.

He didn't know why, and didn't yet understand about menthol. He bought the Oasis because of the cool name. He was after all just seventeen and a half years old. He remained standing and gazed around the hotel lobby, not really looking at about fifteen other young boys, all also likely joining the navy, but just trying to come to terms of why he was there.

It was the last day of May, 1964.

The war in Vietnam was heating up.

Brice Wesley Moser had never heard of Vietnam.

But he knew it was time to do something besides milk cows, throw hay bales, and fix fence.

He took another drag, hated the taste, and swore the next pack would be straight Camels, just like the occasional ones he had stolen from the cupboard farthest to the north. His dad's personal stash, where all important papers, mementos, and other things important to his dad, were stored, and his dad's cigarettes. Now *those* cigarettes tasted good, like a cigarette should.

He chuckled as he realized he had just said a cigarette commercial in his head, but had no idea what brand. It didn't matter. His next purchase would be Camels, just like his dad smoked whenever he had to dress up to go somewhere. At home his dad smoked a pipe filled with Prince Albert tobacco carried in his shirt pocket. For just a second he pictured his dad filling his pipe with that flat red can with a picture of a bearded guy dressed in a long coat on the front. But when he went somewhere important he smoked the straight Camels.

And he was pretty sure his dad never missed the few he stole…well, maybe that day after school when he stole three, so he could share with two other boys younger than him. He smiled at the memory. They had gone into the deep Boxelder trees of the pig pasture and all lit up and coughed and choked and finally were smoking nearly just like professionals.

Yeah, that time his dad might have figured it out, but never said anything.

His dad was like that, rarely a cross word with his son. In the coming days Moser would come to realize and fully appreciate his parents, the rest of his family, the Iowa farm he was raised on, and a certain neighbor girl named Leah who he was secretly in love with. Oh yeah, and his little sister, eight-year-old Geri, who worshipped the ground he walked on.

"You tryin' smokin' for the first time too?" asked a guy he hadn't seen coming.

"Well, it's not my *first* time."

"Close though." The guy took a drag of his own cigarette and coughed, lightly, "Right?"

"Yeah." *No reason to lie*, he guessed.

"It's *my* first time though—oh, I got an occasional one from my older brother, but it wasn't strong, like *this* one."

"What are you smoking?"

"The guy pulled a mostly-white package from his shirt and looked at it, "Lucky Strike."

"Yeah, I've heard that's a strong one—good though, I bet."

"Yeah, if I ever get used to it—how about you?"

Moser pulled his own pack and showed it proudly, "Oasis."

"Menthol! God, I don't know how you can stand it!"

"I can't. Next pack will be straight Camels."

The guy laughed, then held out his hand, "Guess we all have to learn sometime—my name's Terry Hamm, from Dubuque."

He shook the hand, "Brice Moser, Ridge, a little town south of Des Moines here."

"Farmer?"

"Yeah, how did you know?"

Hamm grasped Moser's right hand and turned it palm up, "Calluses. You must have worked hard. I grew up helping my dad in his office, and I never had to work for a thing in my life, so I got no calluses." He dropped Moser's hands and turned up his own palms, "See?"

He didn't know what to say.

"So, did we make a mistake signing up? I heard there's a war going on, somewhere."

"Oh?"

"Yeah, somewhere in Southeast Asia—but I don't care! I hated what I was doing—which was *nuthin*—so I figured it was time to do *somethin'*. Anyway, navy guys don't have to fight on land."

*Right.* Moser guessed he hadn't thought that far ahead, and he certainly never hated what he was doing on the farm…he had gotten tired of it, *that* was true, but he never hated it. and right that moment he truly wondered if he had made the right decision—

"Listen up, guys!"

Moser and Hamm jerked toward the sound of the voice, an older young man that neither had yet noticed, but who did get the attention of everybody lounging around at tables and on chairs.

"I'm cadet Mortensen from the university here in Des Moines and heading for boot camp same as you. From now, until we land at San Diego, if you have any questions or problems, you can come to me."

"What happens at San Diego?" somebody asked.

Mortensen smiled but didn't laugh, "Don't worry, somebody will tell us what to do, just like tomorrow. After we get to the induction center, again, somebody will be telling us—including me—what to do."

"That guy will never make it," Hamm said,

"What, who?" Moser asked.

"The idiot who asked that question." Hamm just shook his head.

"Okay," Mortensen continued, "If there's no more questions, you each have a room here, so enjoy your last night of freedom for at least nine weeks."

His stomach tightened a bit after that pronouncement, and again he wondered if he had made a good decision.

****

The next morning came early.

At four a.m. there was pounding on Moser's door, "Let's go, Moser, breakfast downstairs. You got ten minutes!"

*Ten minutes?* Sounded like Mortensen—*Jeeze!*

Ten minutes wasn't even enough time for a shower, so he just splashed his face good, dressed, and headed downstairs.

Hamm already had a plate, and waved. Moser returned the wave, then went to where they were handing out plates already stacked with fare, got his, then joined Hamm, "Mornin'"

"Mornin'" Hamm was shoveling the food in fast, "Mortensen already gave his speech about no time to eat so you better get to shovelin.'"

"Shit, he just woke me!"

"You were spose'ta have a wakeup call—didn't anybody tell ya?"

"No. Christ...." He wondered how much more he didn't know, and again wondered about his decision, but did start eating.

Time passed in a blink.

"Let's go, guys, there's a bus waiting to take us to the induction center."

"Shit, I'm only half through."

"Just grab that slab of sausage and put it inside your toast," Hamm said, "And eat it on the way."

"Won't Mortensen get mad?"

"Don't let'im *see* it, ya...Christ!" Hamm was already leaving.

He did as Hamm said, wrapped it in a napkin, shoved it inside his shirt, then joined the others boarding the bus, and, luckily, saw Hamm holding a seat for him.

Hamm jumped up, "Take the outside seat, and keep that sandwich down till we get going."

He did as told. Once they were moving he bit and chewed and choked and swallowed the sausage sandwich in about one quarter the time he would have liked.

They arrived at the induction center while he was still chewing the last bite, and about to vomit.

The bus's door slammed open. Mortensen stood up, "All right, boys, I'll be leaving you here. They induct us cadets a little differently. Maybe we'll see each other again, maybe not, so, no matter what, good luck, and keep your head up!"

Then he stepped down and was gone. Nobody moved. Finally the driver turned, "Let's go, boys!" He pointed toward a nondescript door leading to a really bleak-looking gray building, "They're waiting for you right there."

Again Moser wondered, *what the hell am I doing here*? But he joined the others heading for that door, down the steps of the bus, then the sidewalk, then that door. They weren't even all in yet when came a commanding voice, "Line up, boys, one line, drop your trousers and shorts, bend over and spread'em!"

*What the...*? But he did as told, and could kind of see a guy dressed in white coming down the line. What the guy was doing he didn't know, but could hear latex gloves being snapped as they went on and off a hand, so he had a pretty good idea. When the guy in white got to him...all doubt was quickly removed..

"Stand tall, get dressed, and stay in line!"

Which took just seconds, as everybody was glad *that* ordeal was over.

"You might as well find out today, boys," the guy in white doing the shouting continued, "When you're in a line—I don't care what kind of line, medical, vaccinations, chow—it's asshole to bellybutton! So close that line up and keep it there! We need to get you boys inducted and tested and to the airport for your flight to San Diego! Your flight leaves at four p.m. and I have a date at three-thirty. Everything here needs to be finished at three. So, if you boys just stay in line and cooperate fully you'll make me happy, and everything will be hunky-dory."

The guy started to leave, then snapped his fingers and stopped, "Just about forgot. When you get to San Diego, there's gonna be guys yellin' at ya from the time you step from the plane for the next nine weeks, so ya might as well get used to it. Believe me, in a couple more days you're gonna wish you had me again."

Next came physicals: temperature, blood pressure, heart rate, electrocardiograms, weight, height, and endless health-history questionnaires. Finally, at one-thirty—dangerously close to three o'clock—they filed into a room with a long table for a written IQ test.

"Here they'll get rid of at least one guy," Hamm said as they were taking chairs, "I'll bet you it's the idiot who asked that question earlier."

"What? Oh yeah, do you know him?"

"No, but I've seen him around Dubuque. He's a numbskull, period. Better he gets dumped here than there, because they might even hurt him in bootcamp."

"You seem to know a lot about a lot," he ventured, uncertainly.

Hamm pulled out a chair, "I've been around, and I reckon I'm at least a year or two older than you."

"I'm seventeen."

"And I'm twenty." Hamm sat.

And Moser sat, feeling glad he had a mentor, of sorts. He had felt that way in school too, all eleven years worth. Any kid a year or two older he had looked up to, even sometimes considered the older kids heroic, and always smarter than him. Had he gone on to be a senior, he too would have reached that pinnacle of being the older, *smarter*, kid, but he quit high school after his junior year. Didn't know why for sure, just felt he was ready to get a job, maybe just simply figured he was ready to move on.

And he *had* moved on, definitely, right from the quotable frying pan to the fire. He hoped he could stay with Hamm, at least keep him nearby…he didn't feel quite ready to be the older, smarter, heroic, kid.

Not yet.

**** 

At the end of the test, at two-forty-five, everybody was told to stay in their seats while the tests were checked with lay-over answer sheets. It wouldn't take long.

Moser hoped so, because he wanted that guy to get to his date.

Only about ten minutes passed.

The same guy in white appeared, "Stand tall, boys, and push your chairs back under the table." Then he handed a note to another guy in white, who then walked down the line, tapped one boy on the shoulder, and took him from the room. After a door closed, "The rest of you passed your physicals and the written test, so, in a moment or two you can head back the way you came. The same bus will be waiting to take you to the airport." The man hesitated, then looked down the line, "Attennnn—shun!"

The line came to attention for the first time.

For the first time he noticed the man in white had two silver bars attached to his shirt collar.

"That's a pretty good first time, boys. By the time they're through with you in San Diego, you will know how to snap to attention and stand proudly for your country—now I'm going to swear you in with the Oath of Allegiance. I'll say the whole thing first, then we'll come back and you boys will say it, a little at a time, so listen up! *I*—" The man stated his name. Moser heard it but forgot instantly. "—*do solemnly swear that I will support and defend the Constitution of the United States against all enemies, foreign and domestic; that I will bear true faith and allegiance to the same; and that I will obey the orders of the President of the United States and the orders of the officers appointed over me, according to regulations and the Uniform Code of Military Justice. So help me God.'* So, raise your right hand and repeat after me… *'I*—and state your full name!' I'll wait for you. Okay, we'll begin. *'I*—'"

And the oath was stated and repeated. Moser listened carefully and repeated each word, but still wasn't really sure what was happening. Even so, at the end he felt good, as if he was standing a little taller.

"Remember," the man in white went on, "You are entering the military service for God, country, and your family. Good luck and Godspeed!"

"Was that…did we just…?" He was uncertain what he wanted to say, but finally finished, "Are we in the navy now?"

"Yes, we just took the oath of allegiance to this country, a much stronger oath than that *'Pledge of Allegiance to the Flag,'* we used to say back in school every morning."

"Yeah, I s'pose."

Hamm tapped Moser's shoulder, "Let me tell ya something, Moser. You can consider yourself lucky that I took you under my wing."

He looked back, "Yeah, I guess."

"But be careful who you rub up against. It so happens I'm a nice guy, I won't try ta con ya or anything else, but there's guys out there who will."

"Yeah, I reckon."

They reached the bus and started loading. This time Hamm took the inside seat because Moser reached the seats first, "Do you want the outside seat?"

"Naw, you can have it, and it's not that far to the airport—but look!" Hamm pointed toward a guy walking with his head down, "That's the idiot who asked that stupid question this morning. He must have failed that written test, and that's why they took him away earlier than the rest of us."

"Wow, you sure called it, Hamm."

"Yeah, nuthin I'm proud of, though, but, believe me, he was better off failin' here, cause now it's over. He can go home—if he has one—and say he gave it a shot."

Moser looked after the boy, and thought in a very narrow-minded way, *better him, then me,* then instantly felt guilty, but maybe Hamm was right. Maybe the boy was destined to fail, and truly, better here then out there, and still again, *what the hell did I get myself into?*

Already, the macho oath of allegiance he had just taken had slipped to the back of his mind.

About ten minutes later they entered the Des Moines International Airport, and soon stopped close to the front passenger entrance.

Again, Mortensen stepped up to the door, "Well, guess what, guys, I'm going to the same company as you where I will serve as RCPO, which means, Recruit Chief Petty Officer, which means under the chief we get as Company Commander, I'll be in charge, so, you might as well start getting used to it. In uniform I'll have three what's known as birds right here." He tapped his upper left arm, "Birds because they look like the caricature of a bird in flight. They're also called *'crows,'* but you'll soon be learning plenty of navy terms. Our flight will leave in twenty minutes, so we'll have about ten minutes in the waiting room. If somebody's hungry, use the vending machines. We won't have time to go to the café—and there'll be no cafes—or vending machines—for nine weeks. So start getting used to that, too, plus it's possible we'll get a meal on the plane, at least a small lunch." He looked up and down the two rows of seats. "Any questions?" He waited about ten seconds, "Okay, let's get in there, and stay together!"

On the way into the airport waiting area Hamm asked, "What's a caricature?"

Moser glanced at him, "I don't have a clue."

## 2
## Pan American

Soon the boys were at 30,000 feet and soon to reach the mountains.

Since Hamm had flown before, he insisted Moser take the window seat, and he was glad of that, "Nothing but cottony clouds out there, Hamm, it's like flying over a marshmallow mattress."

"Yeah, well, that happens—ah! Here comes our lunch!"

"What would you boys like to drink?" the quite pretty and nicely plump stewardess asked.

"Coke for me," Hamm answered.

"And you by the window, sir?"

Moser was busy filling his eyes with this young woman. Not that he had never seen a pretty girl before, well, at least not as pretty as *this* one. There were plenty of pretty girls in the small town high school he attended, but they all seemed to have boyfriends. And all went *steady* with those boyfriends, kind of an unwritten small town rule. If a girl was going steady with some sports-jock one didn't mess with her, not if he liked his good health anyway.

There was the one girl he really liked, though, Leah, and of course she had a boyfriend, but at least he wasn't an athlete, big though, damn big…

"Sir…?"

He had examined the woman from her chipper stewardess hat all the way down to her well-rounded mid-section—

Hamm finally elbowed him, "She needs to know what you want to drink, Moser!"

"Oh! Yeah, sure, a Coke!"

The stewardess nodded and sent him a nice smile, then left to get their drinks.

"Maybe you'd rather have the aisle seat, Moser. Then you can ogle the stewardess all you want!"

"Ah, no thanks, Hamm. I s'pose we need to start getting used to no girls too."

"That's right, buddy."

Minutes later the stewardess returned with a cart carrying several lunches and drinks. When she got to Moser's she first lowered the tray from the back of the seat before him, then placed his lunch, then leaned in farther than necessary with his drink, and sent another gorgeous smile, which he ate right up.

After she left, "Damn," Hamm said, "If we were on a normal flight I'd say you have a roommate for tonight."

"Really?"

"Oh, right. Like you didn't understand that smile she gave you."

He felt surprised, "She was just being nice."

"*Extra* nice! Jeeze, she sure didn't give me much smile, if any."

"Really? She's older though."

"Oh, if you ain't the dumbest fucker! Her age don't hurt her! Maybe in another twenty years it might, but surer'n hell it don't hurt'er now—you better learn to read women, my man— gawd! You're lucky to have me!"

Moser laughed it off, then started on his lunch, a sugar cookie, peach sauce, and a small brick of cheese. Wow, was Hamm right? Did that gal really like him? No girl in school ever had, well, not the pretty ones anyway, and this gal certainly was pretty. He tried to imagine what they would do, saying they actually got to have a date. He didn't know. He had never gotten to even first base with any woman, so had no idea what he would do.

He stabbed the peach with the plastic fork and ate half with one bite.

One of his older, *heroic*, friends, had once tried to explain to him about girls, but he really hadn't gotten it. He of course had witnessed bulls doing things to cows, and boar pigs with sows, and even roosters doing it with hens—which he *really* didn't get, as there didn't even seem to be a penetration. Cats and dogs were the craziest. He had seen the big tom cat capture the mother cat and just hold her down, and she would just start meowing and almost screaming, and dogs were worse yet, as it always looked to him like the boy dog would just drop his ears like he was embarrassed or something, and let the bitch dog drag him around, like he couldn't even get away from her— lot'a screamin' with dogs too.

He bit into the sugar cookie, then sipped his Coke, then more sugar cookie.

Nothing with the livestock looked very romantic, most even looked painful, and it sure as hell got over in a hurry, well, except for the cats and dogs. They seemed to stay attached for quite a long, painful-sounding and looking time.

Finally he picked up the brick of cheese. Probably should have eaten it first—wait, he was in the navy now, and his own boss. He didn't need to adhere to anything he had learned before, so took a bite, then the other half of the peach, then the rest of the cheese, then sipped the juice from the peach sauce.

Done.

So he wasn't so sure he wanted to even *experience* the sex act. Of course humans probably did it a lot differently. He couldn't imagine doing it if the woman were to start screaming—like a female cat—and he also suspected it probably shouldn't get over so fast.

A few more minutes passed.

The stewardess arrived to pick up their dishes. Just as she smiled for Moser and leaned in to get his plate the plane dropped—

Her smile disappeared but experience had prepared her for such things at the most inopportune times. However, Moser, who had left his seat belt on the whole time, was not affected and grasped the bottom of her lower arm, and held on till the plane stabilized and she leaned back straight, "Thank you, sir." She smiled richly again, "May I ask your name?"

"Moser. Me and my buddy here joined the navy this morning and we're heading for bootcamp at San Diego.

"What about your first name?" she asked.

"Brice. Brice Moser."

"Well, Brice, I want to thank you again for what you did, and I did know you boys were heading to the navy bootcamp. Every so often we deliver a bunch of new recruits to San Diego. Sometimes for the Marine Corps too, and I believe your bootcamps are located close together."

"I don't know about the bootcamps, and you are very welcome, Ma'am. Glad I was here."

She let go with another gorgeous smile, then went to a pocket on her well-fitting uniform and came out with a card and handed it over, then pulled back, wrote on the back, then placed it in his hand, "Good luck in bootcamp, Brice, and your friend too." She sent a light glance toward Hamm, then right back at Moser, "I believe your camp lasts for nine weeks, give me a call when you're free…if you want."

He felt his eyes nearly explode as he accepted the card, "Yes, Ma'am…!"

"And please don't ever call me '*Ma'am*' again."

"No, Ma'am—I mean…." He looked at the card, then back up "*Morgan*, I…I, I will—I mean, I won't!"

She smiled again, "Okay, Brice, I'll look forward to it. I'll be working in First-class for the rest of the flight, so you boys please take care." She waved, and left.

"I will." He barely got the last words out above a whisper.

"A goddamned buckwheat I'm sittin' with!" Hamm said it in a humorous way, "And *you* get the girl!"

Moser was too flabbergasted to even answer.

He looked out the window.

The clouds were gone. He saw snow-covered mountains ahead, and plastered his face against the window as they were passing, enjoying the view, and really enjoying the memory of that gorgeous stewardess…what? He wasn't even sure what had happened, and visions of Leah began to pass before him— Leah, then Morgan, back and forth, but of course he suspected he had no chance with Leah…all he knew for sure was that he had Morgan's name and her phone number on a business card, and had *nothing* from Leah. And since he didn't really want to speak with Hamm right then, he left his face against the window until he felt the plane begin its descent…

Into a white fog like he couldn't even imagine—*how the hell can the pilot even see?!*

Still looking out the window he saw the wing flaps go down and heard and felt the instantaneous slow-down, then he was sure he felt the plane touch, gently, the runway, then came another roar—he was pressed against the seat belt, "What the hell? Did the pilot shift down?"

Hamm laughed, "I think he reversed the engines so we could slow down."

The plane slowed quickly, turned, then came to a stop.

He let a breath go and his shoulders drooped.

Hamm already had his seat belt off and turned to him, "What the hell? Were you scared?"

"Let's go, boys!" came the voice of Mortensen, already standing tall by the exit, "And remember! When you get out there, just do what you're told and you'll be fine."

*Yeah, right.* He didn't answer Hamm, just shook his head as he threw off the seat belt and stood.

# 3
## Company 299

As Moser passed through the exit door, the most humid air he had ever felt hit him. Halfway down the ladder he saw what looked like a school bus coming. It stopped not far from the bottom of the ramp. A school bus all right, already with a bunch of guys on board, and painted an ugly gray with black letters and numbers on the side. The side door snapped open. At the sound he felt something leave him. He wasn't sure but it felt like his stomach…or maybe just the concept of freedom.

Mortensen led the way, then stopped at the open door, and didn't speak, and, really, what else was there to say?

Moser stuck close behind Hamm, again feeling glad he had a buddy, as several others of the guys appeared to be totally alone. As he entered the bus that feeling of something leaving him intensified. He glanced at the driver. The driver faced stoically ahead. *Nine weeks*. He hadn't yet considered the fact of those two words, but just suddenly it was clear: His freedom was gone and his life was over for *nine* weeks.

Luckily, he was able to again sit in the same seat as Hamm. Had they gotten separated…well, they didn't, so he didn't want to think about it.

Nobody said a word during the ten-minute ride. As they passed the gate to the base he saw an armed marine standing by the guard shack, and saw the sign.

**Naval Training Center**

His stomach felt like the three words left the sign and entered his stomach. His fists tightened—*what the hell have I done?*

Two more minutes passed.

To Moser it was only a blink until the bus stopped and the door swung open. Mortensen stood up immediately, went to the door, glanced back as he left but didn't say anything.

Nobody moved—

From outside came that voice they had been warned about, "I want four lines and I will have four lines—move it!"

Everybody jumped up but still managed to leave the bus…somewhat, mannerly.

He hadn't noticed but two buses—plus a third arriving—already there, also had guys streaming out and lining up facing a black sailor wearing a white hat, with two red stripes on his shoulder that looked something like flying birds.

It took but two minutes before everybody was out, lined up, and standing tall. Then he noticed a different group lining up, also being yelled at.

"Right!—*Face!*"

Most everybody turned the correct way. The ones that didn't jerked one way, then back again, looked around crazily, and finally everybody was correct.

"Forwwwwward!—*March*! Left! Right! Left! Right! Come on, you dumb fuckers, get in step!—Left! Right!"

Nobody was speaking except the black guy calling cadence.

"Left! Right!..." The black guy made a move and suddenly was marching backward, "Okay, boys, we're coming up to a right turn corner! When we get there, when I give the command, you boys on the right will march *In Place*! That means you'll keep marching but you won't be going anywhere except to vaguely be turning, so that when everybody is turned you'll be facing the correct way too!—Left! Right Left! Right!"

That right-turn corner kept coming. Moser was telling himself—focus! *Focus!* Focus, as he was on the right side right behind Hamm—

"Company!—Right Turn!—*March*!"

He stopped going forward and kept his feet going in step with the other—

The guy behind walked into him and stepped on both his heels!

He went down!

"Companyyyy! *Halt*!" The black man came around the ranks so quickly. Moser got back to his feet just as he arrived, "Well, we do have a dumbass here—where you from, boy?"

"Iowa."

"A farmer from Iowa!" The man said it with a tone that made him feel he had just been insulted, "Well, son, I'm not going to be your company commander. You won't get him till we get to the grinder, but you can be damn sure I will tell him that he has at least one dumb fuck to deal with, but don't worry, there'll be more!"

*But it wasn't my fault!* Somehow he knew it would do no good to say that.

The black man returned to the other side of the company, "Companyyyy! Forwarrrrd! March!" Again the man made the maneuver and suddenly was marching backward again, Moser guessed the better to talk to the marchers, "We have two more turns before we get to the main grinder! They're both *left* turns—think you can handle that, farmer boy?"

He was uncertain if he should answer—

"Farmer boy, are you *deaf* too?"

"No, sir—I mean, yes, Sir! I mean...."

"Just shut the fuck up, farmer boy." The black man shook his head, turned back to forward marching, and said not as loudly, "I will pray for your company commander."

Which brought some laughter.

"Silence in the ranks!"

The laugher stopped, but he knew—as well as he knew his name—that he had just been labeled a fuckup. He didn't deserve it but had no choice but to accept it. The first chance he had he would take a good look at the guy behind who had stepped on his heels.

****

After they reached the main grinder and halted, a new guy wearing a hard-brimmed hat and khaki-colored clothing started doing the shouting, "These will be your billet numbers! I'll call your name out, then a number, then you double-time, find that number and stand tall, and that will be your always position in ranks! The first numbers will be for your squad leaders—Jessup!"

A tall, kind of gangly guy broke ranks and ran to the head of the billet numbers.

As Jessup was running, the new guy called out, "Squad four, Jessup!"

The five other squad leaders were called, then began the others

As the numbers were called Moser took the chance to look behind him. A guy shorter, blonde hair, and quite a bit heavier stood there. A smirk appeared, "Iowa farm boy, huh?"

He jerked forward just as his name was called, "Moser! Billet number six, squad four!"

As he double-timed to the painted number six on the grinder he noticed the black guy who had brought them approach the new guy, speak to him, then both looked toward him and the black guy pointed, just as he reached his number.

The number calling went on. Hamm ended up closer to the front of the ranks, number five in squad three, so not too far away. Nobody yet stood to Moser's left—

"Durban! Billet number seven, squad four!"

The heavy-set guy started double-timing. He could not believe his eyes. The same guy would march behind him for the whole nine weeks! The guy arrived on billet seven and said barely aloud, "I see our new CC got the word about *you*, farmer boy."

He faced straight ahead and ignored the comment, but knew sooner or later it would probably become impossible.

The billets were all filled. They were now Company 299.

"Listen up!" the guy in khaki shouted, "My name is Master Chief Claremont, and for the next nine weeks I will be your mother, your father, your preacher, however the fuck you want to think of me. Listen carefully to all instructions, and keep your nose clean! We don't want any fuckups in this company—Mortensen!"

"Yes, Sir!"

"For today you will march in front of the company."

"Yes, Sir," Mortensen said calmly.

"For the rest of you fuckups, I will call the commands from the left side of the formation, which from now on is *Port*! Your right side is Starboard! Okay, boys, we'll first march to the barber shop where you darlings will lose those glorious hippie locks and tresses—believe me! It'll be easier keeping your presently lice-infected heads clean! Then we'll head over to supply to pick up your ditty bags and uniforms."

The chief stopped shouting and looked them over, then said calmly, "Keep your eyes forward, boys, you never make eye contact unless you are damned certain what you want to say, and if you *are* certain, and say it as if you *are* certain, then I might just let you get away with it— looking at my eyes—that is. Sometime tonight we will march over the bridge to the island—called Hell's Island by some—where you'll spend your first 4 weeks!" The chief, somewhat heavyset, looked them over again, then, "Attennn—*shun*! Right—*face*! Forwarrrrrd—*H'arch*! Heeeey-lep! Heeey-lep!—That's when your left foot hits the grinder, goddamn it! Get in step! Heeey-lep!"

Already Moser liked the idea of marching, and felt every left foot hitting the grinder…just so that asshole behind him stayed off his heels, but was pretty sure he wouldn't.

# 4
## Hell's Island

Hair freshly cut right down to the skull, learning about the chilly San Diego night air, and loaded down with their full uniform, the boys of Company 299 started across the bridge to what they had heard referred to as Hell's Island. Moser was pretty sure that reference would be correct, as he felt like every step was taking him farther from the land of sanity—

"Heeee—lep! Heeee—lep!...." came the voice of their new Company Commander, Master Chief Petty Officer Claremont, marching farther ahead of them than usual.

Maybe the man was giving them a break: By being farther ahead he wouldn't be able to hear all the groaning going on, and there was plenty of that. And nobody was any longer in step. The goal now was just to make it over that bridge to their new barracks and hopefully go to bed—

An extra grunt came from behind—

"Shit!"

He glanced back. His antagonist, the boy named Durban, had just fallen on his face, and most everybody was just going around him. One other new recruit helped him up…but his gear was strewn far and wide, and marching feet were trying to miss everything but mostly unsuccessfully, caused in part by darkness, except for widely-separated bridge lights.

Even though Moser was carrying about all he could, he just couldn't leave another guy in need, so stopped, plopped his own seabag down and hoped it would stand, then helped gather up Durban's uniforms. When he got to Durban he saw the problem. The guy must not have listened—or for sure hadn't understood—the instructions of how to quickly store a seabag. The seabag was full, and would not take what he had collected.

With big eyes Durban just looked at him, then hoisted his seabag, "Got no more room."

Cussing to himself, he returned to his own seabag, which Hamm, who also had heard the commotion, had returned and was holding Moser's seabag up, "Thanks, man!" He took stock of what he had of Durban's, a set of undress blues and three white T-shirts, then shoved the items into his own seabag, hoisted it, and ran to catch up to the company, which Durban had already joined.

*What a dumbass!*

The chief was waiting, "What are you doing out of rank, sonny—whoa! Aren't you the farm boy that was pointed out to me?"

"Yes, Sir, but I was helping a fellow recruit—"

"I don't care what you were doing—get down and give me ten pushups!"

"Sir, I—"

"Do it! Right *now!*"

Moser again plopped his seabag, hoped it would stand, dropped to his hands and knees and gave his new company commander ten pushups, then jumped up and stood at attention.

"Now get your ass back to your company—double-time!"

He grabbed and hoisted his seabag to his right shoulder in one movement and started running.

"Faster!"

He *was* going fast—*how can that fat fuck even keep up to me?* But the chief was, with no problem—

"Faster! Faster!"

They arrived at the marching company—everybody suddenly in step again—maybe scared of raising the ire of their new company commander.

"Now get into your billet number and see if you can stay in step till we get to your barracks!"

Moser, puffing, slipped into his spot and thanked his lucky stars it was open.

Minutes later:

"Company—*Halt!* Right—*Face!*" The chief moved to the front of the ranks and pointed backward with his thumb, "There's your new home, boys. Sorry, but you don't get to go to bed yet—you have to empty your seabag into your brand new locker, and use your brand new padlock that came in your ditty bag, to lock that locker and make damn sure it's *always* locked! *Always*, boys, as what's in your locker is your life. If you lose something, consider yourself fucked, because it won't be replaced—"

"The farmer boy's got some of my uniforms!" Durban cut in.

*"What?!!!"* The chief came stomping to where Moser—his stomach absolutely gone—stood.

The chief came right into the ranks and faced Moser, his angry face about six inches away, "You, boy, have about one more fuckup before I send you back over that bridge to hope to join up with another company…if anybody'll take you—*why do you have Durban's uniforms*?

"Found them, Sir, right where the dumb fuck fell down and dropped them." Moser held his breath as he tried to keep from looking the chief in the eye and waited for some response….

The chief executed a move to his left and then faced Durban, but said nothing to Durban, "Please return this man's uniforms, farm boy."

Moser swept his hands into his seabag, came up with the five items and handed them to Durban to his right. Durban accepted them and put them under his left arm.

The chief turned smartly to his left and walked back to the front of the ranks, "One last thing, boys, I will be right here in this same building with you for the next four weeks—*Pray*! That you all get to march back over that bridge at that time, and not before." The chief looked them over, "Now get your asses in there, get your lockers stowed, and *maybe*!...You'll get an hour's sleep before breakfast, which is four a.m.—Fall out!"

\*\*\*\*

Moser woke to the sound of somebody pounding on the cover of a metal garbage can. He tried to keep his eyes closed and ignore the sound…until it was at the foot of his bed—

"Out of that rack, farmer boy!"

He didn't see who had made that pronouncement, but knew he better accept that he wasn't having a long-running nightmare and move.

He pushed himself up partway, then swung his legs out. The guy in the upper rack landed nearly on him, and glanced back as he moved to his own locker, right above Moser's, "Sorry," he said, "Ya better get moving."

He did. He stood and stretched, "Do we get to go to the bathroom?"

His bunkmate, already nearly dressed, first laughed, then, "I wouldn't take the chance, farmer boy, it's nearly four o'clock, and if I were you I'd start callin' it the head."

"What...?"

"The *head!* Your bathroom back on the farm is now the *head* here!"

"So you're gonna ride my ass too?"

"I don't know—what the hell happened, anyway? Or wait! Tell me another time, and get yourself dressed—*Jeezus*!" The guy, a couple inches taller than Moser's five-eight, put on his hat, pushed past him, and left.

Then it suddenly occurred to him that the guy was right. He was in the navy now and needed to focus, and, he hoped, somehow shed the *'farmer boy'* title.

Two minutes later, having taken a ten-second break in the head, still buttoning up, hurried down the stairs to join the forming company, and stepped into billet number six, right next to antagonist Durban—

"Farmer boy!" the chief shouted, "Where the fuck are your leggings?"

Leggings? He didn't even *have* leggings. He looked around. Everybody else had tight brown leggings clasping their shins to their shoes. He heard the stomping sound coming.

Again the chief stopped right in front of him—

"Answer me, Farmer boy! Where the fuck are your goddamned leggings?"

Best to be truthful? "I don't know, Sir." The strange stomach-leaving-him feeling came back, really serious this time.

"I told you before, farmer boy, you are about one more fuckup before you're kicked out of this company, but you need to eat, so I'm going to let you by this *once*! And get your goddamned shit together!"

The chief returned to the front of the company, "Company! Attennn—*shun*!"

After the chief left he heard snickering coming from his antagonist, and nothing he could do about it—

"Boys, we're going to march over to the chow hall, we'll halt on a specific set of grinder numbers, you eat fast, then get your asses back out to the grinder number where we will form up and return to the barracks. You boys have a lot of shit to do and learn today, so we need to get at it!" The chief looked them over, "Right—*Face*! Forward—*H'artch*! Your-lep, your-lep, your-lep, riiiight *left*!"

Again the feeling of his left heel hitting the grinder on every left-call made him feel good, like he was definitely in the navy. But truly, he really needed to get focused and get his shit together!

*I'm in the navy now!*

# 5
## Chow

Once they got in the chow line the chief disappeared—

"Asshole to belly-button!" A guy in a white sailor suit with three red stripes on his shoulder that—again—looked like birds flying, "Come on—close up this line!"

"That's the Master-at-Arms," somebody in the line said, "A First Class Petty Officer—three crows on his arm."

Moser wondered how that guy already knew navy terms, then picked out the speaker, the guy who slept above him in the barracks. First chance he got he would introduce himself, and maybe have a second mentor, along with Hamm—he hadn't even *seen* Hamm yet that morning.

The line kept moving, rather quickly, he thought, and no time till he reached the plates and trays, grabbed one of each, then reached what looked like scrambled eggs and presented his plate to a kid wearing a white T-shirt behind the counter.

The kid slopped a spoonful on. He jerked his plate toward him again.

"You only get one," the kid said, "Move it along!"

He wondered if that was true but moved along anyway to the meat.

"You get two choices," another kid in a white T-shirt announced.

"Bacon and sausage."

The kid gave him three bacon slices and one paddy of sausage.

Then hotcakes, very small. He was certain he could eat four or five, "Six, please."

Another kid grinned, delivered four, then poured syrup over the whole plate.

Then fruit. He held his plate forward.

A kid dumped one small spoonful. Strawberries, melon chunks, grapes.

The end of the line arrived. *No coffee?* Having been raised on the farm he was accustomed to coffee, at least three times a day. Breakfast, morning lunch, and afternoon lunch. He thought about asking somebody, but who the hell would he ask? And he remembered the chief saying to *'eat fast!'* So he looked at the tables, hoping to see somebody he recognized, but nobody, so just went to an empty spot and sat down, and started tossing the food down. Eat fast. Right.

Suddenly his plate was empty. *Did I eat too slow? Is my company still out there?* Even though full, his stomach again took on that leaving-him-feeling. He looked all around and saw many guys going in the same direction, stopping at certain places and going on, then placing their hats on as they went outside.

He got up quickly and hurried in the same direction, hoping he was doing right, and wondering when the hell somebody was going to start telling him what the fuck was the right thing to do?

He reached the first stop and saw—thank God—that he was right, scraped off what little remained on his plate in the garbage can, then placed knife, fork, and spoon in the correct spots, then a place for cups and glasses, neither of which he had, finally the tray, then the door, grabbed his hat and slammed it on...and met—what he would find out in another second, was an officer, who he was required to salute.

The officer stopped and gave him a very dirty look.

Way late he spotted one gold bar on the man's shirt collar, and threw his right hand to his forehead and said nothing.

The officer returned the salute, "Carry on, sailor."

"Yes, Sir! Thank you, Sir!" He dropped his salute and hurried outside...and saw four different companies forming. He hurried down the line looking—desperately—for somebody he knew.

But *nobody*!

"Moser!"

He heard his name, and continued looking everywhere...and finally saw his friend Hamm waving. He rushed to his billet number and stood tall, just as their chief arrived.

"All present or accounted for, Sir," Mortensen said, then saluted the chief.

"Very well!" The chief returned the salute, "Company! Atennn—*shun*! About—*Face*!"

He had no idea what that command meant, so just waited and watched what others were doing, then just quickly turned himself one hundred and eighty degrees. And suddenly he was behind his antagonist, and considered stepping on his heels so *bad*...but no, he couldn't do that, and wondered why everything was backwards—

"Forwarrrrd *Hart'ch!*"

They moved forward about forty feet—

"Company *halt!*"

The chief walked to their port side, and Moser applauded himself for remembering left was port. He was pretty sure anyway.

"That's right, boys. When we march to chow, and classrooms, and other activities, we will halt facing the establishment. Depending on where, and whether or not a street before us is available to leave going forward, as there isn't at the chow hall, then we will do an *'about face,'* march a short distance and do another *'about face'* to get back into position. When we leave here we will head for the main grinder where we will do calisthenics and practice commands, which I saw almost none of you did *'about face'* correctly!"

One kid quickly spun around again.

The chief, of course, saw it, "Not now, dumbass!"

The kid then spun back around. For a second the chief stared toward the kid, then he looked them all over, "When we come back to the chow hall for the noon meal, I can guarantee you will all know how to *'about face.'* correctly—About—*Face!*"

Again Moser just very quickly turned himself around—

"That was a little better, but I saw what you did, Farmer boy—Forwarrrd—*Hart'ch!*"

Again came the snicker from Durban.

His fists doubled for a few seconds, *sooner or later I'm gonna have to nail that guy*, then relaxed, lest anybody see his fists doubled.

# 6
## Drilling

Chief Claremont had just done his maneuver to march backward, "Company *Halt!*"

Two extra steps, left foot joining the right at the heels, and they halted.

Moser felt amazed that a man of the chief's size—not just big and strong but actually could be considered a bit fat— could do the move so well. He guessed it was pure military prowess, and hoped he could learn to march and drill as well.

"Okay, boys, for the next four hours we will do calisthenics and learn how to march and drill. After that we'll spend a half hour in class to learn about the piece you will carry here in bootcamp, an M1 with the firing pin removed, then we'll go to the armory and get one for each of you." As usual the chief looked them over, then, "First calisthenics! Mortensen, take charge!"

"Aye-aye, Sir! Jumping jacks—Begin!"

For the next thirty minutes they went through the main exercises, including sit-ups, push-ups, crunches, and then more jumping jacks.

"Those are your main calisthenics, boys," the chief said, "Eventually we'll do pull-ups, but we can't do that out here on the grinder. Next we'll learn the in-ranks and marching drills. Mortensen, you lead the company. I'll call the commands from out here."

"Aye-aye, Sir."

"To start," the chief went on, "I will just call the commands. You boys who learn faster, help the dumbasses, and if you're fucking up too bad I will, again, describe the drills in detail— Right—*Face!*"

Everybody did that nearly perfectly.

"Left—*Face!*"

Also, nearly perfectly.

"About! Face!"

Not so perfect. Moser hesitated and watched what others were doing. At least three times, finally he thought he had it. *Right toe to left heel, spin, and bring left foot back into attention.* He tried it, and didn't see the chief move to where he could see him…but he was pretty sure his move was correct.

"Good job, Moser," the chief said.

Eyes wide, he jerked toward the chief, and nodded, barely.

The chief returned the nod, then walked away again, "That's enough! Company! Attennnn—*shun!* Forwarrrd— *Hart'ch!* Hey-lep! Hey-lep! Hey-lep, riiight, left! Hey-lep! Hey-lep—okay boys, we're going to do a right flank! That means you take one more step with your left foot, then spin yourself to your right, and suddenly you're following the man who normally marches on your right side…Hey-lep! Hey-lep—Right! *Flank!*"

Moser took one more step with his left foot and spun to his right—right into his neighbor in Squad Five, which nearly knocked them both down. He grabbed onto the guy's left shoulder, which stabilized them both, and he saw plenty others screwing up too—

"Enough, Goddamn it!—Company! Attennnn-*shun!*"

Everybody clambered back into their correct billet locations, without the billet numbers.

"That wasn't as bad as I've seen before. Some of you boys must have done some marching somewhere else, so, again, help your neighbor to learn these drills—that's called *teamwork*! Something you'll need when you get out on a ship somewhere on that big goddamned ocean out there, and something you'll need for the rest of your life…so spend the next two minutes talking with your neighbors."

Moser turned to his neighbor. He hadn't yet met the guy so extended his hand, "I'm Moser."

The guy grasped his hand and shook.

"I'm Nudell, Elvin. I'm from—"

Moser cut him off, rudely, he knew, but, "Just your last name, Nudell—shit, this isn't a get-to-know-you party."

"Well," Nudell came back, "You're quite the asshole too, huh?"

He heard Durban snicker, "Look, the chief just gave us two minutes to get this right—look…!" He demonstrated the right flank, then the left flank, then had Nudell do it, and he did it correctly.

"Quite the smart ass, too, huh?" Nudell added, "So, you gettin' some kind of kickback?"

"Company! Attennnn-*shun!*"

"Yeah," came the word from behind from Durban, "Didn't you hear the chief earlier? Told the farm boy he did a good job."

"No more talking in the ranks! Forwarrrd—*Hart'ch!*"

And they marched for the next half hour, practicing left and right flank, then expanded into left and right obliques, which caused even more confusion, even after the chief not only described the move but demonstrated. So, again, it fell to the recruits to help other recruits, which Moser willingly did, but only received more smart remarks and comments from both Nudell and Durban.

They continued marching until the chief headed them toward the armory classroom. Moser was glad and looked forward to the expected break, and again felt good marching, his left foot hitting the grinder with all the rest of the recruits correctly in step—again his heels began getting stepped on!

*Enough!*

He jumped ahead, spun, then sent his right fist into the center of Durban's face. Instantly blood spurted from his nose and the guy went down, all the way to the grinder.

Moser spun back into formation, but too late—

"Company *halt!*" The chief stomped back to where Durban still laid on the grinder holding his nose, "Moser hit me!" he cried.

"I saw what happened, Durban, and I know what happened before. After the noon meal you will be escorted back out here under guard to clean up your blood, Now you get your ass up and back into formation—and no more bleeding on the grinder—by *any* of you dumb fuckers!"

Moser would have loved to turn around, but kept facing forward. When the chief started back to where he normally walked, through peripheral vision, he saw the chief slow down directly to his left. He didn't see the chief's expression but could *feel* it.

It felt good. Maybe now he would get some respect, and maybe even lose the *'farm boy'* nickname—not that he hated the nickname—or maybe just the tone some used would change. He didn't know what the future held, but was pretty sure Durban would never step on his heels again.

# 7
## 3-5-day Test

How many days had passed? Two? Three? Had he even slept yet? He thought, *'yes'* probably twice, for about a total of five or six hours. Moser wasn't sure, but he did know each event that happened gave him a little more confidence about his new place in life.

The weeks passed. They did a lot of marching, calisthenics, exercises with their pieces, which he especially liked, and spent a lot of time in classrooms learning about basic *navy*. He even passed two written tests, and felt *really* good about that.

Then came the day they got to march back over that bridge to the regular navy bootcamp, where it was even rumored being easier. He doubted that but didn't argue, just kind of gloried in the sound of his left foot hitting the bridge grinder just a little harder then the right, telling him *'yes'* he was in step!

****

Almost right away they got hit with another written test, the so-called 3-5 day test, meaning if they passed that they had been in the navy four weeks.

Moser wasn't worried. He had already passed three tests, including the one back at Des Moines, so no need to worry about this one…the questions *did* almost seem to be a little harder, though.

One day went by. He wasn't worried, exactly, yet he didn't feel confident either.

That afternoon he saw the yeoman coming down the barracks lane between the centerboard table and the row of bunks. They *never* saw the yeoman in the regular barracks. True, he was a recruit, same as the rest of them, but the guy even had his own office where he kept track of every other recruit's business.

He didn't mean to but made eye contact with the yeoman, then stepped back between the bunks. He didn't know *why* he did that, but just suddenly he felt more uncomfortable then he ever had in his whole life—

The yeoman stopped at the foot of his bunk, and did not smile, "Moser—"

His heart sunk right into the bottom of his stomach—

"You didn't pass the 3-5 day test."

He couldn't believe it. There had to be some mistake—sure, he wasn't certain of every answer but—

"You'll need to get your gear together and march back over that bridge yet today and find your new company," the yeoman went on, then handed over one sheet of paper, "This is a checklist to be sure you don't forget anything. When you're ready to leave stop at the office and I'll give you your orders."

He just stared. There was absolutely nothing he could think of to say, and hardly noticed a second sheet of paper in the yeoman's hands.

The yeoman started to leave, then glanced back, "Oh, and you're not going alone. Seaman Recruit Hamm is going with you, so be sure you two get together and leave at the same time."

Then he walked on. Moser settled onto his bunk, still nearly in shock. Finally he looked at the sheet, the list...he skipped quickly over his uniform, ditty bag, personal effects...blanket? Sheet? Piece...! *Jesus! That's too much stuff to carry in one trip!*

"Bad luck, Moser," the guy from the upper bunk said.

Fuck! He didn't even know his bunkmate's name yet!

"Thanks, man." He looked at his bunkmate and saw an expression of...what? Indifference? Yes, total indifference, and why not? The guy was probably just thanking his lucky stars it wasn't him going back over that bridge. He folded the paper and stuck it in his dungaree shirt pocket, then stood, opened his locker, shook out his seabag, and began packing it, knowing everything had to go in correctly or he couldn't close it.

A half hour later he was ready and left to find Hamm, who was even a little less happy then himself, "Hamm, ya okay, my friend?"

"Fuck no!" Hamm turned, then turned away again and wiped his face, then came back. The guy looked like he might even have been crying.

Moser felt like it too, and if his heart fell any lower into his stomach he just might, "Anything I can do to help?"

Hamm shook his head, "Naw, I'm just about ready." He turned away again, "Meet ya over by the yeoman in about five more minutes, okay?"

"Yeah, see ya then."

He returned to his bunk, checked everything again, then hoisted his seabag to his right shoulder, shoved the blanket under his left arm, grabbed his rifle, and knew he better start seriously using correct terminology from then on—*my rifle is a piece!*

As he walked toward the office it occurred to him that, other than Hamm, he had not met one other guy that he felt close to, not close enough anyway, to go to the trouble of seeking out and saying goodbye.

That would have to change. He was in the navy now. Going back across that bridge was a setback, yes, but not the end of the world. In his next company he would make friends, he would, as Chief Claremont said, learn about and practice teamwork.

He reached the yeoman's office. Hamm had just arrived. The yeoman appeared with two large brown envelopes.

*Shit! Now where the hell am I going to carry my orders?* He plopped his seabag down, blanket on top, and lay his piece to lean against it.

The yeoman handed one brown envelope to, "Moser, your new company is 321. They just marched over the bridge yesterday..."

*My new company? We're not going to the same company?* He felt his heart heading down again—*Jezus! How much more?*

"Hamm, your new company is 323. Your barracks are not next to each other. There's another in between." The yeoman didn't smile, but an expression of compassion possibly swept his face, "I'd recommend carrying your orders pushed down in the front part of your dungarees, guys." He then demonstrated, "It's a long walk, and it's up to just you to make it, so…well, good luck."

The yeoman turned back to his office.

# 8
## Back to Hell's Island

Still on the mainland-side of the bridge, Moser and Hamm stopped and plopped down their gear.

The empty bridge leading back to Hell's Island reminded Moser of a war movie he had seen a couple years earlier. The soldiers had stopped because the bridge had a slight hump in the middle, preventing them from seeing *exactly* what lay ahead. Was an enemy company approaching? Maybe a tank? They didn't know. The only way to find out was to keep going and hope for the best, and that *'best'* in the movie didn't turn out well.

No hump existed in this bridge. They could see the other side. No enemy patrol was coming, yet the world seemed darker over there. They were stepping back into their own recent pasts, but with a second chance to do better.

"Well, ya ready?" Hamm asked.

"Yeah, We might as well get over there and get started again."

"Sorry we're gettin' separated, Moser, you're about the only guy I knew well in Company 299, and now we both have to start over with a bunch of strangers."

"Well, we were all strangers back in Des Moines too."

"I guess." Hamm lifted his seabag onto his right shoulder, blanket under his left arm, piece in his left hand.

Moser did the same, "Lucky the yeoman told us how to carry our orders, huh?"

"Yeah, lucky us."

Halfway across the bridge he could see that Hamm—actually bigger and stronger-looking than him—was beginning to show some stress.

"Gotta stop, man." Hamm stopped and dumped his load, "Jezus! This is such bullshit!" His seabag tipped over, dumping the blanket. He threw his piece against the seabag. "Fuck! I'm so damn tired!"

About ten feet ahead, Moser stopped and plopped his load too, and felt surprised that Hamm was having trouble. *He* was too, but maybe his farm-upbringing was helping him. Physically, yes, his farm-upbringing *was* helping. Emotionally, well, he couldn't think of anything that would help that. He had never felt so alone, and worthless, in his whole life. His heart and stomach both were on the very bottom.

He walked back to Hamm, "Let me carry your blanket, man."

"You would do that?"

"Yes, we need to help each other. Teamwork, ya know?"

"Yeah, I guess the chief mentioned that—he could of said *'goodbye'* ya know, could of treated us like we were worth something."

"He could have, Hamm, but he didn't. And I guess, right now, maybe we *aren't* worth much. It's kind of another test, maybe, to see if we can handle it."

Hamm straightened up, grasped his blanket and handed it over, "Thanks, man, I'll take it back as soon as I can…ya know, the truth is, I didn't want to go around saying a bunch of tearful goodbyes. It's just that I kind of *liked* that chief."

"So did I." Moser agreed, and wondered—*hoped*—that he would get another chief as good, and fair, in Company 321.

Hamm hoisted his seabag and grabbed his piece, "Let's go."

Moser returned to his gear and did the same, except with two blankets he had to double them over, cradle them under his arm and carry his piece pressed against them and his chest.

Ten minutes later they arrived back on the Hell's Island grinder. At the first barracks a couple dozen recruits in dungarees were out scrub-brushing their laundry on concrete tables and hanging them on clotheslines, something like his mother used back on the farm. For just a second a homesickness pang hit him in the stomach, and a picture of Leah, but he brushed the visions away and called out, "Hey, guys, we're looking for companies 321 and 323!"

A really big guy in a white uniform sitting near the door stood up. He had two small black birds on his upper left arm that he had learned to recognize as signifying recruit officers—to a point at least. This guy was likely a recruit Master-at-arms. The guy pointed to his right, "Three-twenty-one is next door topside. Three-twenty-three is the third barracks over. Topside or ground floor I don't know."

"Thanks!" he shouted, then to Hamm, "Let's go. I'll set my stuff down then help carry your stuff over two more barracks."

"Thanks, man!"

# 9
## Company 321

Halfway to the other barracks Moser's stomach did a flip, *Jezus, I shouldn't have left my stuff just laying there!*

He was right.

When he and Hamm arrived he quickly handed Hamm his stuff, slapped him on the shoulder, "Take care, man!" and double-timed back to his own barracks…and his new chief was waiting, arms folded.

It of course was not the first black man he had ever seen, but it *would* be the first he had really ever spoken to. He slid to a stop, stood tall, and saluted.

The chief returned the salute but didn't speak.

He dropped his salute and pulled out his orders, "Moser, Sir, reporting for duty in Company 321."

Quietly the chief answered, "Take your orders topside to the yeoman, Moser. Take all your gear topside, get everything stowed properly in your locker, and don't *ever* leave your piece—or *any* of your gear—laying around like this again."

"Yes, Sir!" He saluted again.

"Carry on!"

"Yes, Sir!" He dropped his salute, grabbed his gear and headed for the door. Luckily, another recruit in dungarees was there and opened it for him.

"Thanks!" He suddenly had the strength of two men as his feet carried him up the steps and into the barracks. Without even stopping he found the office and the yeoman and handed over his orders. Then he stood there bent under the weight of his seabag and gear, and noticed the yeoman had only *one* black bird on his left arm.

Quizzically, the yeoman looked at him, "Something else?"

"Ah, yeah…I need a bunk and locker."

"I'm kind of busy right now, ah…," The yeoman looked at the orders, "Ah, Moser…ah, could you come back later?"

"*Later?* Are you shittin' me?"

"No. Come back later."

He plopped his seabag down, his blanket on top, his piece against it, then took two steps into the office grabbed the yeoman's white uniform in two places, and jerked him partway off his chair, "Goddamn it! I need a locker now!"

The yeoman's eyes got big, "Okay…."

He slammed him back down and stepped back out of the office…and noticed the yeoman getting up and reaching for the door. For one more second he held back, but the yeoman started closing the door, so he crashed back and got his shoe between the door and the casing, then slammed the door fully open again and started toward him again.

The yeoman cringed back, "Talk to the master-at-arms—Jeeze, he takes care of the bunks."

"Okay, prick, and you couldn't have just *told* me that earlier?" He stepped back again, "So where'll I find him?"

"Right behind you, Moser."

He spun, and there stood a giant of a man in a white uniform with the two small black birds on his upper arm. The master-at-arms. About twenty guys in dungarees also stood around, watching, some grinning.

"Follow me." The master-at-arms started away.

Moser gathered up his gear and followed.

As he passed those standing around and watching, one moved closer and said quietly, "Good for you, man, that fuckin' smart ass yeoman needs his ass kicked!"

He glanced and acknowledged but hoped his new company commander would think that too, because his new chief absolutely would hear about this little fracas.

At his new bunk, he had just gotten started stowing—

"Hey, man, you're my new bunk-mate, huh?"

He turned and saw the same recruit who had praised him for standing up to the yeoman, with his hand stuck out—

"My name's Cordegan, from Texas."

Glad to have a new acquaintance, he grasped the hand, "Good to know you, Cordegon, I'm Moser, from Iowa."

"Whoa! Nearly straight up from Texas...." Cordegon began talking and kept on nearly nonstop. Moser acknowledged or agreed as necessary, but knew the most important thing was getting his uniforms and locker squared away.

An hour later he had everything properly stowed.

From out of nowhere arrived the recruit second-in-command under the RCPO, and Moser still hadn't remembered what to call him, but the guy had two of the black birds on his left arm, same as the master-at-arms.

"Chief Brecker wants to see you, Moser."

"Where is he?"

"You'll find the office through the main door to your right."

"Good luck with the *'choker,'*" Cordegon commented, then grinned.

"Thanks." He nodded to the recruit second-in-command, then glanced at Cordegon—wondering what the hell the guy meant by *'choker'*—then walked quickly through the aisle, dreading this meeting. In a brand new company and he had screwed up twice already. He reached the main door, passed through, and saw an important-looking door to the right. His fists doubled automatically, then relaxed as he started forward, and stopped.

The door was closed.

*Do I knock?*

Yes. No way could he just barge in. He knocked, and waited.

*Do I knock again?*

He didn't think so, and he didn't need to screw up a third time...so he kept waiting.

*Maybe I didn't knock hard enough the first time.* Maybe the chief was hard of hearing.

He raised his hand to knock the second time—

"Come in!"

*Jesus!*

He opened the door, entered, and stopped about two feet from the desk.

"Next time you have a problem with another recruit, Moser, you come to me. Do *not* take matters into your own hands—is that clear?"

"Yes, Sir."

"I've gone over your service jacket. It appears you were doing fine until the 3-5-day test. What happened?"

"I...don't know, Sir."

The chief looked at him for another few seconds, then turned to a different page of his service record, read a bit, then looked up "Seems you bashed the nose of the recruit behind you while marching…. Care to fill me in on that, Moser?

"I…." He didn't really want to say…to *tattle*, so to speak.

"All right, Moser, your company commander detailed what happened on this notepaper sheet for extra comments, but here is how it is: if the guy ahead of you is out-of-step, you step on his heels until he comes to his senses and gets back in step— so, do you want to add anything?"

The chief again drilled him with the calmest eyes he had ever seen.

"I…was…*not* out-of-step, Sir."

"All right, Moser." The chief closed the file and said calmly, "You are starting all over at day one. You will think you're smarter than the others because you've already been here, but you *aren't* smarter, Moser, and when we march back over that bridge, again, you are going to find there's a whole lot of stuff you don't know at all."

The chief waited, then added, "I'm going to watch you, whitey, I'm going to watch you much closer than any other recruit. Don't fuck up again. That is all!

*Do I salute him? Inside? Without my white hat on? Jesus!*

He didn't know, but did know whatever he did in the next second would be either right, or wrong.

"Yes, Sir! Thank you, Sir!" He didn't salute, just turned, walked quickly through the door—wondering what the chief meant by *'Whitey'*…his very blonde hair?—and closed it…and hesitated about two seconds waiting…but no further command came.

He must have done right by not saluting, and hurried back to his new bunk.

**** 

The three weeks of marching, calisthenics, rifle training exercises, and lots of Hell's Island inspections again went by. He failed one personnel inspection, a vague yellow ring in the sweat band of his white hat. It would be his *last* inspection failure while in bootcamp.

Chief Brecker met him halfway up the ladder, grabbed his white hat, flipped it inside out, stared at it for about one second, then slapped his face with it, "Yellow ring in your white hat, Moser—that's your third fuckup, and it had better be your last! Tomorrow morning we're marching back over that bridge—don't make me send you back here *again* to Hell's Island!"

Feeling some fear, yet a growing respect for his new company commander, he accepted his white hat back, "Thank you, Sir."

# 10
## Back Across That Bridge

Zero seven-forty-five arrived. Moser had learned the military time up to noon. Just add a zero before every number until getting to ten, then it was ten-hundred, eleven-hundred, and twelve hundred. Pretty easy. After that it got a little harder, and became thirteen-hundred, fourteen-hundred, and so on. To figure it out if he had to be somewhere at a certain time he started at twelve and counted forward on his fingers. Still pretty easy, but time-consuming, and he doubted he would ever fully memorize the military way.

He had just finished plopping his seabag at the foot of his bunk and felt ready to cross that bridge. He had clean dungarees on, white hat shoved under his belt in front of him, shoes shined like diamonds, leggings holding his jean dungarees down tight—he was ready!

Staring straight ahead at attention, he could feel them coming down the aisle for one last check. He heard the chief speaking softly to each recruit, but couldn't be sure what he was saying. The RCPO arrived first, glanced in, made eye contact, moved on. Then Chief Brecker, who stopped, "Make me proud, Moser!" then said the same thing to his upper bunkmate, right beside him, "Make me proud, Cordegan," and moved on.

Wow, he didn't remember his first chief being so personable…in fact, he couldn't even remember his first chief's name.

The inspecting party reached the front of the barracks. The chief turned around, "Company 321— We are heading out to cross that bridge! fall out, and line up in your billet number positions! *Move it!*"

Somehow he had gotten everything—even his blanket—into his seabag, so all he had to do was throw his seabag to his right shoulder and carry his piece, which he did, to the barracks front door, down the ladder, and out the door to his billet number. Then he plopped down his seabag and stood with his piece at attention while the rest of the company mustered.

Only about three minutes passed.

"Company! Atennn—*Shun*! Right! *Face!*" The chief looked them over good, "At ease. Okay, boys, once you have your seabags on your shoulders you'll want to space yourselves out a bit. Just be glad you aren't marching with the marines next door. They have to carry their gear regularly, the only difference being it's in a backpack, so a little easier. I know it's going to be a tough march carrying everything, but we are as tough as the marines, and we are going to look sharp marching over that bridge! Okay! Get'em up there!"

The chief waited all of ten seconds while eighty-two seabags went to eighty-two shoulders, "Company! Atennn—*Shun!* Forwarrrrd—Hart'ch!"

As the chief in his first company had done, Chief Brecker also marched on their port side and often backward, only he made the movements front-to-back look much easier and looked really professional. Even though somewhat afraid of his new company commander, Moser enjoyed watching him and believed the man loved his military role. He was even more amazed to hear the chief begin a marching song.

"Eeny-meany-miney-moe, let me hear that left foot go— hey-lep!...Hey-lep!...Hey-lep, right, left! That was swell, that was fine, let me hear it one more time—hey-lep!...Hey-lep!...Hey-lep, right, left!—Stand tall, you guys! Hey-lep!...." And the beat went on.

With every left call he increased the slam of his left heel. Everybody was. It became a wondrous sound along with the chief singing—what a man!

They reached the end of the bridge and came to a street.

"Company—*Halt*! Road-guards *Out*!"

A recruit from the two outside squads fell out and double-timed into the street, then went to Parade-rest to block any traffic, whether there *was* any or not.

"Company! Right turn—Hart'ch!"

The company made the right turn, then continued marching in place.

"Road-guards In! Forwarrrd—*Hart'ch*!"

He could see the barracks ahead, and hoped they would soon get there. He was getting tired, and noticed a couple of the guys ahead of him leaning forward and stumbling a bit—

"Straighten up, men!—stand tall!—Don't any of you mutherfuckers fall down on me or I will have your ass!"

The two guys he had noticed, straightened up. If their legs felt like *his* legs he didn't know how they could have.

They reached the barracks, then the second barracks, then the third—

"Company, Halt! RCPO, Take charge!" The chief disappeared into the barracks.

*Thank God!* He was all but collapsing himself but waited.

"At ease, men. We're on the ground floor this time. The master-at-arms has already issued bunks. You'll find your names on the aisle-side of the bunks, so, concentrate on getting your gear stowed, one squad at a time. Squad Six—Fall out!"

\*\*\*\*

An hour later Moser had everything stowed, he hoped correctly, as locker inspections could happen at any time.

His bunkmate was finished too, "What now?" Cordegan asked.

He was surprised to be asked that question.

"You've been over here before, man, so what now?"

"Well, yeah, for a couple days—Christ, I don't know anymore than you, but I guarantee they will soon tell us."

His bunkmate grinned,"Right."

"Company 321!" the RCPO shouted, "Gather down here at the front of the barracks men, and stand at ease. Chief Brecker wants to speak to you."

Everybody headed there and waited. Only about thirty seconds passed before the chief arrived.

"Attennnn—*Shun!*" the RCPO shouted.

Everybody, even though not in ranks, snapped to attention.

"Stand at ease, men," the chief said, "I'm going to give you men a little inside information. You already know my last name, which is all the name you need to know, but you don't know my rate. I am Master Chief Brecker, Boatswain's Mate. I joined the marines at age sixteen. I made two Pacific landings during World War II before they discovered I was underage, but they didn't kick me out. The Powers-that-be said I could stay in but I had to go over to the navy. I agreed. Now I have made it to the top of the enlisted men's ranks and I'm due to retire. You boys will be my last bootcamp company."

The chief looked them over and made several eye contacts, including with Moser, "This company is also going to be my best. We carry a company flag at the front of our ranks. I have already picked from among you somebody—and two substitutes—who will *always* carry and snap that flag smartly. At the end of each coming evolution the company who did the best—meaning good class grades, no failed inspections—just plain no *fuckups*—earns a gold star on that flag."

Again the chief looked them over, "At the end of your bootcamp stay, on Graduation Day, when we pass in revue before the stands filled with the big shots, I want our flag to have four gold stars." Again a hesitation, "So be forewarned. If any of you become a regular fuckup I will first punish you with extra calisthenics. If that doesn't bring you to your senses I'll give you calisthenics until you drop—you *will* be first-rate recruits when you leave my care."

The man's eyes seemed to actually burn as he gave them one last once-over, "So don't let me down, boys. That is all."

"Attennn—*shun!*" ordered the RCPO.

Everybody snapped to attention.

The chief returned to his office.

Moser felt himself relax inside, and sensed a collective sigh move through the crowd.

"We have one free hour before chow time, guys," the RCPO said, "Use it for laundry, shining shoes, cleaning your piece, writing letters home—whatever is needed, and now I'm going to give you another piece of inside info." The RCPO looked them over, not quite as scary-looking as when the chief did it, but his message *was*, "Some of you maybe already know, but our CC has a nickname among the other company commanders." Again, the look, " *'Choker'* Brecker. He *wants* those four gold stars, so, if any of you feel you just can't make it, I'd request a transfer out right now."

So he finally heard what Cordegon had meant by *'choker.'* It added a little twitch in his stomach, but, *fine, I just won't fuck up again.*

Still again, the *look* from the RCPO, "One more thing. For each gold star we get an on-base picnic. Okay, fall out and get to work."

# 11
## "Those who can, Swim…."

While waiting to fall out for breakfast, Moser was getting his usual earful from his bunkmate, "You're a farm boy and you don't know how to swim?" asked Cordegan, beginning to chuckle, "I thought all farm boys got thrown into the river by your brothers, and then you sank or swam."

"No brothers." He grinned back, and wondered what lay in store for him that day.

"That's what my brothers did to me," Cordegan exclaimed, "I got two older brothers—mutherfuckers—and I think my dad was behind the whole shenanigan, cause he was there. When we got to the river my dad said, *'It's time, boys!'* and I didn't know what the hell he meant, but my brothers wrestled me to the ground, got hold of my hands and feet swung me back and forth a couple times, and threw me at least twenty feet out into the Rio Grande!" Cordegan had been mostly grinning, but for a couple seconds his demeanor changed, "Bastards!" came out much lower, "And I sank all right, and swallowed a ton'a the Rio Grande River, finally struggled back to shore—an' those mutherfuckers—all three of'em—were laughin' like hell!"

Moser felt a little shocked at the story. He had *heard* of such things, but felt the experience had stuck with Cordegan and not in a good way, "But I guess you learned to swim, huh?" He grinned, but only half-heartedly.

"I learned all right, made sure that would never happen to me again, and I caught my brothers one at a time, the same night, and beat the fuck out of both of'em!"

He felt his eyes enlarge. He couldn't even imagine treating siblings like that, or friends—or *anybody*—

"I wanted'ta do it to my dad too, but I guess my brothers warned'im, cause I could never catch'im alone after that, and as soon as I was old enough I joined the navy here."

Instead of laughing, or even grinning, Moser felt sympathy for the boy and put his hand on his shoulder, "I'm sorry that happened to you, Cordegan."

"Ha! Learned to swim, didn't I?"

"Yes."

Cordegan chuckled, "Kind'a makes me wonder how they're gonna figure out today who among us can swim, or not."

"Won't they just ask?" He immediately felt stupid asking such a stupid question.

"Ha! I doubt that—Moser, I think you're the kind of a country boy who ain't never been anywhere before, so you better stick with me!"

"Thanks, man." Cordegan seemed to have some real street-smarts, and Moser liked him, and needed a friend, "I will."

An hour after breakfast Company 321 arrived at the swimming pool complex—

"All right, men," Chief Brecker shouted, "When you fall out, go into the dressing rooms—and I hope everybody brought their swimming trunks, but if you didn't you're going into the pool naked! So get in there, get changed, and line up at the deep end. There'll be instructors around to direct you from there—Fall out!"

Changing didn't take long.

Only about six minutes passed until Moser was in line, waiting his turn. There were four lines…but nobody was jumping in—

"Okay, boys," a bald instructor yelled, "When I give the signal, just jump in and swim to the other end! If you can't swim, just do your best to get to the surface, then I or one of the other instructors will reach out to you with a bamboo pole. Just grab on and we will pull you out. Remember! Just grab it and hold on! If you start going hand-over-hand, like you really want that pole, then we will let you have it, and back to the bottom you'll go—first line in!"

The first four recruits jumped in and started swimming for the other end.

"Second line in!"

And on they went. Over half the company had jumped in before somebody tried going hand-over-hand, and, yes, the instructor let him have it, and right to the bottom the recruit went. The instructors then stood at the edges of the pool and watched the recruit struggle.

His turn was close, p*lease, God, let me just hold on…!*

Finally one of the instructors dived in and pulled the recruit up and out.

When it came to his turn he jumped in, sank, struggled back to the surface, and looked for the pole. It was there. He grabbed it, hung on, and was pulled out.

"When everybody was done the statistics were given by the main instructor, "Company 321, you did well. Just three of you have to come back for lessons."

*Great, now along with every other fucking thing….* He didn't know how to finish his irritated thought, but decided if he was going to be in the navy he had probably better know how to swim.

# 12
## Punishment

The weeks went by. They marched, did calisthenics, practiced drills with their pieces, went into a closed space with gas masks, then had to get the mask on when the tear gas came—many, including Moser, were very slow, so got to experience the burn of tear gas first hand. On another day they went into another closed space with a fire hose to put out a diesel fuel fire, and the gold stars continued to appear on Company 321's flag.

The flag that soon would belong to the retired Choker Chef Brecker.

One week to go.

Hair was growing out, sunburns were turning into suntans, skinny guys were gaining weight, fat guys were losing weight, recruits were relaxing and letting their guards down, and fuckups were beginning to happen regularly. *Too* regularly. And Moser's buddy, Cordegan, was leading the pack in fuckups.

Fuckup number one happened when they were returning from church one Sunday. Because of the number of recruits all going in at the same time and then coming out at the same time there was no attempt to form into one's regular company at the end of church, but still it was necessary to form into a company to return to the barracks, even if you knew no one. Then the ill-formed companies had to march beyond the barracks to another grinder in order to fall out, and double-time back to their home-barracks. Cordegan usually followed the rule. Then one time, as his company marched past their barracks, he and several others snuck out of the ranks. Unfortunately, Cordegan and two others got caught. Then it was two days of extra calisthenics and cleanup.

This didn't affect the chief's gold star but it did point out a recruit—Cordegan—to watch more closely.

The second fuckup came when his shoes failed personnel inspection. More punishment and a warning.

Already two recruits had been sent to the hospital because of back problems brought about by the ultimate punishment, that of doing sit ups on the narrow centerboard, a long table through the center of the barracks with seats on both sides and an eighteen-inch-wide table for writing letters, shining shoes, etcetera, but not meant for exercises.

Smoking, when the smoking lamp was out, was a major fuckup, and Cordegan loved to smoke when he wasn't supposed to. One day he and another got caught, by the chief himself, "All right, boys, get rid of those cigarettes and find two empty garbage cans."

Moser was nearby, busy with his laundry—

"Moser! Find the RCPO and tell him to get the company out here! On the double!"

"Yes, Sir!" He found the RCPO and gave the message.

"Company 321!" the RCPO shouted, "Fall out to the front of the barracks!"

By the time Moser returned, both Cordegan and his buddy had returned, each with a 50-gallon metal garbage can. In another minute it appeared the whole company was outside.

"All right you two smokers, sit yourselves down right there and there." The chief pointed to spots about five feet apart, "Cross your legs because you're going to need the room."

The two recruits did as told.

"Show me your cigarette packs."

Both obeyed. Both packs showed half full, at least.

"Good, you both have plenty of smokes, so light up!"

Both recruits appeared confused, but lit up.

"Master-at-arms, place the garbage cans over these smokers. We want them to get good and full of tars and nicotine! The rest of you idiots, stand fast and listen to'em cough and choke, so you'll know what to expect if you don't respect the smoking lamp! Master-at-arms, leave'em covered for ten minutes." The chief walked away.

The coughing and choking soon began. Tough as Cordegan thought he was, he couldn't breathe all that smoke and not cough and choke. Moser waited for the ten minutes to go past, even thought about asking the master-at-arms to let them out sooner—

At least six minutes had passed. The coughing and choking had escalated to constant, "What the hell, master-at-arms!" he exclaimed, while taking a step closer to the can his buddy was under, "Let'em out!"

Unknown to him, the chief was still at the door, and nodded to the master-at-arms, who immediately stepped forward and removed the cans. The cloud of smoke released turned the whole area temporarily blue.

He stepped past the master-at-arms and knelt by his buddy, "You dumb ass, Cordegan, what're you trying to prove? We just have a week left!"

Cordegan was fairly blue, and still coughing.

"Step away, Moser!" the chief shouted, "And get back to whatever you were doing—leave those scum where they lay, and hope they will have learned something—everybody! Back to work!"

Moser stood and hurried back to the concrete table and his scrub-brushes, and couldn't help the feeling that Cordegan was not going to make it.

**\*\*\*\***

The next days went by. Cordegan no longer talked, about anything, didn't even answer when Moser, or anybody, spoke to him, but Moser, while folding his daily laundry, kept trying, "I know, bootcamp is the shits, man, but we're almost done, for Christ's sake! Tomorrow we get another picnic, the chief gets his fourth gold star, and two days after that we march in review—don't you want to be a part of that?"

Cordegan just looked at him, then crawled up into his bunk.

"Jesus, man, we can't be in our bunks this time of day." He looked quickly around to see if anybody had noticed. Two other recruits were looking that way, but weren't running off to tattle. He lifted his mattress, then stepped on the metal frame and pulled himself up, "Man, you can't be in your bunk—now get the fuck up! Before somebody sees you!"

"Too late, Moser." He recognized the voice of the RCPO, "Tend to your own work—Cordegan, on your feet!"

Moser was not sure what was happening, but felt sure some weenie-ass had squealed to the RCPO, and now the RCPO had no choice but to turn Cordegan in. Cordegan didn't argue, just crawled off the end of the bunk and jumped to the floor, then glanced back at Moser, his expression saying...*he knows he's done.*

About thirty seconds later—

"Moser!" the chief's voice, "Bring Cordegan's piece! Double-time!"

He grabbed his buddy's piece and had no doubt what was coming, just hurried to where everybody was gathering and handed Cordegan's piece over.

Cordegan took the piece, stepped up on the centerboard, sat on the table part, placed his feet under the seat on one side, his piece behind his neck, held onto both ends, then leaned back until he hit the other seat and right away came back up—

"Well," the chief said, "That was way too easy. Moser, bring your piece over here."

He felt his mouth fall open—

"Do it! Double-time!"

He soon returned with his piece.

"Master-at-arms, tie those two pieces together, then assist Cordegan to get them behind his neck."

The master-at-arms, stoically, did as instructed, but Moser was pretty sure the man was also feeling sympathy.

"Okay, Cordegan, I know you're tough but let me see you do a sit-up with *two* pieces!"

"Chief, Sir," Moser said, "Can't he just say he's sorry?"

The chief's eyes nearly burned a hole in him, "Shut the fuck up, Moser, or you'll be up there beside him! Cordegan, do it!"

Cordegan did it, and again, and again.

"Stop!" the chief exclaimed, "RCPO, get another piece!"

The third piece appeared.

"Master-at-arms, tie all three together!"

For maybe two seconds the master-at-arms hesitated, then did as instructed, and helped Cordegan get the three pieces behind his head.

"All right, Cordegan," The chief said, sounding almost sympathetic also, "This is going to finish you. If you go down and think you can't go up, then just stay down and we will help. No use you destroying your back. Okay, begin."

Cordegan looked one more time toward Moser, then began leaning back…and touched the seat, then began going up, but slowly, straining, but made it up, then went down again, and started up.

The chief nodded to the master-at-arms, who stepped forward to be ready to help.

Cordegan made it up again, and down again, and got halfway—and screamed and dropped the pieces. Instantly the master-at-arms was there and held him, while Cordegan continued groaning but evidently refusing to scream again. The chief signaled the yeoman, who must have called the ambulance, which ten minutes later arrived.

When Cordegan was on the stretcher on the way out, Moser approached the chief, "I want to say goodbye to him."

The chief waved to the ambulance crew to wait, "He wanted out, Moser. This is what he chose…." For one second the chief looked down, then said lower, "He could have stopped."

Moser stepped up to the stretcher and grasped Cordegan's hand, "Good luck to you, man, and take care." He patted Cordegan's hand, then stepped back.

Cordegan sent one small smile, then was out the door.

The next day the on-base picnic happened. Everybody enjoyed their hot dogs, burgers, potato salad, baked beans, and pop. Nobody mentioned Cordegan. Moser vaguely *thought* about him while enjoying his eats…but the guy had asked for what he got. The chief gave him a chance to quit and even stay in the company, but, no, he had to go to the limit and hurt himself. Now he would probably medically discharge.

Not a good way to go home, but then he didn't think Cordegan had much of a home or family either, not like the home and family *he* had. So he just shook his head and kept eating.

# 13
## Graduation

Graduation Day arrived. The recruits got up and had breakfast, then had free time until noon, when they ate again, then dressed in their best whites, their shined-like-diamonds shoes, tight leggings, grabbed their piece and mustered outside ready to march to the parade grounds.

Moser stood on his billet number, and while waiting, looked both ways to see the other close companies forming up. He felt—glad to be done, yes—but he also felt taller, and stronger, and proud to be associated with the United States Navy—

"Company 321!" the chief—also in whites and looking so damn sharp, even wearing a shining-like-gold sword— shouted, "Attennnn—*Shun!*"

The sound of the other close by company commanders giving orders sounded almost like music—they were done!

*I'm in the navy now!*

"Right—*Face!*...Right shoulder—*Arms!*...Forwarrrd— *Hart'ch!*"

And they were off.

He heard every left foot hitting the grinder as they marched. From the corner of his eye he watched the chief marching, going from front to back, turning so gracefully—*the man must be so proud!*

Time passed. They reached the parade grounds, then formed the companies into battalions and then regiments, then waited for the signal to go, for the companies to leave one at a time and march, right turn, and march, and another right turn and march.

To the stands full of civilians and officer's families—

"Company!" the chief shouted, his sword raised high, then down to his shoulder, "Eyes...*left!*"

They passed the stands.

"Company! Eyes...forward!"

They returned to their barracks.

Then it was magically over.

Moser received a second stripe, automatically making him a Seaman Apprentice, was chosen for Torpedoman School, had the option to go home on leave, but didn't, deciding he would rather get the schooling over first, so stayed in San Diego and headed over to Class A Weapons School.

# 14
## Weapons School

First choice, photography school. Second Choice, meteorology. Third choice, weapons. So he got weapons. Moser wondered what would have happened had he put weapons as his *first* choice. Likely he still would have gotten weapons, as probably very few photographers and weathermen were needed in the navy.

He didn't mind.

At the gate he crawled out of the cab, paid, held onto his orders, got his seabag out, plopped it on the sidewalk and gazed at the fenced school, wondering what lay ahead. Most everybody likely would be like himself, fresh out of bootcamp. And like the naval training center, the school was right on the ocean, probably closer, as he didn't ever remember seeing the ocean while in bootcamp, not even in the far distance.

He shoved his orders down in front of his dress blues uniform, threw his seabag to his shoulder, and walked to the gate, where a marine waited. Strange they couldn't have navy guys on their own gates. Sometimes the marines kind of scared him. Upon arrival he plopped his seabag down, handed over his orders, and waited. The marine looked them over, then pointed, "Check in there at Administration."

The marine looked so damn sharp he wondered if he should salute. Probably not, and the marine might even take it in a negative way, so he just said, "Thanks!" Then he shoved his orders back into the front of his uniform bottoms, threw his seabag onto his shoulder again and hoofed it over to Admin.

****

Near the entrance Moser met another sailor with the two black slanted stripes, just like his, "Hi, where do I take my orders?"

The other sailor stopped and gave him a look, "Weapons or Sonar? They teach both here."

"Weapons."

The sailor pointed to the open, well-lit front door, "Right in there, second door on your right," then gave another look, "Good luck," and walked away.

Wondering what the guy meant by *'good luck,'* he walked to the door, plopped the seabag next to it in the hall, pulled out his orders and—

"Well, hello there, young man!"

Taken back a bit, he kind of froze. This would be his first real exposure to a real sailor out in the real navy world, and he hadn't quite expected such a friendly greeting. It almost made him think he was back in Iowa and had just entered the local hardware store.

The man in white behind the counter quickly came and shoved out his hand, "I'm Signalman Second Class Hornstall, I should be out on a ship sending messages by flags but they put me in this shore duty instead."

Still feeling vaguely like he was back home, he accepted the handshake, a powerful one, "Nice to meet you, Sir."

"Oh, man, didn't they tell you anything?" The man's shining smile almost hurt his eyes. He finally noticed the two black birds on the left upper shoulder, much bigger than those in bootcamp, "The onlyiest people you have to call *'sir'* now are the officers—well, until you know'em a bit, you might want to call your class instructors *'sir,'* for awhile, anyway."

The man dropped his hand and went back behind the counter, "Now, how can I help you?"

His orders still just half out of the front of his uniform, he finished pulling them and handed them over, "Just checking in."

Hornstall grabbed them, took one look, "Ha, a tubesucker from Iowa, hey?"

" *'Tubesucker?'* "

"Yep, that's your new nickname!" The man's wild smile continued to almost hurt his eyes, "Those in the sonar school are called *Sonargirls.*"

Kind of wishing this interview would get over, he shook his head, "So what now? Who or what do I report to?"

"The master-at-arms over in Building Eleven will get you set up in the barracks—come on!" The man left the counter again, grabbed behind his left elbow—which Moser didn't exactly like—guided him to the front door, and pointed toward a building maybe an eighth of a mile away, "That's your barracks. You'll find the master-at-arms in the ground floor office. He'll assign you a bunk and a watch section, and…soon as I get your orders sent in, somebody will find you and let you know what class and when."

"Thanks." He started to leave.

The hand still on his elbow tightened, "Say, ah, Moser, some of us are gettin' together tonight for a little down-homin'."

" *'Downhomin'?* "

"It's a prayer group. We don't just sit around praying though; we also talk, about anything you want to talk about."

"I—"

"Now don't automatically say *'no,'* Moser, It's a nice group, about a dozen of us, and maybe a half dozen right from the base here, so you'd be among friends already."

"I don't know if I want to leave the base so soon—"

"Nonsense!" The elbow-squeeze tightened, "You could come right back here, about seven—and wear whites! Lose those dress blues! Nobody wears blues around here, and that's my car right over there, the Cadillac. I'd take you there and bring you back."

"How far from the base?"

That brighter-than-Hollywood smile disappeared. The elbow-squeeze tightened even more. He felt his trust of this guy—nonexistent from the start and now even more nonexistent—going right out the window.

"I'm not sure, maybe a mile or two."

*Jesus, you should know.* No way did he want to go anywhere with this guy, and he didn't know *why* he didn't want to…just a gut feeling…and he had always listened to his gut…but things had changed.

*I'm in the navy now….* "All right, man, I'll be here."

That blazing smile came right back. Hornstall gave a stronger squeeze, then finally released the elbow and slapped his shoulder, "Seven o'clock! Now go get your bunk and locker squared away—but don't eat! We'll have plenty of food at the meetin'!"

*'Don't eat?'* That sounded a bit strange, but, what the hell? *I'm in the navy now.*

## 15
### Hornstall

Seven o'clock arrived. As Moser approached the Admin building, dressed in his whites, just like Hornstall had told him, he couldn't help thinking of the warning Terry Hamm had given him back in Des Moines about rubbing elbows with the wrong guy, but then he had no real reason not to trust Hornstall, that is, except for his gut feeling, which he didn't recall ever being wrong.

Hornstall, dressed in civilian clothes, that smile just burning up the world, waited by his car, "Hey, guy, you're right on time—did ya eat anything?"

"No, well, I had a candy bar. It was a long time to seven."

Hornstall opened the door to the passenger side of his car, "Well, I guess a candy bar won't hurt…but, next time…."

*Next* time? That had almost sounded like an order. His stomach twitched. What the hell was so important about not eating? And why the civvies when *he* had to wear his uniform? Double twitch. He had half a mind not to get in that car. And why did the guy stand there holding the door open? What the hell? Triple twitch!

"Well, should we scram?" For just a second or two the smile changed to *coldness*, an expression he had never seen before during his well-sheltered life—then the smile came right back, maybe even brighter…but the eyes remained cold—*what the fuck?*

Quadruple twitch!

He stepped back, or tried to, as Hornstall again gripped his arm right above his elbow, "Come on, guy! They're waiting."

"*Who's* waiting?"

"My friends!" The smile stayed lit up, the eyes stayed cold, "You'll *like* them, I guarantee it!"

"Let go of my arm."

Hornstall's expression changed to that of an embarrassed child, and did release his arm, "I'm sorry, I just get overly-excited sometimes I guess."

The man's demeanor had changed radically. His stomach twitching stopped immediately, but then that's how folks from Iowa were. They were friendly, *trusting*, people.

He slid into the car and Hornstall closed the door.

****

They soon turned onto a quiet street in a friendly-looking San Diego neighborhood. Two blocks later they arrived at a ranch-style house where several cars were already parked. Nobody was in the front lawn.

"They'll all be in the fenced back yard," Hornstall said, "Let's head on back there."

The moment Moser was out of the car he wished he had worn anything but his uniform, but all the civvies he had were one set, and not exactly clean. Approaching the front door he saw himself in reflective glass, and absolutely knew he would be the only one in uniform.

Hornstall opened the door. He hesitated. He had money; it would be no problem to get out on that main drag and catch a taxi, but his thoughts were interrupted when Hornstall's hand gripped his left arm and guided him—a bit forcibly—into the front room, a large room with many cushioned chairs, about a dozen guys and not one uniform.

"I thought you said the back yard, and that a half dozen of these guys were from the base."

"They are."

"Where are they?"

"Guys, this here's a brand new seaman apprentice fresh out of bootcamp—from Iowa! His name's Brice Wesley Moser!"

"Hi, Brice!"

"How ya doin,' Brice?"

"How'd you know my name?" The stomach twitch came back, tenfold.

"Why, I just looked at your service jacket. Is anything wrong?"

The ten-story smile was gone. The expression now was that of a stranger—

"How about a beer, there, Moser?"

He turned to see a really tall guy holding a bottle of beer, and his face looked the same as Hornstall's, expressionless.

"No thanks."

"What? Don't Iowa farm boys drink beer?"

"We drink as good as anybody…I'm just not in the mood…first night on the base and all."

Hornstall spoke up, "Why don't we just get started, guys?"

"So we'll finally get something to eat?" he asked, innocently, which brought a round of laughter.

"We'll eat later," Hornstall said, then did a wave with his hand.

Immediately a hum began, and the tall guy with the beer set the beer down, then opened a Bible and began to read, "This is from Matthew 28: 19, *'Go therefore and make disciples of all nations, baptizing them in the name of the Father and of the Son and of the Holy Spirit,'*"

Several *'Amens'* went around the room.

Moser had been raised in a Congregational church, and felt very, *very*, out-of-place among these…people.

The tall guy passed the Bible to the first person sitting nearby on a couch, who read, "John 5: 39, *'You search the Scriptures because you think that in them you have eternal life; and it is they that bear witness about me,'*"

Finally the Bible reached Hornstall, who read, "John 8: 32, *'And you will know the truth, and the truth will set you free.'*" He looked at Moser and handed the Bible over, "Just read the marked verse, Moser."

He took the Bible and looked, then read, "1st Corinthians 3: 18, *'Let no one deceive himself. If anyone among you thinks that he is wise in this age, let him become a fool that he may become wise.'*" He liked the sound of that verse, but wished he were in a much different setting. So far these people had done nothing against him, nothing wrong, but he just somehow didn't trust them, or *like* them either.

Then the humming began again, just a low sound from every guy present and he felt every eye in the room looking at him—*what the hell?*

"Get down on your knees, Brice Moser," Hornstall said.
*"What…?"*

"Please! Down!" Hornstall removed his white hat and pushed down on his head. Then, as he dropped to the floor,

Hornstall threw the hat to land by his knees, and began speaking in monotone, "Lord, God, we have in our presence tonight a new child of yours, *'Brice Wesley Moser,'* from the farming state of Iowa, and we have found him to be a sinner just like all the lowly humans on earth. Please accept his praise and love for You, and please take him into Your loving arms...."

A few seconds passed, then from Hornstall came...he didn't know what, "Huskscotaba-youbereignement-muchgartbata...," and on and on, for a full two minutes the man spoke in a jumble of unknown words, then Hornstall grasped his head by the back and forehead, squeezed, and almost shouted, "Be *healed* and *saved!*—now and forever—Be born *again*!—*thank* You, Lord God!" Then he released Moser's head and pushed.

He hit the floor, as if receiving the Spirit had been so overpowering that he had lost physical control.

Hornstall immediately dropped to his side, "Let me help you, son. How do feel after receiving the Lord?"

*I didn't feel anything, you fucking moron!* "I feel great! Are we going to eat soon?"

Hornstall laughed, "Yes, after receiving the Spirit one often feels overwhelmingly hungry, so we shall return to the base." He helped Moser up, then reached and grabbed the whitehat, brushed and shook it off, then handed it over, "We'll stop at a restaurant, son. You and I need to discuss your new direction in life."

*What I need is to leave here and never see you and your crazy fucking bunch again!* "Fine, let's go!"

As they left a half dozen of those present sent farewells, "Good to meet you, Brice!"

"See you next meeting, Moser!"

*Not if I see you first, you crazy fuckers!* He turned and waved, "You bet'cha!" then ducked through the door, and walked, almost marching, to the car.

Hornstall passed him, got there first, opened the passenger-side door, then stood there with a really stupid look on his face…not entirely stupid, but…triumph…?

It crossed his mind not to get in, but to just walk the two blocks to the main street. Certainly a taxi or a bus would soon go by. Certainly buses and taxis serviced the naval centers, but what the hell? This idiot had brought him there; he sure as hell could give him a ride back!

So he got in.

Hornstall, that stupid look starched on his face, closed the door.

*Triumph…?*

# 16
## Pretty Boy

On the way to that meeting, they had passed at least two restaurants that looked to Moser like all-nighters. Hornstall, not saying a word, passed one—and, yes, it was open with a full parking lot—drove on for another three blocks, then turned onto a street with few lights.

"What the hell, Hornstall? Where are you going?"

"Just sit tight, young man."

"*Shit!* I don't want to sit tight—where the *fuck* are you going?"

"You can talk like that after being born again?"

"I was hoping I wouldn't have to tell you this, Hornstall, but you are a fucking *idiot!* Now turn this car around and let's get back to the base!"

Hornstall turned all right, onto a street with *no* lights, and finally stopped.

*I'm all through screwing around with this guy!* He reached for the door handle—

Four pops! He had never seen electric door lockers, had not even *heard* of them, and now he was locked in a car with…what? A mad man? A criminal? A fellow *sailor*?

He turned toward Hornstall.

The man remained behind the steering wheel, grinning…triumphantly, "I like boys, Brice Wesley Moser, and you are one pretty little boy."

"You are nuts! Unlock my door!"

"Where do you want it, pretty boy? In your mouth or your ass?"

That's when he noticed what Hornstall held in his hand. In his life he had *heard* the word *'queer,'* and had *some* idea what it meant, but he had also heard that there were very few of them, consequently had never in his wildest imagination ever figured he would run into one, and now he was locked in a Cadillac with one, "Open my door, Hornstall."

"What? After all I've done for you today you think I'm going to let you go without getting me off?"

"Open my fucking door, you crazy bastard!"

Hornstall's eyes turned a little wild-looking, "You get right over here, Moser, and get that cherry mouth of yours down right here!" He pointed toward his penis, quite a large one, and sticking out like an ear of Iowa corn.

The man outweighed him by at least fifty pounds, and most of it *not* blubber. He hadn't even considered the man's weight before, and that he likely wouldn't have a chance if it came to a fight, and why on earth would he ever have considered having to defend himself from this, what he didn't even understand? He could think of only one out, licked his lips, focused on the penis—now showing up brightly and very white in a rising moonlight—and began slowly moving toward it.

"That'a boy." Hornstall reached toward Moser's head and began to arch his back and hips, "Come on, be nice and sweet now."

That hand touched the back of his head and pulled, slowly, and forcefully.

Knowing the pain from getting hit in the testicles, and figuring he wouldn't have to hit too hard—but would hit hard anyway!—he reached open-handed for the penis, then changed it to a fist, drew back quickly and slammed it into Hornstall's groin, *twice*, then reached across the man and flipped the switch for the door locks.

He barely heard the four pops over Hornstall's screech, but was back across that seat in a blink, got the door open, and was out, running into the darkness.

*Thank God for the moon!* He ran on, dodging trees and bushes and swing sets, and decided he was in a city park, but not a big one. He soon reached a street, a better-lit one, and stopped and pushed himself against a tree, as he had learned how to disappear while hunting deer…and listened.

Barely a sound.

He doubted Hornstall would follow, and suspected the man knew next to nothing about moving through trees in the dark, yet, if he *was* following, as his eyes too acclimated to the moonlight darkness, his white uniform soon would stand out, probably quite brightly. But was it worth it to the idiot to even consider following him? Was he so horny for a boy? Christ, he wasn't the only one lonely for a little loving. *He* was too, but *not* for another man!

He continued listening, and finally heard a car's engine start, and about the right distance away. A second later he saw headlights. They started moving, and stayed on the street. Had the idiot thought he could have swung the car toward him and the headlights would have located him right now, but evidently the idiot *didn't* think.

Probably too sore. That double punch had to have hurt him and he *knew* he had connected right where he wanted on the soft little testicles. *Twice!* Yes, that *had* to have hurt!

He kept watching the headlights. They soon turned onto the other street, went a block, then onto the main street...but the other direction. So he wasn't going to the base. Maybe a second class petty officer didn't have to live on the base. Good! If he had started walking toward the base the idiot could have parked anywhere and maybe caught him.

A long breath finally left him. He stepped away from the tree and started toward the main street, and felt glad he was in a park, and not on a well-lit street where people lived, and where people would have wondered what on earth a sailor in uniform was doing walking down their quiet neighborhood street at night. He decided it would be a time before he left the base again, and hoped he would never have to go to the admin building again, and wondered if he should report Hornstall?

Probably not. It would be a second class petty officer's word against his, a seaman apprentice fresh out of bootcamp. So, fine. He just hoped he would never see the guy again.

Now to just focus on his upcoming weapons classes.

*I'm in the navy now!*

17
Dokken

Two days later Moser ran into and recognized the young sailor he had met near the entrance to the Admin Building, who told him where to go and wished him *'luck.'* He now was pretty sure what the guy had meant.

"So how'd ya do with ol' Hornstall?"

He stopped and let out a breath, "Well, I got away from'im…you could have told me what you meant, ya know."

"I could of but you wouldn't have believed me."

"You're probably right. The last thing I was expecting was to run into my very first queer."

"First one, huh? You were lucky." The young sailor stuck out his hand, "My name's Dokken, from Oregon, what class ya head'n' for?"

"I'm Moser, Iowa." They shook hands, "Weapons—you?"

"Weapons too. Class fourteen is startin' in a week."

"So we'll be together."

"Yep! They got ya on a duty yet?"

"Yeah, cleaning barracks."

"You're lucky. I got stuck on mess cookin,' not that it's a terrible job…I get all I want to eat for sure."

He chuckled and shook his head, "Say, what'd you mean when you said I was *'lucky'* to get away from Hornstall?"

Dokken's turn to chuckle, "Cause not everybody gets away. Word is, that idiot puts the moves on almost every new guy who arrives. One guy who *didn't* get away, got back to the barracks and cried half the night. Bleedin' too."

"Can't something be done about it? Hasn't anybody ever reported him?"

"Uh-huh, and who's gonna do it? You? You gonna tell command what happened, when ol' Hornstall can just turn the table on ya and say it was *you* who went after *him*."

He didn't answer.

"Right it'd be your word against his. The scuttlebutt is that a long time ago somebody actually *did* report him, but nothing happened, and not long after, the guy who reported him flunked out of school. You gonna tell me that a top student suddenly started failin'?"

"So Hornstall won that one."

"Damn straight he did. I don't know how he did it but he did—but just know this, Moser, there's a few queers in the navy, so ya have'ta look out for'em yourself. They probably aren't all like that asshole, Hornstall, though."

"So, what do they look like?"

This time Dokken just broke out laughing, "Boy, you really ain't been around, have ya?"

"I guess not."

"Look, there ain't no way'ta tell what they look like. Hornstall's the only one I ever met—that I know of anyway— how'd you get away from'im, anyway?"

"I pounded his nuts—*twice!*"

"No shit? Man, that's the best I've ever heard—say, the weekend's about here. I'm going over to visit the Naval Station, the biggest navy base on the west coast. I'm gonna volunteer for submarine duty, and they got a mothballed sub over there for folks'ta visit."

"'Submarine'? 'Volunteer'?"

"Yeah, man! Ya get hazardous duty pay on the boats—ya want'ta come along?"

"Yeah, ah—you ain't one, are ya?"

Dokken laughed, "What? Queer?"

"Yeah."

Dokken laughed even harder, "No! And I kicked that asshole's ass even harder than you did, and he let me out of that fancy Cadillac right now! But I made'im bring me back to the base anyway!"

"I didn't. I got away and had to walk all the way back. No taxis, and the two buses wouldn't stop."

"They don't at night, man—so! You gonna join me at the Naval Station?"

"Lookin' forward to it!"

"Great!"

# 18
## USS Charr SS328

The weekend arrived. Moser and Dokken rode the city bus to the main gate at Naval Station.

"How come they have marines at all our gates?" Moser asked.

Dokken laughed, "Ha! Saves on us, man, and, I don't know—get your identification card out."

They got through the gate and began walking toward the very open sky to the west. The open sky meant the ocean, "We'll get to the piers," Dokken said, "Then we'll have to ask somebody for directions."

"Yeah, wow." He felt amazed as he stared toward the piers and the rows of ships in both directions, "A hell of a lot of ships here."

"No shit—ah, here comes an officer. We'll salute him and then ask him where they keep the submarine."

"Can we just...*talk* to him?"

"Come on, man, officers are people too—good! He's a boat sailor!"

"How do you know?"

"He's wearing dolphins—I'll explain about them later."

They came even with the officer and both raised their hands in salute. Dokken stopped, "Lieutenant, Sir, I see you ride the subs. I'm planning to volunteer and we came down to look at the one here in mothballs."

The officer, with two silver bars on his shirt collar, stopped and dropped his salute, "That's good. Both of you?"

"I haven't decided yet, Sir," Moser said, "That's why I came along with Dokken here, just to look."

"Well, you two take a look, and remember this. The boat we have in mothballs here is from World War II, not saying there isn't plenty of those older boats still out there. In fact, most new volunteers—after sub school—do their first training and qualifying on the old boats, then many transfer to the nukes, which requires a lot more schooling." The officer pointed, "It's three docks down, just beyond that cruiser."

Both Moser and Dokken said "Thank you, Sir."

"You're welcome, and good luck to both of you—by the way, what are your ratings?"

Both answered, "Torpedoman."

"A good rate, and definitely needed. Again, good luck!" The officer waved, then walked away.

"Ya see, Moser? They're human too. Ya don't need to be scared of 'em!"

"Right. So, what about dolphins?"

"It's what ya get after you're qualified, sorta like wings for the air force, or anybody who flies planes, I guess, but in the sub navy everybody gets to wear dolphins…after they're qualified."

"I tried to look at the officer's dolphins, but didn't want to stare."

"I'll show you when we get back to the base. I've seen at least three instructors wearin'em. They're two dolphins with the front of a boat right between'em. Real neat!"

"Thanks, my friend, and now let's get over there."

****

And there it sat, quiet in the Pacific Ocean water. Black, or a real dark gray, not a sickly light gray like so many vehicles of the navy were but a rich, dark, almost-heavenly color. The sail with masts and the periscope stood tall at amidships, and that was about all Moser knew about submarines.

"See that what looks like kind of a folded wing about twenty feet back?"

"Yeah."

"That's the bow planes, there's one on each side, controls the depth, and way in back, below the fantail, underwater, is the stern planes. They control the up and down angle. And on the very end, the rudder, is controlled by the helm."

Moser imagined the sleek warship sliding like a snake through the water, far below where any enemy ships sailed.

"See up there where the front of the sail is lower than the rest?"

"Yeah."

"That's the bridge, where the officer-of-deck and the lookouts will stand when they're sailing on the surface."

For just one second he was ready to ask *'What about when they're underwater?'* but, thankfully, he came to his senses first. Of course they wouldn't be there underwater—*dumbass!*

"Can we go on board?"

"I don't see why not."

They were half way across the gangplank when a sailor in a white uniform wearing a duty belt with a holstered pistol appeared.

"Hey, man!" Dokken called, "Can we go belowdecks?"

"Yes, but wait till I get to my post." The guard then continued walking until he reached what looked like an old school desk on a pole, except it likely was aluminum. He stopped just forward of it, and waited.

"He's waiting for us to salute," Dokken said, and then saluted first the flag flying back on the fantail, then the guard, then Moser followed suit.

The guard returned both salutes, "Got to sign you in here, guys." The guard opened the desk, removed a log book and signed them in, "Be sure to let me know when you leave. The belowdecks watch will show you around. But wait for him." He pointed forward to an open hatch, then leaned over what looked like the school desk, and flipped a switch, "Belowdecks, Topside, we have two guests coming down to the forward torpedoroom. They'll wait for you there."

"Topside, Belowdecks, aye."

Dokken went first. Moser followed, and the moment his feet touched the padded deck and he saw the absolute smallness... "Holy cow! How can anybody *live* down here?" He stared at the torpedoes, three on each side, maybe more, with sleeping bunks above and below, two more right up by the overhead.

Dokken had already went farther and opened a door, "Come and get a load of the head, man."

He looked into a very tiny room with a metal toilet and tiny sink, "Wow. I don't think I could do this, Dokken."

"Sure you could, all it takes is a little belief in yourself."

"You boys seen enough of the torpedo room?"

"Yeah," Dokken answered.

"Come on this way, then." The man, dressed in dungarees with three birds on his left shoulder, stepped back, then waited, "I'm first class Engineman, Starsky. We'll just walk along and I'll explain things as we go. Any questions, just shoot. This here is the forward battery, which includes the officers' mess, Captain and Executive Officer staterooms, and junior officer sleeping quarters."

Starsky ducked and stepped into the next compartment, "This is the control room, which includes the air manifold to blow the tanks in order to surface."

"'Tanks'?" Moser asked.

"Yep, to dive we open the vents and let those tanks fill up with sea water and down we go, and to surface we need to blow'em out again." He touched one of the silver T-valves protruding from the manifold, "Bow Buoyancy, Main Ballast Tanks, and Fuel Ballast Tanks, and the most important, maybe, Safety. If we really have to get up in a hurry, blowin' Safety'll get us there." He pointed toward the starboard corner but would actually be the port side of the sub, "Over there, to port in the corner, are more controls for tanks. There we pump sea water back and forth from one tank to another to control our trim."

Moser felt proud that he had gotten port and starboard correct, but then felt confusion too. He glanced at Dokken. His new buddy also looked confused.

Starsky must have noticed, as he added, "...our *balance*," then went on and pointed to large steering-wheel-like wheels about three feet in diameter, "That's where we operate the bow and stern planes."

"Remember?" Dokken asked, "I told you about it while we were on the pier."

"Right."

"Moving on," Starsky said, starting toward the next compartment.

"What about the Conning Tower?"

"Yeah!" Starsky said, returning to a ladder, "We can go up there too." He went up.

The boys followed.

Starsky first pointed out the helm.

Dokken nodded to Moser, grinned, and pointed.

Starsky then moved to a small table with a built-in map under plexiglass, "This is where the navigator and quartermasters keep track of where we are when at sea, with black, erasable markers."

"And signalmen?" Dokken asked.

"Yes, I suppose signalmen could be up here, but I don't know if there's a billet for signalmen on the older boats, nukes, maybe, but they're mainly for the surface craft."

"Did you go to sea on this boat, Starsky?" Moser asked.

For a second or two an expression of nostalgia seemed to come over Starsky's face, "Yes, I spent three years on this old girl, kept her engines working, and requested this job."

"Which you do well," Moser added.

Starsky smiled, "Thank you." The man then started down the ladder.

Dokken put his hands on a really shiny tube about eight or ten inches in diameter, "Periscope?"

"Yep!" Starsky continued down the ladder, was followed by the boys, and stopped briefly before ducking and stepping into the next compartment, "This little puka here is for the yeoman, and the yeoman we had for the last year was one big muther, but he had no trouble squeezing himself into that space, and that's something you'll learn, boys, even the biggest man—

during an emergency—can fly through these compartments and hatches as well as the smallest man."

*'Emergencies'?* Moser wondered what they could be, but wasn't sure he wanted to know right then, as he was still considering whether or not he would want to live in such a closed environment, where he was pretty sure two guys couldn't even meet in some places, without one of them backing up.

"This here is the galley, where the ship's cook prepares your chow—best in the navy, by the way—and there are four tables where you'll enjoy that chow, or play cards, or Acey-deucey, or whatever." Starsky moved on, described the cramped sleeping positions in the After Battery, then to the Forward Engine Room, then the After Engine Room, where he stopped and put a hand gently—with that look of nostalgia again—on a big valve wheel, "This is where I spent my time for the last three years, boys."

"Can you tell us some of the history of this sub?" Moser asked.

"During World War II she saw a lot of action…she rescued two downed aviators, escorted a badly damaged Dutch submarine to Australia, and the biggest action was a spread of torpedoes into the Japanese cruiser, Isuzu, which sunk it, and later she sunk a coastal freighter by gunfire. You maybe noticed the deck guns."

Both boys quietly uttered, "Wow."

"And after all that, well, I don't know what her future holds…could be sold for scrap, or, a better death *I* think, she would be towed to sea and sunk…practice for new officers and torpedomen."

"We're both going to become torpedomen," Dokken piped up, and we're both volunteering for submarine duty."

Starsky smiled, "Good for you! Well, we have two compartments left, Maneuvering Room, where all those volts for running the batteries when we're submerged, is controlled from, and the After Torpedoroom."

They went through the last two compartments. At the ladder leading topside, Dokken turned and offered his hand, "Thanks for the tour, man."

Moser did the same, "Good luck to you, Sir."

Once topside and walking forward to the gangplank, "Hey, Dokken I never said for sure that I was volunteering for sub duty."

"You will." Dokken smiled, "And that guy appreciated hearing that."

At the gangplank, this time they saluted the guard first, and then the flying stars and stripes back on the fantail.

Walking down the pier, Moser asked, "What the heck is that acey-deucey thing he mentioned?"

"Ya got me, man, reckon we'll find out though." Dokken then brought up something not very surprising, "It's early, ya know, how about we find a bar somewhere and some friendly chicks?"

"I'm not old enough to drink."

Dokken laughed, "Oh, you are one sorry farm boy, man. You better stick with me and I'll show you all the ropes a sailor needs to know when he's on Liberty."

## 19
## Liberty

At the gate they waited only ten minutes for a city bus to come by heading downtown. Again, Moser felt fortunate to have someone a little older to follow along with. First there was Hamm, way back at Des Moines, then Cordegan in Company 321, and now Dokken in Class A Weapons School.

They climbed on and paid their fare, "Let's go clear to the back," Dokken suggested.

They sat, "Now we can have a good view if any cuties come on, although I doubt the cuties ride the buses."

"Why not?"

"Oh, they ride the buses all right, but probably not the ones that usually overflow with brand new sailors. They're people too, Moser, and they probably like their meat a little more mature than the boys just out of bootcamp."

"Really...."

Dokken laughed, "Okay, I can tell by the look on your face that you ain't buyin' it, and there's likely plenty of babes lookin' for the cherry sailors, but those gals're older, not the kind you and me are lookin' for."

They rode in silence for about two minutes.

Dokken pointed, "Up here's our Weapons Base. Now just watch this bus fill up with fresh-faced sailors."

The bus stopped. At least twenty more sailors climbed on board.

"You're right, Dokken, they all look like…children, almost."

Dokken turned and grasped Moser's face, then turned his face toward him, "Just like you look, my man, and you look all of eighteen."

"I'm seventeen."

"Ha! I knew it, and that's why you're gonna stick with me, my man."

"Fine. I will, but how come you know so much, and about the sub too?"

"For one reason I'm twenty-one. I've been around the block a couple times, and about the sub…I *don't* know so much. I was tryin'ta impress the guy, plus I found an official-lookin' book lyin' around about submarines."

"Can I see it?"

"I went through it kind of fast and left it layin' there. Anyway, you and me are gonna soon have our hands full with our schoolin. Basic Electricity, then Basic Electronics, and then the torpedoes themselves. We'll have plenty'a time to learn about subs after we get to sub school back in…New London, Connecticut, I think."

The bus soon stopped and picked up another five sailors.

"These guys look older," Dokken offered, "They must be in from the fleet…maybe we'll watch and see where they get off…they've probably been here before, and know where to go."

"I thought *you* knew."

"Ha! I tend'ta talk kind'a big sometimes, especially around a greenhorn like yourself." He grinned, "But this is my first time off the base in San Diego too."

The bus turned onto what looked like a main downtown street and soon stopped. Most of the younger crowd got off.

They moved on another three blocks, then the older sailors got off.

"Let's go!" Dokken said.

They got off, and watched the older group head out.

"They don't look *that* old, Dokken."

They aren't. Probably about the same as me, but they've been *in* longer."

"Let's not follow them. Let's pick our own place…then we'll always have it to go to.

Expressionless, Dokken looked at him for a few seconds, then, "I like your idea, man." He shook his head, "What say we go a block further and *then* turn and go our own way?"

"Let's do it."

They started out, and for the first time since he had said *'I do,'* to joining the navy, he felt like he was stepping finally into newness and adventure, and he wasn't uncomfortable— well, maybe a little, as Dokken had mentioned alcohol, but if he just drank *some*, in moderation….

Soon, up ahead a blinking neon sign said *'The Brightlight.'*

Dokken nodded, "There's our new home away from home, my friend."

\*\*\*\*

Dokken pushed through the door first and walked right in.

Moser followed but stopped short, waiting for his eyes to adjust to the dimness of a bar. It would be his first time—*ever*—in a bar.

Dokken glanced back at him, "C'mon, man," then continued on to a booth.

As his eyes adjusted, as he followed Dokken, he noticed a number of women just sitting, together, and beyond them he noticed couples were dancing...he *loved* to dance, and he made eye contact with a red-headed woman who so reminded him of someone that his mind went flying back to his sophomore year when he had finally asked his favorite girl of all time, Leah, to dance. His attention was so taken that he walked into a chair pulled out from a table—almost as if it was put there just to trip him and embarrass him...but he didn't fall down, he got his balance and again made eye contact with the red-headed girl...or, woman...he wasn't sure. She looked young and she maybe looked...older.

She smiled.

He smiled back, then hurried to join Dokken already sitting.

Their waitress arrived, a well-endowed blond, "What can I get you cute sailor-boys?"

"Ya got Olympia, gorgeous?"

"You bet, how about your little brother there?"

"Yeah," he piped up, "Olympia for me too."

The waitress smiled and left.

"Wow, she didn't even ask how old I was."

"She knew, but she also could see this was your first."

"Hey, Dokken...." He nodded toward the women sitting on the other side of the room, "Why do you spose those girls are just sittin' there like that?"

"I dunno. Why don't you ask our waitress when she comes back?"

That quick she was back.

"Ah, miss, I'd like to ask you a question."

"Go ahead." She set the two bottles down, then leaned in with her well-endowment, "And no, I ain't takin' such a young boy as you, home with me."

He grinned and nodded, "I meant those ladies sittin' over there."

She straightened up, "You want'ta dance?"

"Yes, very much."

"Which one?"

"The one with the red hair."

"Oh no." The waitress wrinkled her nose, "She's old. You should pick one of the cute young ones."

"Well, I like her with the red hair."

"Okay, sonny, that'll be twenty bucks."

"What? That's almost all I got."

The waitress put her right fist on her hip, "Take it or leave it."

"I'll take it." He pulled out his wallet, removed the twenty, looked at it, then handed it over.

The waitress snatched it, "So wait for the right song—or go ask for it—and then go over and ask her."

"What? You mean she can say 'no?'"

"She sure can, if she doesn't *like* you."

He sent his eyes back to the redhead, and she sent hers right back, "I'll take the chance."

"Have a ball." The waitress left.

"Twenty bucks?" Dokken wrinkled his nose too, "For one dance with that skag?"

He couldn't believe his new buddy would say such a thing, "Come on, man, I *like* her."

Dokken looked again, "She's old, though."

"Not *that* old." Right then the song changed, "*Sleepwalk!* That's my song, man." He got out of the booth in a blink, looked toward his girl and she was looking back. He was halfway there when another guy came out of nowhere, blocked him, grabbed her hand and pulled her to her feet.

He didn't stop and tapped the guy on the shoulder, "This is *my* dance, buddy."

The guy turned, and he didn't even see the fist coming. He only saw stars, then everything went black.

\*\*\*\*

Moser didn't wake up until the taxi hit a pothole and jarred him.

"Whooo—*boy!*" Dokken said, "That guy dropped you like a sack'a spuds from Idaho!"

"What happened?" He felt his forehead, which now sported a black-and-blue, good-sized bump.

"You got to learn when your enterin' harm's way, my boy—you should'of *expected* that guy to slug you!"

"I *'should'* have?"

"Yes, anybody could'of seen that was *his* woman, just by the way he beat ya to'er."

"But why the eye-contact?"

"What? She gave you eye contact? That's why you got so goofy and paid twenty bucks to dance with'er? Course, we didn't know her man was even there."

"I want to go back."

"No, you ain't goin' back. At least not until that bump on yer forehead is gone."

"You're not my boss!"

"Yer right, I ain't, but us sailers've got to take care of each other. You go back there and I wouldn't guarantee anything."

"You're probably right about my forehead though, but the moment it's gone…."

Ten days passed. Starting the night they got back to base, Dokken had helped and put ice on the bump, three times a day after that, and the bump finally went away.

One day he looked in the mirror, "It's gone. I'm going back."

He approached Dokken, "All right, man, I'll go with ya, but if she ain't there, then that'll be the end of it."

"Good enough."

They arrived back at the same bar. Dokken went to a stool by the counter to wait while Moser walked back to where the girls sat waiting for dance partners. The redhead was there and immediately made that delicious eye-contact.

He glanced around for any big bruiser lurking, saw nobody—and wouldn't recognize him anyway, as he saw no face that night, just that huge fist coming. For some strange reason his favorite song began, *again*, just as he approached. He stopped in front of the redhead and held out his hand, "May I have this dance, Ma'am?"

She smiled in a way that showed true appreciation, then stood, "You may."

Hand in hand they walked to the middle of the dance floor, then stopped and faced each other. He lifted his left hand and slipped his right hand and arm around her waist. She put her right hand in his and her left high on his back. They moved nearly together as the gentle sounds of *Sleepwalk* took them slowly into each other, until not much space remained between them.

The song of course had to end. They stayed together until some instinctive signal pushed them barely apart…but their eyes remained connected, then closed as they kissed.

It was his first kiss.

His head spinning, his main goal right then was to remain standing.

"Dance with me again, please?"

"I will, but you might have to help hold me up."

She smiled, "I can do that." She leaned back a bit and gave a signal to the DJ.

Again the rapturous strains of *Sleepwalk* filled their beings. That mi-nute space between them during the first play of the song disappeared as the two filled themselves with each other. A movement from one or the other, honestly perceived or not, started the movement of their lips to again connect, and stay connected for the duration of the song.

At the end, "What is your name?" she asked.

"Brice."

"Brice, please don't come again. That man who hit you was my husband. He is viciously jealous, and is not supposed to even come here. If he sees you again…."

"What is *your* name?"

"Here I go by Miss Crawford."

"Thank you for this dance, Miss Crawford, I will never forget you."

She leaned in and kissed his cheek, "Thank you, Brice. Goodbye, and God go with you."

He escorted her back to her seat, then, still kind of dizzy or *something*, he held onto her and waved to Dokken, who came immediately and took charge of this young man drunk from his first true love experience. Miss Crawford remained standing as they left, their eyes never leaving the other's until the front entrance door closed.

Riding back to the base, his body was on the bus's seat, but his head was in the clouds. His friend, Dokken, must have somehow understood because he didn't try to disturb. Once they got off the bus, though, he was ready, "I'm in love, man."

Dokken laughed, "You poor dumb fucker. She's married, she's ten years older, and the waitress—you remember her?"

"Yes."

"She recommended we never come back, cause that gal's husband is one mean muther—she said the guy takes drugs, and might even possess a gun!"

"Oh, I know, man, but I'm just enjoying the moment. I've never been kissed before—and what do you mean by *'drugs?'*"

"I dunno, marijuana, probably...heroin...I hear some even take prescription meds."

"What? What the hell for? Cause they're sick?"

"To get high, man, *Jesus! * Where the fuck—*no! 'Never been kissed?'  How* the fuck did you even ever grow up?"

"My mother has kissed me, and my aunts, I suppose b ...but I've never been kissed on the lips."

"You never had a girlfriend in school?"

"No. I liked a couple girls—one especially, but she's hung up on some rich guy...she danced with me a couple times though."

"So you still have your cherry, huh?"

"Yes, I suppose."

"Well...." Dokken slapped his shoulder, "We can't have a sailor hang onto his cherry."

"So, my new friend, do *you* take any of those drugs you mentioned?"

"Fuck, no! I don't even when I'm sick!"

## 20
## Morgan Rhodes

During the days and then weeks following, Moser not only buried himself in his studies, but had made the decision to volunteer for submarine service and put in his request. Basic Electricity was fairly easy, but Basic Electronics took a little more of his time for studying. He didn't forget the red-headed Miss Crawford, though, but quite often, Leah, from high school would slip in and take her place. Maybe when he went home on leave he would drop in on Leah. Couldn't hurt. He'd wear his uniform; maybe that'd impress her.

But that leave was still weeks away, and his eighteenth birthday was coming up, time for him to spread some of those wild oats his dad and uncles had mentioned, but Miss Crawford was out-of-the-question, although he felt sure she would be a good and gentle lover—

And then he remembered. He bookmarked his text on Basic Electronics, pulled out his wallet and began to dig. Buried in the junk one sometimes stores in a wallet a dog-eared business card finally appeared with the PanAm logo.

*Morgan Rhodes.* He remembered admiring the girl's name as much as her body. Wow. He read the phone number, then got up and hurried to the payphone by the candy machines, dropped in a dime and dialed…

"Pan American Airlines…how can I help you?"

*What?* "Oh, may I speak to Morgan Rhodes?"

"Sir, is that someone who works for the airlines?"

"Yes, a stewardess."

"I'm sorry, but we don't have any connection to the stewardesses."

"Oh, well, thank you." He hung up and, totally downcast, returned to his room shared with six other guys…*why would she have Pan Am's official number on her card? Was she just screwin' with me?* He wished he had Dokken there to ask, but Dokken lived in one of the other barracks, plus he doubted Dokken would have answers for everything!

He sat down and re-opened his workbook, and returned the business card to his wallet, wondering why he was bothering to even keep it. The instant the card disappeared his mind showed him a picture. Inadvertently he had turned it over, and there was some writing. Then he remembered! She had written on the back! He pulled the card back out!

There was her phone number in living color! He slammed his workbook closed again and hurried back to the phone—*no dime!* He hurried back to his room and scoured his locker, and found a nickel and four pennies…!

He jerked around looking at his bunkmates, three other aspiring Torpedoman's mates and two aspiring Sonarmen, "So who's got a dime for a nickel and four pennies? I need to make a phone call, guys!"

One of the sonar guys finally answered, "A girl?"

"Yes!"

"Local?"

"Yes!"

"Do I get to meet her?"

"No."

The sonar guy laughed, "I don't blame you—here's a dime, and keep your change."

"Thanks!" He grabbed the dime, hurried to the payphone and dialed…just one ring and a recording: "I'm sorry, but that number has been disconnected."

His heart dropped right down to his feet.

He hung up and returned to his room.

The sonar guy piped up, "Well?"

"Number disconnected." He plopped on his bed.

"Sorry, guy. Girls are like that."

"Thanks—ah!" He rose and walked over, "Here's your dime back."

The sonar guy accepted the dime, "I'm truly sorry, man. Girls jerk guys around all the time."

"Yeah." He returned to his bunk and again plopped. No more studying would happen that night. Instead, now he had pictures of three different women in his head, Miss Crawford, the gorgeous and exotic Morgan Rhodes, and of course, his girl back home—*Ha!*—Leah, who probably not only didn't *miss* him but probably still didn't even know he was in the navy—probably didn't even know he was alive!.

Then his mind clicked. Morgan had written her address on the card too! He jerked it out and looked. Sure enough!

Twenty minutes later he had showered and put on his dress blues, and headed out—

"Where ya goin'?" shouted the sonar guy.

"I'm going to her address."

"Not a good move, guy," the sonar guy said, "A disconnected number could mean a couple things."

"Like what?"

"Like she moved, or maybe she had to change her number cause some guy was harassing her…maybe it was *you*."

"Me? No, I met her only once, on my flight out here."

"A stewardess?"

"Yeah."

"Wow, well it still ain't a good thing'ta just show up, but…ya gotta do what ya gotta do, guy."

"And I need to see her." He waved, "See ya later."

Payday had just passed. He had plenty of money for a taxi, and the taxi found her apartment complex with no problem, and dropped him off.

And there he stood, staring at the richest-looking building he had ever seen. On the ground floor, beyond floor-to-ceiling windows, an inside-swimming pool.

His heart gave an extra loud beat, and then kind of hurt. He felt his chest…yes, he was still alive. Shit, what was he *doing* there? *She probably won't even remember me…if she's even home*…but he couldn't forget that delicious smile she had given him as she was leaning toward him past Hamm to be sure she—and her lovely endowment—got as close to him as possible.

He let out a held breath, and felt surprised; he had actually been holding his breath. Why? She was just another human being…though a gorgeous, lip-smackin' human being.

He sucked in an extra large breath, held it, then let it out, and started toward the door.

The mail boxes…*Morgan Rhodes*…it was right there. 211.

He touched the door knob. Probably locked. It wasn't. He turned it and climbed one set of stairs. A sign pointed him to his right. He took another breath and went, and soon stopped at…

Apartment 211.

Another breath left him. His fists doubled. Without thinking any further he knocked.

No answer.

He knocked again…and heard stirring.

A peephole. He hadn't noticed before. *She'll see me and then not open the door.*

She opened the door. There she stood…in a robe. Had he woke her?

Her hand went to her mouth as her eyes registered recognition. She stepped out and closed the door to a crack, "The boy heading to navy bootcamp."

She smiled, the most wondrous smile he had ever seen, he was certain, "Yeah, I made it."

"I see you did. You look very brave in your uniform." Her smile kept up. Then she asked the last question he was hoping to hear; in fact, he had no idea *what* he had expected to hear.

"What can I *do* for you?"

Her lovely face continued to smile. He saw layers of sheer material under the robe that somehow—he thought so, anyway—had opened a bit. He saw the jutting prominence of her breasts. He saw just the very slightest of stomach, and imagined her body lying, waiting for him—

"Brice, I wish you had called first."

"I—did, and got a recording…."

"That should have told you I wasn't here."

"But—"

"Brice, I'm sorry. I was wrong to give you my card, but at the time…well, I'm just sorry. I encouraged you and I'm sorry. I'm with my boyfriend."

"Your…?"

"Yes, Brice. He's waiting for me in my bed."

He let go a breath. His shoulders slumped forward.

"Brice, you are a good man." She leaned forward and kissed his cheek, "But there's nothing here for you." She stepped back into her apartment and looked down as she closed the door.

And closed the door on his heart.

The weeks at Weapons School went by. His birthday came. He got a card from his parents, and another from little Geri, where she wrote in her third-grade penmanship, *"Hurry home, Brice, 1 miss you a lot, and 1 love you a lot too—love, Geri"* His heart brimmed over. Well, if he had no other woman ever in his life he knew he would always have his little sister. The navy had a gift for him too. Guard duty, the very night of his birthday, with an M1 rifle and two loaded clips of live ammunition.

Midnight to four in the morning he had to walk back and forth along the ocean front. He would never forget it. Never forget the chill, the loneliness, the spooky sound of heartbroken foghorns talking to each other…forlorn ships passing each other in the night. After two hours a third class petty officer armed with a handgun came around and relieved him so he could step inside and warm up and smoke a cigarette. And he smoked that cigarette like there was no tomorrow, sucking deeply and nearly constantly, and when he went back out he was so sick and dizzy from it he almost fell down.

At graduation there was no marching in review, no parade in full dress uniform…in fact, at the school they had never marched at all, did no drills with pieces, and only one personnel inspection happened, which he passed.

No problem, but some of the glory for the navy had left his mind.

Then he got his orders, and Dokken got his.

At the gate near the Admin Building where they had first met, Dokken waited for a bus to take him to the train depot for the straight up trip to his parents' home in Oregon, and Moser waited for a bus to take him to the airport for his very first military leave.

The time passed mostly in silence, as both boys knew they were again leaving a buddy. As Dokken's bus approached he stuck out his hand, "Well, Moser, my fine farmer-boy friend, it's been real, see you later at Sub School."

"Not me." He handed over his orders.

Dokken read, "GMU10—what the hell?"

"Yeah." He took the orders back, "Some fuckin' missile base there at Pearl Harbor. I don't know what the fuck happened to sub school!"

"Sorry, man." The train depot bus stopped. Dokken threw his seabag to his shoulder, "Well, good luck anyway. Maybe we'll meet again." He stepped into the bus and the door closed.

And he had lost a third good navy friend. How many more he wondered. Now he had thirty days leave at home on the farm, and wasn't sure if he even wanted to go. Right then he wasn't sure of anything.

## 21
## First Leave

"Fasten your seatbelts, please," came the captain's voice over the intercom. Moments later, the plane banked to Moser's right. He saw Des Moines in the near distance; he even saw the airport's runway. The city looked small compared to where he had just come from. At least there was no whiteout fog like when they had landed at San Diego…how long ago? Six months? Yes, he had been away from home for six months. It didn't seem that long.

The plane leveled out. The flaps went down. He could feel the plane descending and slowing down…the city appeared, just buildings and houses and trees…they hit the runway. He listened for the squeal of the tires as he had heard on television shows, but heard nothing—then he was thrown slightly forward against his seatbelt as the plane reversed its engines and *really* began slowing down. He wasn't sure the plane reversed its engines, but doubted it was tire brakes.

Was momentum moving them as the plane continued to slow, and turned, and finally stopped? Certainly they didn't use jet engines on the ground…maybe the wheels had little motors and remote steering wheels? He laughed. His thoughts had gone completely corny. He threw off his seatbelt, stood, opened the overhead compartment, helped an older lady get her bag down, then returned for his, grabbed the small overnight bag, pulled it down, and joined the line of passengers departing.

His mom would be inside that depot, waiting to kiss and hug him, and his dad probably, but Leah would *not* be there. Did she even know he had been gone six months to the navy? Would she even care? Was he really, seriously, planning to drop in on her? Would he find her in bed with her boyfriend, too, as he had found the gorgeous *Morgan Rhodes*? No. Leah, still a junior in highschool, wouldn't do that. He *hoped* she wouldn't, but if that rich guy she thought she was in love with asked her to, maybe she would, and that guy was two years out of highschool, so would be as ready for sex as he himself was.

He reached the airport terminal, and sure enough, there stood his mother at the head of the line, her face shining in pride, her hands and arms desperate to hug her son. She stayed back, though, until he had gotten to her, and then it was all over. She threw her arms around him and held him for a full minute. When she pulled back she was still smiling but toned down a bit, "You started smoking, didn't you, Son?"

He pulled her back into the hug and patted her back, "Yes, mother, but I don't smoke very much."

That seemed to satisfy her, somewhat, anyway. He then shook hands with his dad.

"Good to see you, Son."

Nostalgia and homesickness swept over him right then. He hoped it wouldn't last, and wouldn't affect him too much.

Then the third person waiting to welcome him home came from behind his dad, his little eight-year-old sister, Geri, who ran right into his arms, "Hi, Brice!"

He swept her up and held her tight, "How's my little sweetheart?"

Geri squeezed his head and neck for several seconds, then leaned back, "Leah's engaged."

Of course. His little sister that adored him would know. He hadn't ever, *exactly*, told her how he felt about Leah, but nevertheless, everybody in the Moser household—*somehow*—knew *exactly* how he felt about Leah, their neighbor's daughter who lived two miles away and also on a farm.

Continuing to hold Geri, he glanced at his mother.

"It's true, Son. She's going to finish school though…first."

"That's good," was all he could think of to say, but his thoughts went right into overdrive. Did that asshole get her pregnant? And if he did, would he follow through and actually marry Leah? Would he be good to her? Would he love her like Brice Wesley Moser would? No! He wouldn't! The guy wasn't capable of such love…*I'm going to go see her*, "I'm going to go see her. Can I borrow the car after we get home, Dad?"

"Of course, Son, but we wish Geri could have held off telling you."

"I'm sorry," Geri said.

"It's okay, Sweetie!" He gave her another strong hug, then set her down, then pulled her into still another hug. He could never get enough of his little sister, "I'm glad you told me."

"Well, let's get out to the car," his dad said.

Dad led the way. He walked between his mother and little sister, and kept his arms around them both, his mother's waist, little Geri's shoulders.

On the way to the farm nobody talked. He was glad, and sat in the back seat with his arm around his little sister, and she had both her arms around his waist. That's how they had always been with each other, from the day his parents brought the charming little bundle of baby girl home. He remembered standing sometimes for many minutes at a time, just looking into the bassinet at his brand new little sister.

Nothing had changed between them, and nothing ever would.

They arrived home, just forty minutes south of Des Moines.

He got out of the car, his little sister right behind him, "Are you going to ask Leah to marry you instead of that other guy, Brice?"

He swept her up again, "No, Sweetie, I couldn't do that."

"Why not? If you love her...you do, don't you?" Her face showed the concern of an adult.

"Geri, I can't." He held her even closer, "I'm in the navy now. It wouldn't be fair to her, cause I'd be gone all the time." He felt her sob and leaned her away. Yes, tears were flowing. He pulled her close again, "But I do have to go see her, Sweetheart."

He set her down, but the tears weren't past.

"Geri has made friends with Leah, Brice," his mother said, "I didn't know it was happening...but I wouldn't have stopped her either. If she wants to be friends with Leah, well, someday Leah might just need a good friend like your little sister."

"Thanks for telling me, Mother." He leaned down and hugged Geri again, and kissed her tears on both cheeks, "I'll be back soon, Sweetie, and then you and I will do something together."

"Like *what*?"

He thought she had sounded a bit sarcastic, maybe payback for not doing better with Leah, who, evidently, she had wanted for a sister-in-law, "That board game you like, Chutes and Ladders...okay?"

"Okay." Geri stepped back and went to his mother, but didn't stop looking at him as he got into the driver's seat and left the yard.

*Boy, I guess I really didn't know how little Geri felt.*

## 22
## Leah

At Leah's driveway he stopped and shut off the lights. Dusk seemed to have fallen quite quickly. He was glad though, to have a couple more minutes to gather his thoughts, not that even an hour or two would make a difference—hell, his whole life wouldn't make a difference!

He clicked the lights back on, went a little farther, and turned into the yard.

Somebody—Leah's mother he thought—appeared in the window, then a light on the porch by the door came on. He stepped out, and Leah's mother appeared, "Hi, Brice! We heard you were coming home! Come on in!"

Wow, he hadn't expected such a good greeting. He didn't know *what* he had expected. The story of his life, just plod along and sometimes things come out right.

Not this time.

He got to the door.

"Come in, Brice, I told Leah you were here! She'll be glad to see you!"

Wow, he hoped Leah would have just half the enthusiasm of her mother.

"Sit down right there, Brice." She pointed to the kitchen table, then went into the other room and called, "Leah! Brice Moser is here to see you, and just wait till you see how handsome he is in his uniform!"

The sound of another voice seemed to answer, but, no, not with even a quarter of her mother's enthusiasm. *I shouldn't have came—*

"Hi, Brice."

And there she stood, the girl of his dreams. She smiled. Her green eyes reached out and touched him. He stood, "Hi, Leah. How are you?"

"I'm fine, and...I guess you've heard." She looked down, then up again.

"Yeah—I'm glad you'll finish school though." Then his thoughts just left him, "Leah, I...."

She kept her smile going, "Brice, even though November, it's so nice out...shall we go sit in the swing set?"

*"Yes!"* His quick answer appeared to startle her—hell! It startled *him* too!

They went out, and walked into mostly darkness away from the porch light.

"I think you look nice in your uniform, Brice."

"Thanks, Leah, you look really nice too."

They reached the swing. He sat down, then Leah sat down also, and fairly close to him.

"Will you be gone a long time?"

"At least four, I...enlisted for four years."

"That's a long time."

"I know...Leah...."

"Yes...?" The most charming and gentle face turned and her eyes looked right into his eyes.

"I...will always love you, Leah." There, he had finally said it, finally told her how he felt.

She looked away, and looked sad, "I've always known, Brice, but I've been with..." And she said the name. He heard it but locked it out, then picked up what she finished saying,

"…for so long, well, I guess I've always known I would marry him…some day."

*But at least now she knows how I feel too.*

They then sat in silence for at least ten minutes. Neither moved, but somehow their bodies began touching, creating warmth where there had never been before been warmth. He wanted to turn toward her and wrap his arms around her, but knew it would not be the right thing to do, so…"I…guess I should go…."

"All right…will I see you again?"

"Yes…but I don't know when. I have to soon report to my first duty station. It…might be years." That was something of a lie. He had thirty days of leave, but he doubted he could stay home very long—not after *this* conversation. Leah almost sounded like she felt the same as him, but that seemed so impossible, but the warmth coming from her body…but she had never given him even the tiniest clue.

"I better go."

"Brice, please kiss me."

His heart almost stopped; his breathing absolutely did. He turned more toward her, and moved his arms to surround her but barely touch her, yet he certainly *was* touching her. The reality of her nearness began sending gentle shock waves throughout his body, and she not only allowing it but even seeming to *want* it. He held her just close enough to balance and support himself, then he leaned forward, and she did too, and their lips touched…and time stopped. Her lips were the softest most sensitive things he could imagine. He turned his head ever so slightly and she did the same, the better for them to merge their tasting, and sensing of each other…and the locking in of the memory. Then a little gust of wind from limbo moved the swing and they parted.

He felt his head nearly pounding, his short breaths giving him not nearly enough oxygen, or so it seemed. Leah, too, was not her normally totally sensible and steady self, "Thank you, Brice. When you come home again, please, come to see me."

"I will."

They stood, then walked back to the porch, to the door. Her hand on the door knob Leah turned to him, leaned, and kissed his cheek, "Goodbye, Brice."

Then she entered the house. Gone.

*Goodbye, Leah.*

## 23
## Dear Little Geri

For the next days Moser's mind and heart were filled with Leah. What had happened between them that night should have happened long, long, ago, but didn't. Leah was strong on his mind, but he also spent hours on end with his little sister who loved him unconditionally. They played checkers and Chinese checkers, other board games, he taught her to play Cribbage—which he had just recently learned himself—and got her promise to teach their mother and dad, and they spent more hours walking along the coolies and the shelterbelts, or just on the field roads.

He also helped his dad haul in the third cutting of alfalfa, and help repair all the fencing for the milk cows, but he was *so* getting ready to get back to the navy.

Finally, after just ten days, he could wait no longer. He took little Geri in to their nearby town of Ridge, to the Dairy Queen, as he knew she loved their chocolate malts. They both had one, and shared a bag of M&Ms, which he showed her about dumping them in with the malt, which just made her squeal with joy eating the frozen M&Ms!

When they arrived back to the farm they went out to the yard's main shade tree, a huge spreading American elm. Once they got comfortable and had discussed their day, "I'm gonna have to go back soon, Sweetie."

Geri had worn a huge smile ever since he'd been home, every day, every hour, every minute, but it disappeared instantly and she turned away, "When?"

"Soon."

"*How* soon?" The question came out with a sob, then another, then she ran for the house and disappeared inside.

About to cry himself, he followed.

"Brice," his mother said as he went inside, "Geri just ran upstairs, crying her eyes out."

"I know. I just told her I have to leave soon."

"How soon? You just got home." His mother looked about to cry too.

"I know, mom, but...."

"You've always called me *'Mother.'*"

"I know *that*, too. I'm sorry, Mother."

"It's all right. You're older now."

He let out a breath, "I've already checked. I can get a flight out tonight."

His mother's hand flew to her mouth, but she didn't say anything.

"Dad can take me in, and you and Geri can stay home. I'd rather say goodbye to the two of you here, then there."

His mother's hand dropped and she took her son into her arms, "Please take care of yourself, Son."

"I will."

During the next hour he took a shower, shaved, dressed in his uniform, packed his seabag and overnight case, attached his orders to the overnight, and took everything out to the car. He had already spoken to his dad the day before. Finally ready he went up to his little sister, and knocked on her door.

No answer.

"Geri…I know you're in there. Can I come in?"

No answer.

He pushed the door open. She lay on the bed, her back to the door.

He walked to the side of the bed where she lay, sat down, then gathered her up and into his arms. She came to life then and wrapped her arms tightly around his neck. They sat that way for at least five minutes, finally, "I love you, Brice."

He felt her gasp, then more sobbing, "I love you too, Geri, I will *always* love you." He leaned back from her, "Go visit Leah sometimes, will you?"

"I will."

"And take care of Mother and Daddy, will you?"

She smiled, then sobbed again and took a big shaky breath, "I will."

He held her for another minute, then lay her back down and kissed her forehead, "Just Dad is going to take me in."

He had half expected an argument but none came. He walked to the door, turned, waved, and she waved back, then she rolled over again and covered her face.

He hurried down the stairs, gave his mother another hug, and out the door. His dad, understanding his son's need to leave, waited in the car.

At the terminal he plopped his seabag and overnight down outside the door, "You don't have to wait, Dad. It'll be easier for me just waiting alone, and it's not long."

"All right, Son." His dad offered his hand.

Suddenly he felt more love for this man, his father, then he had ever known existed, or knew even *could* exist. He took the hand, squeezed it, but then took his father into a hug, the very first time he had hugged his dad, and his dad hugged him back.

Then they parted.

"Take care, Son, and you write to your mother and Geri."

"I will."

They parted. He entered the terminal, checked on his ticket, then sat down to wait. He was leaving his parents and little sister back on the farm. He had lost Miss Crawford, *Morgan Rhodes*, the gorgeous stewardess, and now he was walking away from Leah, the only girl he had ever loved when he maybe could have told her—and won her—long ago. He also had lost three navy buddies, Terry Hamm from his first bootcamp company, Cordegan from his second company, and Dokken from Class A School, he had been denied submarine service and was headed for dry shore duty at Pearl Harbor, Hawaii.

What more could go wrong he wondered, and what the hell else lay ahead?

But what the hell? He might as well get *to* it.

*I'm in the navy now.*

Part 2 In Mission

## 24
## To Pearl Harbor, Hawaii

Flying over the Pacific Ocean was a little different from flying over land. All Moser could see was endless blue water, and occasionally a puffy white cloud far below the plane. Flying above the clouds seemed kind of weird too. Appeared they were flying toward the sun too—yes, they were flying west, where the sun sets. And it did appear to be getting darker, but not very fast. He wondered, if they kept flying west, would the sun ever set?

Not much to look at, so he spent his time reading some boring inflight magazines, partook of the lunch, appreciated looking at the stewardesses but made no attempt at communication.

In the love-category he was pretty much fresh out. Leah had a warm and solid place in his heart and always would, but he knew it would be pointless to spend too much time and effort beating himself up over not moving on her years ago, when very likely she would have been available. It just made no good sense to dream about what *might* have been. He had to focus on the future, and what the heck his new command would be like. He had figured out that they worked on missiles, but his training was on torpedoes…not that he was an expert on torpedoes, either, but at least that's where his training was.

He pushed his seat back a bit. He then could see out the window better but there remained nothing to look at. He took a deep breath and let it out—

"That almost sounded like pain, Mr. Sailor."

He sat up and looked to his left across the aisle. The blond he had noticed earlier when he first arrived at his seat, was sending a disarming smile. She had blue eyes, bright and sharp, like they were looking right *into* him. He had seen her when he first arrived at his seat. She had smiled earlier too—which brightened the whole plane, and temporarily charmed him. He had returned the smile—as strongly as he felt, which wasn't much—and then gave no more attention, "I'm just bored, I guess." But now he looked a bit closer. She wore some makeup, eye liner for sure, a white top and black skirt; she was small, smaller than him at least

"We have a few hours yet, you know." She kept sending that disarming smile, "Say…," she said, standing up and coming over, "Would you mind if I sat here." She pointed and then sat down without waiting for an answer.

"I…," was all the farther he got.

"So," she continued, "Why are you bored? I've always been told it was only us women who got bored."

He felt his eyebrows raise, and his mouth kind of fall open, "Just anxious to get back I guess."

"Where are you stationed?"

He just stared at her.

"I'm sorry. I really didn't mean to intrude on you—do you want me to return to my own seat?"

"No." He said it quickly, "I guess I'm just surprised."

"That I would be so forward?"

"Something like that." He finally sent a grin.

"So, you didn't tell me where you're stationed."

"Well I'm going there for the first time. It has to do with guided missiles."

"My!" She looked impressed.

"Yeah, I guess it sounds good, and important." No use bringing up submarines, what he really wanted, "So what about you?"

"I don't have a job, but I'm moving to Hawaii."

"Wow…you've just pulled up stakes and set out on an adventure?"

"'Adventure?' I suppose." Her smile toned down, slightly, "I'm a cocktail waitress. I've heard Honolulu is a big navy town, so…."

"I wouldn't know. I'm just fresh out of bootcamp and school."

"So we can discover the island together, then…."

"Ah, I guess." He hadn't figured on this. Good to meet a woman, yes, but he had hoped to clear his mind of Miss Crawford, Morgan Rhodes, and—to a lesser degree—Leah.

"Or maybe you won't have time for me."

"Sorry, I just don't know. I guess if you write down your name…and where I can find you." He pulled a very small notebook out, "Here, you can write whatever you want, and when I can, I'll come find you."

She smiled, wrote something, then handed it back, "That's a girlfriend's phone number and address. I'll be there until I've got a job and can get my own place."

He looked at it, then put the notebook back into his jumper's pocket, but wondered if he really wanted to get involved with a cocktail waitress, as he was quite sure half her clients would also be after her to go out with them. So he just smiled.

A couple quiet moments went by, during which she looked at him twice and continued her smile. The third look was a bit different, a smile yet toned way down, "Do you want me to return to my own seat?"

"No." He again said it quickly. No, he didn't want this very pretty girl to leave. Yes, she might have a hundred boyfriends once she started working in a bar, but right then she was alone, and so was he. Leah's presence in his mind did not change, did not go to a lower level, and he reminded himself that she was now engaged, but also she had asked him to come see her again when he came home, but still…she was far, far, away, "No, I'd like you to stay." He sent her a somewhat sober smile, "Please." He held out his hand, "I'm Brice."

She sent the disarmer again, "Hi, Brice, I'm Leila."

The handshake opened the floodgates from both. They filled each other in fully on their lives until then. When the seatbelt light came on, and the pilot's voice informing them they would be landing shortly, both were surprised that so much time had passed.

Leila put her seatbelt on, then turned toward him, pointing, "There's Diamondhead."

He looked. Sure enough, then turned back.

Leila was still there, "Shall we seal our bond?"

Very unknowledgeable about the world, and girls, he felt much confusion, but then looked into those deep blue eyes looking right back into him, and suddenly felt pretty sure what she meant, and leaned forward for the kiss.

She met him halfway, and, oh wow, what a kiss! Miss Crawford had given him a *taste* of a real kiss, Morgan only kissed his cheek, and Leah's was just a gentle-but head-pounding touching, but Leila dove right in with all she had…and he did not back away from it.

The kiss continued while they were landing, right up until they stopped, when she finally pulled away, "Don't forget me, Brice."

"I won't."

While on the jetliner's ramp, Leila in front of him, he watched other travelers receiving wreathes of flowers, but hadn't really noticed what they were doing. And he knew 'wreath' wasn't the correct word, and vowed to find out. He felt the warm-cool humid air hitting his face, different from San Diego. It felt good; it felt different. Halfway down the ramp he fully realized he was no longer in Iowa, or even in the continental United States, and also no longer under the protective wing of school, or his parents either. He soon would be approaching the real thing, the real navy. But not what he wanted.

"Those are leis," Leila said, after she received hers.

At his turn he suddenly faced a very pretty and somewhat plump Polynesian girl…and he had no idea what to do.

She smiled, and held the lei with both hands about neck high. Then she tipped her head, a hardly noticeable bow. He grabbed his hat from his head, held it with both hands, and leaned toward her. She increased her smile and placed the lei over his head to settle very gently on his shoulders.

"Welcome to Hawaii," she said, and that quickly moved to the next disembarking passenger.

He felt somewhat let down. In the movies he had seen people get not only a kiss but a hug too, and for sure American sailors did, or *should*. He put his hat back on and followed Leila toward the terminal. At the last second he glanced back. And for some reason known only to God and the Polynesian girl, she looked his way at the same time. He sent a slight wave. She returned it, then turned quickly away. He hoped he would see her again, but was pretty sure he wouldn't…and right then he was with Leila.

At the front of the line of people waiting to greet the travelers was one very pretty girl waving like crazy, "There's my girlfriend," Leila said, "I didn't know if she would be able to meet me here or not. Do you want to meet her?"

"Sure." Why not? It seemed he was meeting quite a number of girls lately.

The two girls hugged for a solid minute. He just stood watching, and feeling glad Leila really did have somewhere to go. Finally she stepped back, put her hand on her girlfriend's elbow and turned them toward him, "This is my roommate, Brice, we grew up together back in Indiana and have been friends forever."

Moser and Leila's roommate—as good-looking and charming as Leila—greeted each other and shook hands. Then they picked up Leila's luggage. He told her he would pick his up later, as it wasn't in sight right then, so they headed out to the taxis.

Then it was his turn. Leila hugged him as if he, too, was a lifelong friend, then gave him another *'oh wow'* type of kiss, then released him and the two girls climbed into the taxi, and both waved wildly as they drove away.

Minutes later he had picked up his seabag, flagged a taxi, and the ride to Pearl Harbor didn't take long. At the gate a marine stood tall and straight. He showed his ID card and orders. The marine waved them on. It was November 16, 1964.

When the taxi stopped close to the piers he felt his heart skip a beat. *This is it.* He paid the taxi driver, walked till he could see them moored about a block away. How dark and silent and mysterious and *deadly* they looked…but that was *not* where he was going. His request for submarine duty had been denied, or something. He didn't know what had happened, and stood only for a couple minutes, then threw his seabag onto his shoulder, and started walking. Eventually he would find where he *really* was going.

# 25
## GMU10

The sun was still fairly high, which surprised him, as he thought it was close to setting when he was still on the plane, then it occurred to him that flying west, well, he guessed time would sort of stand still. He had finally gotten directions as to where the missile unit was, but what was about to happen he hadn't yet experienced.

The sun reached the horizon, and a bugle call began. It surprised him. He didn't recall hearing it in bootcamp or class A school either...but maybe he was always inside when it happened. Then he noticed other sailors stopping and saluting.

*My god! Taps!*

He stopped in the middle of the street, plopped his seabag to the concrete, snapped to attention and saluted, and felt honored at being there, and being a part of it.

The music stopped. He dropped his salute, hoisted his seabag back to his shoulder and moved on, hoping to soon get there.

A chain link fence soon appeared in the distance, about two blocks away.

A gate was open so he walked on in and plopped his seabag next to a door that appeared to lead to the office, pulled out his orders, opened the door, saw a yeoman facing away at a typewriter, and walked in, "Seaman Apprentice Moser, reporting for duty."

The yeoman turned around, waved, looked at some notes on his desk, "Yep, Moser. You're about a couple weeks early."

He opened his hands, "Couldn't stand being home any longer." He handed over his orders.

"Lost your girl, huh?" The yeoman shook his head, "Understood," then took the orders and looked them over, "Well, you can go over to Barracks Nine and get yourself a bunk and locker, and then report back here by 0700. We'll put you to work."

"Thanks." He headed for the door. *'Lost your girl, huh?'* That comment kind of bugged him, but, yeah, that's about exactly what happened.

"Hey! Need a ride? It's about a half mile over there, and I'm about ready to head home."

"That would be great—thanks again, man!"

He got his bunk and locker and changed into dungarees, and did a lot of thinking. He didn't like the looks of GMU10, not that it looked dangerous or anything but it was in port, on dry land. He had hoped to go to sea, and he had no idea what had happened to his request for submarine duty. Was it really denied, or some other reason? While in Class A School he had gotten every tooth in his mouth drilled and filled, just because of future sub-service and then got shipped to shore duty instead.

The next day he reported to work, met another seaman apprentice fresh from school, got challenged to a game of pool, and then spent the next two weeks playing, and did not one ounce of work, except sweep the deck and shine brasswork. Not exactly what he had expected.

Then came the morning when the yeoman came out to where they were playing pool, "Moser, the XO wants to see you upstairs."

Figuring he might be in trouble for only playing pool and doing basically no work, he hurried upstairs and knocked.

"Come in, Moser!" the executive officer called.

Feeling some unease, he entered.

For about one minute they exchanged pleasantries, then the officer behind the desk spit it right out, "I see you have requested duty on submarines, Moser." The XO glanced up.

"That's correct, Sir."

"Well, right now the USS Hagfish is in port, and they have a billet for a torpedoman. Would you be interested?"

He felt his eyes pop, "Yes, Sir!"

"All right." The XO signed a paper and handed it over, "Give that to the yeoman, he'll type up orders for you, and you should be able to get on board yet today. I believe they're getting underway right soon."

He took the paper, didn't even look at it, then stuck his hand across the desk, "Thank you, Sir!"

The Executive Officer stood up and clasped Moser's hand, "You are welcome, seaman. Good luck on the Hagfish."

He flew down the stairs, gave the yeoman the paper, and about five hours later he hesitated, again, at the Subbase piers. The dark sails of three docked submarines stood tall. He trembled; he had never been so excited. The ship to the right was it, he thought, as where the number probably should be, it was painted over. The Auxiliary Personnel Submarine Ship USS Hagfish. He knew he had came to the right place because it was supposed to be moored outboard of the USS Carbonero SS 337. That number wasn't painted over. He wondered why.

Next to the Carbonero, on the other side of the pier, lay still another submarine. He glanced at his notes. Yes, the USS Archerfish AGSS 311, an all-bachelor crew he had heard, and wondered why. He stopped, and for a moment just gazed toward the sleekness of those dark United States warships all named after fish. The Archerfish had an open sail like the Hagfish, showing many masts and other vertical tubes that he didn't yet know the names of, but didn't have topside weaponry. It appeared the Hagfish, his new duty station, had at least one large gun forward of the sail. An anticipatory feeling slipped into his stomach, then pushed through his torso and up his spine. He trembled, again, but just once, and felt himself smile.

*Yes, this is it. This is the REAL thing. The real navy.*
At last!

## 26
## USS Hagfish

Moser took a breath, a really short one, then another, and right then began to really sense his own breathing, very short breaths, and felt there suddenly wasn't a lot of air to even breathe. Having just passed the test while at GMU10, and now with three stripes on his left shoulder, he was a brand new seaman, pay-grade E-3. His one accomplishment at GMU10 was to study for, do the practical factors for, and then pass the test.

He approached the gangplank of the Carbonero, stepped up, then stepped back down, changed his seabag to his left shoulder, saluted the stern flag, then the topside watch, who saluted back, then would have kept going to the Hagfish but—

"Hold it! You got orders?"

He stopped and let his seabag hit the deck, pulled his orders from under his jumper and handed them over, then read the name over the pocket of the Carbonero topside watch: Barnet, a
fireman with three red stripes. After just one stripe for Seaman Recruit, he had gotten the second stripe just for graduating bootcamp, and now had the three stripes. He often wondered

why even one stripe in bootcamp, since everybody got it, no matter what. Probably psychology-related.

Barnett looked over the orders then handed them back and pointed, and didn't apologize, not that he probably had anything to apologize for. Probably should have told the guard right away that he was going to the Hagfish. He shoved his orders back under his jumper, grabbed his seabag and lifted it back up to his left shoulder.

He moved on. About fifty feet away he saw just one slouching sailor on the deck of the Hagfish, also dressed in whites. The sailor saw him at the same time, and straightened up. He stepped up onto the gangplank, walked halfway down, stopped, turned toward the stern and saluted the flag, then faced who he now saw was also a guard with a holstered pistol, and saluted him too. The guard returned his salute.

He dropped his salute and continued down the gangplank, a journey of about ten more feet, and stepped aboard the USS Hagfish, flipped the seabag from his shoulder and guided it down to the deck. Then he again grasped the large manila envelope under his jumper that contained his orders and handed it to the guard, and noticed the guard wore silver dolphins. He didn't have dolphins yet and knew they had to be earned, but he knew what they were, the bow and sail of a submarine with a dolphin on each side, "Moser, Torpedoman Seaman, reporting aboard, sir."

The guard, again with three red stripes making him also a fireman, glanced at the cover sheet of his orders and made an entry in a logbook, "Consider yourself checked aboard, Moser. Take your orders to the yeoman, and you'll find him just forward of the Control Room." Then the guard returned to his slouch by leaning over a metal box about the size of an elementary school desk, which was supported on a metal pipe embedded in a hole in the deck of black wooden slats about two inches wide, which he later would learn were made from teak, a wood so soaked with natural oil that it repelled all moisture, and would *not* float. The guard then pointed to the nearest hatch, the After Battery hatch, he soon would learn, "Head right down there, Moser. That leads to the mess hall."

"Thank you." He saluted.

The guard grinned, then straightened up for a second and returned the salute, then slouched again by leaning over that metal box. He thought about introducing himself more formally, but considered the man's apparent attitude and thought better of it, for right then, anyway.

"Oh, and I'd recommend leavin' your seabag topside till you find out where you'll be bunkin.' I see you're a torpedoman, so it'll likely be in one of the torpedorooms...course, they aren't torpedorooms anymore."

"Oh...?"

"Yep, the tubes are gone and the torpedorooms have been converted to berthing spaces. We're a troop transport now."

After the friendly advice he reconsidered introducing himself and stuck out his hand, "I'm Moser."

The guard straightened up again and grasped his hand, "Reinhold. Engineman."

"Thanks, Reinhold."

"One other thing," Reinhold said

"Yes?"

"We're leavin' for Westpac early the day after tomorrow, and tomorrow we got two special training sessions, just in case you have any unfinished business outside the gate."

Yes, he had some unfinished business, although he hadn't considered Leila to be his business at all until that very moment, "Oh, thanks, Reinhold."

He ended up in the after troop space, received a bunk and locker, then immediately left on liberty, suddenly feeling Leila to be very important to him, and himself maybe even important to her. Why hadn't he gone to see her before, while he was at GMU10? He would never know, but now knew he *had* to.

The taxi took him straight to her roommate's address, a house but not on the beach.

He hurried up to the door and knocked.

In a moment Leila appeared, and it wasn't the same Leila. He had seen dark circles around eyes on television programs but figured it was a lot of makeup, that people in the real world would never look like that. She had lost weight too, a lot, "Brice…hi." She gripped his arm, tightly, with a strength that surprised him, "Come in…please." And she all but dragged him in, placed her whole body tightly against him and attached herself to his mouth. It was more than a kiss, much more, but he didn't know what.

He let it—whatever it was—go on for a couple minutes, then broke away. The first thing he saw was needle marks on the insides of her arms, both of them, "Leila, what the hell are those marks on your arms?"

She took a step back and lost her balance and went down. He moved quickly to her and lifted her back to her feet, "Leila, answer me, please." Then he put his arms around her and gathered her in close. He didn't love her, but felt, right then, that she needed him, that she needed to *feel* loved.

"It's…heroin." She reached her arms around him again and all but merged with him, "I need more, Brice, please." The words then came tumbling out, "I haven't been able to find anymore, and I've ran out of money."

"Sweetheart, I'm just a farmer boy from Iowa, and I don't hardly even know what heroin is."

"I *need* it!" She all but screamed, and started struggling, "*Please!*"

He held her tighter, "Where's your roommate?"

"I don't know!"

"You mean she just left you?"

"*No!* I don't know, Brice—fuck her! Can't *you* help me?"

"No, Leila, I can't help you, and in one more day I'm going to sea."

"What? What about…your missiles?"

"Leila, where does your roommate work?"

"I don't know…leave me alone, Brice." Her strength seemed to leave her. Her eyes rolled and she began settling to the floor.

He managed to pick her up and carried her to what looked like a bedroom, and had to dodge a rug covered with vomit. He sighed, "Leila, what have you done to yourself?" He laid her on the bed and covered her, then began looking for the identification of her roommate, and maybe discover where she worked. He didn't even remember her name.

While searching, he heard the door, and hurried to it, and saw, "Roommate, thank God."

The girl didn't smile, "I remember you."

"Good, I hope you can tell me what the hell has happened to Leila."

"Right, and maybe you can tell me where the hell *you* have been? Leila looked for you every day and every day—and finally she just started…taking…."

"I'm sorry. We had only known each other for a few hours…I guess I didn't think—I don't know what I thought. Anyway, Leila's roommate, are you going to take care of her?"

"What about *you* taking care of her?"

"I'm going to sea day after tomorrow. My orders got changed. I just came here to tell her."

"Oh."

"So, will you take care of her? I don't know when I'll be back."

"I'll try."

"Thank you." He went back to Leila's room. She lay still. He went to her, leaned over, and kissed her forehead, then lay the top of his hand against her cheek, then started away.

The roommate was in the doorway, "When she wakes I'll tell her how you treated her."

He passed her in the doorway, "Brice…."

He stopped, "Yes?"

"Do you love her?"

He felt a breath leave him, and his shoulders drop, "Tell her, when I get back, I'll come see her."

"But, do you *love* her?"

"No." He started toward the door, then stopped and looked back, "Please take care of her."

He stepped through the front door and closed it, and felt his heart give a loud bang. Of the four women he had gotten to know in the last several months, Leila was the most likely to have helped him defeat his cherry. Was that why he had come to see her? He supposed it was; he supposed one thing would have led to another and that's what would have happened.

He would have *used* that young woman even though he didn't love her.

And for that unstoppable bastard-thought he hated himself.

He stopped again, returned, opened the door and walked right in to where Leila's roommate still stood in the doorway, "Let's take her to the hospital." He walked past her, straight to Leila's side, threw the blanket back, slipped his arms under her legs and back and picked her up, then stopped at her roommate, "C'mon, girl. You drive. I'll ride in back and try to keep Leila from any more harm." *Yeah, right, you asshole, you could have treated her better from the beginning, but didn't. Leah and little Geri would really love me for being a total prick!*

# 27

## To WestPac

As planned, they got their specialized training the next day, and the following morning, right after 0700 quarters, they left for Westpac, specifically Japan, where they had a secret mission, at least secret to him. Nobody stood on the pier waving goodbye, no families, no girlfriends, no Miss Crawford, no Morgan Rhodes, no Leah, and no Leila. Since he didn't have anything to do for getting underway, he stuck his head out of the After Room hatch, just to watch the goings-on. Not much. Those on the pier threw off the mooring lines and those on deck stowed those lines in superstructure lockers. Nobody had yet told him anything, but he figured anything he absolutely *had* to know, someone would tell him, eventually.

Several days passed as they crossed the Pacific. His time continued to pass with nothing to do. He hadn't even met his bosses, and was beginning to wonder what he was even doing there, if no torpedo tubes. He spent a lot of time in his bunk, reading, thanking God he had bought a couple spy novels, mainly James Bond thrillers by Ian Fleming. His two books he finished quickly, but then discovered others liked James Bond as well, so his two books went into the community library and he was able to keep reading, and mainly just staying out of everybody's way.

Until they reached port. Then things began to change.

**** 

Moser's first job became topside watch. As such he had been hearing shouting from somewhere in the distance for a few minutes, and getting closer. At first it was just distant noise, maybe even a party. But suddenly it was closer, a *lot* closer, maybe as close as the local street, and no longer sounded like a party. He wasn't just sure how far away the street was, or even what was beyond that alley that went…somewhere, just that it probably led to a street. Then the shouting was *really* close, and shadows—up and down shadows—began appearing on the walls of the far building adjacent to the alley. Then men began appearing, some wearing headbands, Japanese men carrying torches, and shouting…at him…?

At Brice Wesley Moser?

Upon arrival—wherever it was they had arrived—it was 1900 hours local time, and already dark. They tied up at the pier, at what appeared to be a civilian area. Then they immediately had a payday and liberty began for two-thirds of the crew. And he was certain two-thirds of the crew, including the captain and several officers, had left. Then he was given ten minutes of instruction on how to be a topside watch, handed the topside log and a flashlight and told to put the two items in the topside box, which another sailor appeared out of nowhere carrying. It fit perfectly in a metal ring hole in the deck, just like at the USS Char. The other sailor then dropped an electrical cord leading from the box down the After Battery hatch, "That's temporary power for your intercom, Nonqual, but don't use it unless God Almighty approaches."

"Right," he had answered, and gave a quick salute, not that the sailor deserved a salute. He was just another enlisted man. No, he sent the salute in a manner of sarcasm. He couldn't think of the sailor's name but they had met in the After Battery chow line, when this blockhead had jumped the line, and he had challenged him, "Line's at the rear," then he had jerked his thumb in that direction.

But Blockhead didn't go to the end of the line, instead, "You gonna *make* me, Nonqual?"

"Forget it, Bonnet," came a southern-sounding voice from quite a ways back in the line, "He's new."

That was the name, *Bonnet*. He had turned but couldn't make out who had spoken, but knew he'd remember that drawl and vowed to find out. But he hadn't, and nearly a week had passed. But might as well find out where they were, "Hey, Bonnet, where the heck are we?"

"What the hell you wanna know for, Nonqual?"

"Why do you call me that? My name's Moser."

"Cause that's what you are, Nonqual. A goddamn nonqualified puke."

"Fine." He sent another salute and turned away.

But Bonnet wouldn't let it stand, "Until you get submarine-qualified you're a goddamn danger to every other man on board." Then he disappeared down the After Battery hatch.

Moser just shook his head and placed the topside log and flashlight in the box. He had other things to be concerned about and dismissed Bonnet.

Less than three weeks it had taken to cross the mighty Pacific Ocean, but of course it would have taken less time except for that jaunt south to witness the nuclear test.

Other than the nuke test there had been no operations with other navy ships, just an occasional submergence to keep their trim, then they had kept hauling ass for Japan. It had seemed a good time to receive training, on a lot of things, but he had been sent to the After Troop Space, was given a book on seamanship to read, and another about submarines, and told to stay out of trouble. Not exactly what he had expected by joining the submarine fleet, but at least he had learned a lot more about the navy. He had finished everything, plus three James Bond novels just two days before their arrival here, wherever, exactly, *here*, was.

Just as Bonnet's head disappeared down the hatch still another sailor had approached from aft, carrying…a duty belt with a holstered .45 caliber semiautomatic pistol and two loaded magazines, "Still dealing with Bonnet, Moser?"

"No. He…just plugged me in, I guess." Then he recognized the drawl, "You're the one who stood up for me in the chow line."

"You've got a good memory, pardner, and I didn't exactly stand up for you. Just trying to prevent a problem." The man held the duty belt open. Moser turned and grabbed both ends of the belt, positioned it around his waist, snapped it closed, then again faced the man, more than a half a foot taller than himself and he was five-eight. "Bonnet tends to make trouble for everybody, but most folks ignore him. I suggest you do the same. My name's Richards, Electronics Technician, Second Class Petty Officer." Richards stuck out his hand, "You okay with the gun?"

He accepted the handshake, "Sure." But of course he wasn't. He had never touched a 45, but he hadn't worried about it just then. Weren't they in Japan? And wasn't Japan a friend, an ally?

"OK," Richards said, "If you need anything just get on the intercom."

"Ah…before you go, can you tell me anything about that hellava big explosion down by Christmas Island?"

"What do you want to know?"

"Hell, I don't know…was it really an atom bomb? Nobody tells me nuthin, ya know."

"Yes. About 600 kt."

"Kt…?"

"Kilotons. About 600 kilotons."

"Well, man, I'm just an Iowa farm boy. What the hell is a kiloton?"

"I'll put it like this, Moser. Hiroshima was hit with fifteen kt and Nagasaki with 21."

"So this one was big, I guess."

"Purty big, yes. But we've got'em bigger."

"How close were we…to *this* one…?"

"About thirty miles."

"Jesus, what if it had missed?" He remembered the explosion, remembered *feeling* it. No, he didn't get to see it, but he remembered the sensation, what had seemed to him like a slight give on the sub's hull. A few others claimed to have felt it too, but most didn't, and most said Moser and the others were imagining things. Well, he knew he hadn't imagined it. And only the camera looking through the periscope actually saw it, and preserved the image for all to see for all time.

Richards just chuckled, and didn't answer.

"So, how come you know so much about it?"

"It has to do with my rating. Electronics Technician Communications."

"Okay, man." He sent another salute, "Thanks." Richards was just another enlisted man too, but much more deserving of a salute than Bonnet. "Hey, man, where the heck are we anyway?"

"Japan."

"Well, yeah, I kinda knew that."

"It's classified, Moser. We aren't really here."

"Oh...."

"Sorry. The captain will fill us in as we need to know."

"But...you seem to know...."

"I have secret clearance. And I work in communications."

"Gotcha." He sent another salute.

Richards returned the salute and left, and that quickly he had found himself alone. Alone with the nightmare memory of that huge atomic explosion. He had always figured they were a lot farther away than just thirty miles. But something else right then was more important than remembering an explosion. The men approaching through the alley. He knew at least one officer would be still aboard, the below decks watch, and at least one-third of the crew with the

duty, besides Bonnet and Richards. He knew there were three duty sections. He was duty

section three. But nobody else was topside. The harbor water on both sides of the sub was black, barely even a reflection anywhere. The dim pier lights barely showed past the bulbs. The navy didn't appear to have much of a base in this town, if any, wherever the hell they were.

So a fresh sailor from Iowa and barely out of bootcamp and class A school was handed a gun and told to stand topside watch, and really wasn't sure what he should do about the approaching men carrying flaming torches. Before arrival to wherever they were the crew had been told they might experience protests at this port. But they didn't say what kind of protests, and whether they might be dangerous or not. Even *he* had heard *that* announcement.  And these guys looked like they were planning to definitely protest *something*.

His right hand reached for the pistol, then just rested on the holster.  Other pistols, with cylinders, he had fired.  A semiautomatic was different, but it felt good under his hand and at least it was there, available.  He probably could figure out how to fire it if he needed to.  His other hand flicked the switch for the intercom to below decks.  He leaned over, grabbed another shallow breath and could barely believe what he was about to say, then spoke, "Repel boarders, port side!"  His voice cracked; he cleared his throat, then repeated, "Repel boarders, port side!"

## 28
### The Protest

A few seconds passed. Nobody answered.

Moser flicked the switch again, "Goddamn it, there's men up here with torches coming through the alley! Repel boarders! Repel boarders!"

For all he knew the Japanese men were coming just to talk, or maybe just to yell at him, yell at an American sailor and an American submarine. After all, in 1964 Japan, World War II probably wasn't that ancient a history. He reached again for the intercom button—

"Hold it, Moser."

An officer—a lieutenant he knew from the two silver bars on the man's shirt collar, and gold dolphins—appeared…from limbo as far as he was concerned. The officer approached the topside intercom box, leaned into it, "Repel boarders, port side! Not a drill! Repel boarders, port side! Not a drill! Moser, check your weapon!"

He did just that. He unsnapped the holster, pulled the pistol out, and dropped it. It hit the wooden deck, clunked like it weighed a ton, then lay still.

"Moser, goddamn it, check your weapon!"

"Yes, Sir!" He picked it up, held it waist high, stared at it—nobody had showed him a damn thing about that weapon. And the Japanese men were pouring onto the pier.

The officer grabbed the weapon, ejected the magazine, saw it was empty, then unsnapped Moser's magazine holster, withdrew another magazine, saw it was loaded, inserted it into the bottom of the handle, then pulled the slide back, lowered the hammer, and handed it back to him, "Take it, Moser, hold it aimed at the sky. If you need to fire just pull the hammer back and pull the trigger, but, God help us, you shouldn't need to fire."

"Yes, Sir." He took the pistol back and did as told, and wondered why the magazine that had been in the gun was empty, and knew he should have checked. Next time he would, first thing when he relieved somebody. He noticed, through peripheral vision, activity, other men appearing from the After Battery hatch and the Engine Room hatch, but he hadn't really comprehended what they did. Now he saw both Bonnet and Richards were among them, three spaced men on each side of himself and the officer, each holding either an M-1 rifle or a Thompson submachine gun. Those two guns he had fired, the M-1, just once, in boot camp, where he had qualified as marksman, the Thompson, also just once, on a special training session late the next day after he reported aboard the USS Hagfish. He remembered the instructor making something on his weapon click. He didn't know the man had switched it to full automatic, and felt surprised when he felt the instructor's hand on his back.

"Pull the trigger," the instructor had said.

He did. The gun started firing, almost wildly, and his finger froze to the trigger as he emptied the entire magazine. If the instructor hadn't held onto his back…well, who knows what would have happened. That had been embarrassing, but at least he had kept the weapon pointed into the sky.

"Chief Petecksky, Houst," the officer said calmly, "Secure that gangplank. Keep your weapons at port arms."

Moser didn't know what securing the gangplank would do, exactly, so he watched as the two burley men, the chief in kackies, First Class Houst in dungarees, approached the gangplank and stood on either side, right hand holding the stock, finger close to the trigger, left hand gripping the stock on the barrel. He remembered Port arms from bootcamp.

Evidently other members of the crew were pretty well-trained. So, they were ready to repel boarders. So what would happen next?

Seventy or eighty Japanese men, many with headbands who also looked very young, like university students, and all carrying either a sign written in both Japanese and English, or a flaming torch, had lined up on the pier facing the eight sailors. But the shouting had stopped.

The sudden silence was almost painful. Finally, maybe the only man who carried nothing, stepped forward. He was probably less than five feet tall, very, very, slim but not skinny, and wore a yellow headband. His hair, black as oil, was short, longer on top and combed up, reminding him of some styles back in the states. "What does the American Navy want in Japan?" the man asked.

"We're here at the request of your government," The officer answered.

"But why?" the man demanded, "Why are you here?"

"Our mission is classified."

"Yes, always classified…."

"And who are you people? Why do you come here threatening—"

"Who are we threatening?  We have no guns.  Not like you."

So the Japanese man had won that exchange, and he was right.  He could see no weapons on the Japanese men, not in plain sight anyway.

"So if you are not here to threaten us," the officer finally returned, "Why *are* you here?"

"We are here to let the American Navy know that not all Japanese people welcome you, even though our government does.  And if you use your bases that are located on Japanese soil at Sasebo and Yokosuka to make war against Vietnam, we will not welcome that, either."  With the pronouncement the small Japanese man turned to his comrades and spoke in Japanese.

Immediately the signs and torches were lowered and the men started away.

The officer than spoke to Chief Petecksky, "Dismiss the men, Chief."

"Aye, aye, Sir."

# 29
## First Indoctrination

"Moser...."

"Yes, sir....?"

"You can lower your weapon now."

"Yes, sir. Sorry, sir"

The officer approached and extended his hand, palm upright. Moser placed the gun in the officer's hand, then waited.

"You've had no training for the 45, correct?" The lieutenant ejected the loaded magazine, then the bullet in the firing chamber, too quickly for him to even see what he had done.

"Correct, Sir."

"All right. We leave an empty magazine in the gun to keep out moisture, although, after tonight, we might be changing that procedure." The officer glanced at him as if maybe expecting agreement, so he agreed, "Yes, Sir. I agree, Sir."

"All right." The officer handed the gun back, then reinserted the extra bullet back into the loaded magazine, "See that little round button just above the left side of the handle?" The lieutenant pointed, "That's where you eject the magazine." The officer handed over the empty magazine, "Insert it."

He glanced at the lieutenant, then inserted the magazine.

"Now, eject it."

He went through the motion.

"That's good, Moser. You're a Torpedoman's Mate. My name is Lieutenant Williams. I'm the Gunnery Officer, your department head, and, I apologize, but I haven't had time to even welcome you aboard. This trip to…" the lieutenant hesitated for about one second, but long enough for him to notice, "…southern Japan…came up very abruptly, and…things…have been heating up in Vietnam, especially since the Maddox incident, so I've been busy."

"Maddox, sir…?"

"The USS Maddox, a destroyer."

Moser, unfortunately, at his young age, did not yet pay much attention to world news, "What about the Maddox, Sir?"

"The Gulf of Tonkin Incident, Moser. Certainly you're aware of North Vietnam firing on one of our destroyers."

"No, Sir. I've been in school, and bootcamp, and then on an Iowa farm puttin' up alfalfa hay. I always let my dad worry about…whatever, like that Tonkin thing."

"Well, Moser, you're in the navy now, and I would suggest that you try to keep up with world events, since we'll be heading straight into them."

"Sir…?"

"Just start paying attention, Moser. You have to do that on your own. But, for right now, I'm going to show you all about this weapon. I want you to learn and not forget, and don't wait for people to train you. Approach First Class Gunner's Mate Higgins and request training on the 40mm deck guns, and the 50 calibers, and learn how to fire and clean all the small arms. We have only two gunner's mates, so gunnery will be *your* job too. You have to focus, Moser, ask questions, and get qualified on this boat on all levels and compartments. You have to know every other man's job before you can earn your dolphins...." The officer hesitated, then went on, "You just earned your Seaman stripes during your short stay at GMU10. Good job! But earning your dolphins will be somewhat harder, especially since you didn't go to Sub School...."

"I expect so, Sir. But I was glad to leave shore duty. What a boring place that was. Course, I was only there a couple weeks, so I hadn't done much more than play pool, and then the XO called me to his office and offered submarines."

"Right, which you had already volunteered for, and that missile place you spoke of was for the Regulus, a submarine missile for which we had to surface in order to fire, which is being phased out. The newer submarines and missiles won't have that problem...."

The lieutenant talked on for about ten minutes, seeming glad to share his knowledge, but then reached a stopping point, as if he had not meant to get carried away, "All right, so I'll expect you to work extra hard, Moser, and earn your dolphins so that you can also learn and perform all your duties with all our weapons."

"Yes, Sir."

"How do you feel about no torpedoes? After all, you just spent three months in weapons training, specifically for torpedoes...."

"A little disappointed, I suppose, but there's plenty here to learn and do without torpedoes."

"That's correct. There's plenty here to keep you occupied."

"Yes, Sir."

He and the lieutenant then spent another several minutes just talking. After about fifteen, "That's all I have for now, Moser. Get yourself trained, and if you have any questions don't hesitate to approach me."

"Yes, Sir." He reinserted the empty magazine back into the gun's handle, slipped the gun into its holster, then saluted, "Thank you, Sir."

Lieutenant Williams returned the salute, then went below.

He then pulled the weapon from its holster, went through all the motions the gunnery officer had shown him. He ejected the empty magazine, pulled the slide back, flipped the safety on with his right thumb, inserted the empty magazine, and released the safety. The slide slammed forward on its own. If the magazine had been loaded he knew the slide would have carried a bullet into the firing chamber. Ready to fire.

Then he left his right finger on the trigger, placed his left hand over the end of the barrel, pressed, and attempted to pull the trigger. The hammer would not fall. If someone else was holding the gun, threatening him, he knew one of his hands could grab the other's wrist and his other hand would have to go over the barrel end and press. The last-ditch safety, the last-ditch attempt to stop someone from shooting him. Better be damn quick though, and damn sure you know what you're doing, or he knew he would get a bullet through his hand, which probably wouldn't be very pleasant. He then held onto the hammer and pulled the trigger, which allowed the hammer to fall slowly and safely. Finally he holstered the gun, shook his head and smiled. *Will do, sir*. He even considered buying a personal weapon, his own .45 caliber semi-automatic pistol.

## 30
### Richards, Second Class Petty Officer Part 1

Second Class Electronics Technician Richards had been sitting on the stern capstan during Moser's training with the 45. Moser had said he was okay with the pistol but Richards now felt he should have taken that answer with a grain of salt. After all, the boy's naval experience till then had probably only been bootcamp and class A school, and he knew neither offered handgun training, as most sailors would never use a handgun. Most would never use any kind of gun. But the Hagfish was heading toward a war patrol, likely several months in the vicinity of Vietnam, so it behooved all hands to know as much as possible about all firearms. Next time he asked Seaman Moser a question about how much he knew about something he would dig a little deeper. He liked the young Iowa farm boy, though, and felt he would be a good addition to the Hagfish crew.

Richards remembered arriving at his own first regular duty station, also shore duty right there at Pearl Harbor, Hawaii. After about an hour of interviews and indoctrination the old chief had leaned back, smiled, and said, "Now get out there and find yourself a woman, young man, or this shore duty will soon bore you to death. The chief had been correct. Shore duty had quickly bored the life right out of him. Even so he had lasted a full year, then requested submarine duty and quickly got shipped to New London, Connecticut, for the sub school. Upon that completion he had made such good grades that he was quickly offered to continue on into nuclear power, which, then, was the coming thing and more volunteers were definitely needed.

He had considered it, but thought he wanted to ride the old World War II fleet submarines for awhile first. He could always go nuclear later. Qualification came quickly, then third class petty officer, finally second class petty officer and a secret clearance. Richards felt he was quite satisfied with all his decisions, and he always fell back on his dad's saying: *'If you hadn't done that you wouldn't be where you are today.'* Real truth in that saying, but Richards was never sure if the quote was originated by his dad or if his dad had just read it somewhere, and it didn't matter, for it had been his late father's favorite saying. Because for every decision Richards had made in the navy he had always told his parents afterword, rather than asking for their opinion, and his dad's next letter had always came back with that same saying.

Now it appeared Richards would maybe have a student in Moser. He would see.

# 31
## Quarters

Moser didn't get a chance to buy his own weapon. He didn't even get a chance to go ashore on liberty. The very next morning they held 0700 quarters, then made preparations to get underway immediately. Preparations included the loading of an ungodly—to Moser, at least—amount of food, ammunition, and other supplies. At 0730 the topside watch leaned to the intercom and announced "Hagfish arriving, Hagfish arriving." The captain, XO, and one other officer stepped onto the gangplank and walked aboard. They all saluted the topside watch but not the flag, then he realized the flag wouldn't yet be hung, and probably wouldn't be that morning.

After the arrival of the officers the loading of supplies continued. He was first in line after the gangplank, and had just received a box of frozen steaks when...

"Moser, Bonnet here will take your spot," Gunnery Officer Williams said.

Bonnet stepped up and took the box. Moser stepped back to face his department head, "This is Master Chief Tetslow, Moser," The lieutenant gestured to a man slightly shorter than

Moser, about forty or fifty years old, and face filled with rugged wrinkles, "You'll be working directly for him when we get underway this morning, and hang around here as the XO will shortly be briefing the crew."

"Aye-aye, Sir."

Lieutenant Williams then left. Moser held out his hand, "Glad to meet you, Chief."

The chief, with a deep tan and those deep but rugged-looking wrinkles, first gave him a look, then grasped his hand, "So you're a torpedoman."

"Yes, sir, Chief, I studied both the Mark 16 steamfish and the battery-powered Mark 37, but I guess I won't be needing that knowledge."

"Right, I doubt we'll be firing any torpedoes anytime soon, but you will need that knowledge if you hope to advance. You and I are the only torpedomen. I'm in charge of Gunnery under Lieutenant Williams, so if we have to do anything requiring weapons we have gunner's mates and fire control technicians for help."

"Yes, Sir."

The chief gave him another look, somewhat deadly, he thought, "Here comes the XO. Get into your duty section."

The men lined up, three sections of about twenty to twenty-five men each, with the section leader in front of each section. It was his first real quarters since being aboard, and noticed Gunner's Mate Higgins was his section leader. Glad to finally find that out. Then he noticed Chief Tetslow out in front of everything, who shouted, "Atennn-shunnn!" He would find out later that his boss, Chief Tetslow was Chief of the Boat, the top enlisted man on board.

The XO stopped in front of the chief. The chief saluted, "All present or accounted for, Sir." The XO returned the salute, "Thank you, Chief. Stand at ease, men."

The chief stepped aside and faced the men along with the XO, who looked the men over for a few seconds, then spoke, "First, men, sorry for the short port call but we are headed for Subic Bay, which will become our new home port, for awhile at least. At Subic we'll pick up in the neighborhood of seventy-five marines, and all their weapons and equipment. We will probably have at least two days there, and then we will get underway to the Gulf of Siam where we will take part in the operation Jungle Drum III, with a number of other navy ships and in conjunction with the navy of Thailand." The XO looked the men over again, then, "Jungle Drum III is strictly an exercise. Practice for the Marine Corps, because from there they'll be heading for the white sandy shores of The Republic of Vietnam. So let's give those boys all the help we can. That's all, Chief."

They saluted again, the XO left, the chief watched the XO disappear down the forward troop space hatch, then faced the men, "All right, men, fall out, get the rest of those stores aboard, and get to your maneuvering stations."

Moser didn't yet have a maneuvering station so, after helping finish loading the stores, just headed for the After Troop Space.

"Moser!" He turned and faced Chief Tetslow, "Get on the sound-powered phones back in the After Troop Space for your maneuvering watch."

"Yes, Sir!" Glad to have a job, he hurried below decks and then realized he didn't know where they kept the sound-powered phones, when of all people to show up, his new friend second class ET, "Richards!"

"Yo, Moser, how's it going?"

"Okay, man, but I'm supposed to man the sound-powered phone back here, and I don't even know where they are!"

"Take it easy, Moser." Richards pointed, "Right there in the sound-powered phone locker."

He jerked in the direction of the point. Sure enough. A little sign said *'Sound-powered phones.'* He grinned at Richards and gave a weak little laugh, "Wow." Then he opened the locker, grabbed the phones, and then just sort of stared at them.

Richards took over, grasped the phones, put them on Moser's head, ears, and neck, correctly, plugged them into the bulkhead outlet, and headed him the cord, "Just listen to what people are saying, Moser, and when you hear Maneuvering say—" he pointed to the hatch leading to the next compartment, *"—'Maneuvering, manned and ready,'* then you push that little button on the mouthpiece and say it for this compartment."

He gave a thumbs-up and almost immediately heard the men in Maneuvering Room say "Maneuvering, manned and ready." So, as Richards had said to say, at least how his untrained mind heard him say it, he said, "Maneuvering, manned and ready." And thought he had done it right.

Immediately a face appeared in the hatch leading to Maneuvering, "Hey, dumbass, you're in the After Troop Space!"

"Ah! Right!" He brought the mouthpiece back up but didn't push the button. Richards did. "After Troop Space! Manned and ready!"

Richards patted him on the shoulder, "Now just listen to what others are saying and learn from it, and very likely nobody will want to speak to you back here, as this is just a berthing compartment. Okay?" Richards smiled.

"Yes, Sir!"

Richards again patted his shoulder, "Don't worry. You'll get it." Then he went to the ladder leading topside and went up, leaving Moser standing in the middle of the compartment feeling very much like just a farm boy from Iowa. He felt the diesel engines start, and immediately lightly sensed diesel fumes. They always made him feel a little sick to his stomach, but at least he hadn't yet puked from the smell.

## 32
## Maneuvering Watch

The phone cord was plenty long, so Moser was free to move about the compartment looking things over. During the trip from Pearl Harbor he had mostly kept his nose stuck in either his novels or the seamanship book, but now he was free to actually start looking at the compartment where he lived, at things he had simply not noticed before. On the door leading to the restroom, what he had learned to call the *'head'* way back in bootcamp, was a locker labeled *'Oxygen Breathing Apparatus'* or *'OBA.'* He opened the locker and saw what stuck with him the most, the gas mask part, which kind of made him shiver, as it made expressly clear where he was: on board a United States Submarine and possibly heading into— what he had seen and heard in a John Wayne movie— *'Harm's Way,'* in fact, if he remembered correctly, that was the name of the movie: *'In Harm's Way.'*

He shivered again, closed the locker, and moved on. Right beside the hatch leading to Maneuvering was a red fire extinguisher. Right, he better remember where *that* was, and he better locate them in all the other compartments. He turned around and looked aft, and remembered the tubes on the USS Charr. He tried envisioning what the Hagfish's After Troop Space looked like when it was the After Torpedoroom, but found he couldn't, as now there were bunks three to five high everywhere, and a small table. The After Torpedoroom was no longer a *'War Room'* and that made him feel somewhat sad.

He moved to the hatch, could hear them talking up topside, but his attention was drawn to a sign on the hatch tunnel leading topside, and read it—Jesus! The sign basically said if they were sunk in salvageable water, a sleeve inside the tunnel would be lowered and the whole compartment would be flooded and pressurized, the hatch opened and the men trapped back there could escape...*IF we're sunk in salvageable waters.* He felt a major shiver and wondered how deep salvageable water possibly was.

He remembered his own experience of pressure at the one hundred-fifty-foot tower at Pearl Harbor, where everyone had gone to the fifty-foot level for Steinke Hood life jacket training the next day after he arrived, that and the small arms training. The Steinke Hood was a new design and inflatable with a hood that went over one's head where he would be breathing compressed air, which he had to get out of his lungs as the life jacket took him streaking to the surface. That idea had seemed easy enough when first explained, until the details came out, that the air one was breathing was, yes, pressurized air, and *had* to be gotten out, or it was quite possible one's lungs could—probably *would*—explode, which, in all likelihood would cause death.

A chuckle left him, but his thought had not been funny.

But still, it had seemed that it would be easy enough to get the air out. As they said, all one had to do was shout "Ho! Ho! Ho!" three times, grab a quick, shallow, breath, then "Ho! Ho! Ho!" again, all the way to the surface. And, again, it had seemed and sounded easy enough, until it came his turn to do it. Evidently he wasn't "Ho! Ho! Hoing!" enough, as he had been grabbed—probably by a UDT guy—far from the top of the fifty-foot level. He considered that the man probably saved his life and would never forget his face, dark eyes and short black hair that reminded him of the actor Earnest Borgnine, and a real hero.

People started coming down the hatch tunnel. He grabbed his phone cord and stepped back out of the way. Two sailors came down, gave him a look and nodded to him, then went through the hatch leading to Maneuvering. Then he heard the topside hatch closed and a loud click. Then he heard on the phones "Forward Troop Space hatch secured." A second later, from the MC circuit, "Green light on the Forward Troop Space hatch."

Then Richards came down the ladder and motioned, "OK, Moser, press the button on your mouthpiece and say 'After Troop Space, hatch secured.'"

He did as told, then listened for the response from the MC, "Green light on the After Troop Space hatch." then looked at Richards.

"Good job, Moser."

Some chuckling came from behind him and the comment, "Dumbass."

He turned around. Three sailors stood there, Bonnet among them, and all three were looking at him with…his best guess, apathetic smirks, on their faces.

OK, Moser," Richards said, "Stay on the phones until the Maneuvering Watch is secured, which will mean we're well outside the harbor."

Richards waited. He nodded. Richards left, but eyed the other three sailors as he passed them. Once Richards was gone there came another comment, definitely Bonnet speaking, "Find out where we are yet, dumbass nonqual? Or where we *were*—course it don't make a fuck anymore cause we're no longer there." Then he laughed.

Moser glanced at him but made no response, just turned away.

"I've known some dumb fuckers in my time, nonqual, but I have to say you're one of the dumbest."

Again he didn't respond, but felt some time he might have to, so shut off any further comments and just listened to the sound-powered phones-talk. He would learn as he went, and, eventually, he would earn his dolphins.

One half hour later, "Secure from Maneuvering Watch," came over the MC circuit.

They were at sea, bound for Subic Bay, the Philippine Islands, their new home port…for *awhile*.

## 33
### Lookout Watch

"Moser, roll out. You got the watch."

"What?" Moser looked down from his top bunk that was right beside—he had just recently asked and found out—the stern planes motor. He looked down at a sailor he didn't yet know, "Nobody told *me*."

"Well, they want you up there in Control. You go on watch at 1200 hours."

He looked at his wristwatch. 1130. That gave him time, he hoped, to get at least a bite to eat, "What watch?"

"Lookout and planesman. God, don't they tell you anything?"

"No! They don't!" He felt a little irritated, "Nobody has told me hardly a fucking thing since I came aboard!" He grabbed a couple of supported pipes, swung out of his bunk, allowed his body to hang straight, then dropped to the floor.

"Hey, sorry, Moser, I'm Nagle, Third Class Fire Control Technician." The man, about Moser's age of eighteen, stuck his hand out, "It's an unfortunate fact. New people kind'a get kicked around for awhile, but we just came through a crash course yard period to get outfitted as a troop transport, then a hurry-up trip to Pearl, then that side trip down to Christmas for the big nuke blast, then a very short liberty in Japan, and now we're hauling balls for P.I. Truth is, Moser, we've been kind'a busy, and some people ain't taking it as well as they should…am I forgiven?"

"Yes." He accepted the handshake, "I'm sorry too, and I'll get over it."

"Good, and I'll call up there for'em to make you a horsecock and cheese sandwich…and tomatoes and lettuce too?"

"Yeah, and thanks, man."

"That's okay, but find out who's your boss when we're underway. It's probably Chief Tetslow, but I could be wrong. That way you can know what your duties are, cause if you relieve somebody late…well, I'm sure you know that causes the shit to hit the fan."

In the next few minutes he flew into his dungarees uniform and Nagle made the call about the sandwich.

****

At 1149 hours Moser made his way up first the Control Room ladder, then the Conning Tower ladder leading to the Bridge, "Permission to come on the bridge, Sir." Luckily, some compassionate soul had thought to tell him to *'ask for permission'* first, before he stumbled up there without asking and got in more trouble. He would find out later that the Officer of the Deck (OOD) needed to know who was on the bridge in case there would ever be need for a crash dive, which, in peace time wasn't likely. Although some would call the expanding Vietnam War not exactly *'peace time.'* Plus, the farther west they got the more ships they saw of the Soviet navy, especially the electronics-laden so-called Russian fishing trawlers.

"Permission granted."

He finished the climb up, saw the officer, Lieutenant Junior Grade (J.G.) Bostwick, "I'm here to relieve the port lookout, Sir."

"Very well." The officer nodded to the port lookout, of all people…Bonnet….

"About time you're gettin' up here, Moser."

He bit his tongue. He was still early and was not going to let this jerk get to him. Bonnet stayed in the puka—in navy terms he had just learned—meant hole, or cubbyhole,

"Watch closely, nonqual, we're going to be diving in about ten or fifteen minutes." He glanced at the OOD and got a positive nod. "And I'm going to show you this just once, and then you are going to do it and do it right the first time. Remember what I said, you're a danger to every man on this ship until you're qualified, and even then some guys remain not qualified, but that's not up to me to decide who is and who isn't, so watch and learn!"

Bonnet took his binoculars and slipped his arm in so that the binoculars now lay under his arm and against his left rib cage, then he ducked down, made a turn to his right, grabbed the handlebars of the Conning Tower ladder and jumped, placing his feet on the outside of the bars and sliding down, then turned to his right again and did the same maneuver on the control room ladder, then returned topside and handed over the binoculars, "I guess you're not going to get a chance to practice, Moser. Our dive has been upped. So just stay in the puka there, and when the OOD clears the bridge just do the best you can. I'll be waitin' for ya down below."

Then he got the surprise of his life, or at least the biggest surprise since he had been aboard the USS Hagfish, Bonnet took hold of his shoulder, squeezed, then patted, "Don't worry. You'll do fine." Then he performed the same acrobatic maneuvers getting back below decks. Once below Bonnet came partway up the Control Room ladder and called back up, "One more thing, Moser. You'll be coming down first, and the starboard lookout will be about a second and a half behind ya."

He sent a salute, then ducked down and moved into the port puka, glanced at the OOD, then did a sweep of the horizon with his binoculars from the bow, 360 degrees or 000 degrees, all the way back to 180 degrees and dead astern, then looked for a few seconds, then began a sweep back…just passing about 270 degrees—what the hell! He swept back about five degrees, "Contact, sir! Looks like a ship just about amidships, just over the horizon."

The OOD used his own binoculars in that area, "Very well, Moser. Good job."

About two more minutes passed, then, "Clear the bridge! Clear the bridge!"

# 34
## Dive! Dive!

Moser grabbed his binoculars and slipped his arm under the strap, made the right turn, grabbed the ladder and jumped! Amazingly, his feet clutched the outside of the ladder and he slid down and hit the Conning Tower deck! Then he heard the diving alarm, *ARRUUGA! ARRUUGA!*

About one second later from the MC, "Dive! Dive!"

He knew his mind was still up on the bridge, but somehow he made the other right turn, did the same with that ladder and hit the Control Room deck, then saw Bonnet.

"Hit that switch, Moser!" Bonnet pointed. He hit it. "Now hit that one!" Bonnet pointed again. He hit it and stood up straight, and realized he was shaking, and facing the stern planes wheel. It was the second time he had seen it—the first time was on the no longer operating USS Charr. He heard the starboard lookout hit the floor behind him, then felt Bonnet's hands on his upper arms, "Take it easy, Moser. Just take hold of your planes wheel and turn it left."

He did it, then heard the OOD hit the floor, "Full dive! Both planes! Periscope depth!"

From the MC, "Green light on the Conning Tower hatch, Sir."

"Very well."

Bonnet pointed to a gauge that showed two arrows. The one on the left was pointing slightly toward down, "That shows the stern planes in the *'dive'* position." Then Bonnet pointed to a tube about six inches long fashioned into a pouty-mouth, "And that shows you where your bubble is. You're not quite at full dive, so turn your wheel a little harder...."

He did it. The bubble went clear to the bottom!

"OK!" Bonnet said, "Ease off a little."

He did it—or thought he did! But the bubble went streaking back in the other direction.

"Bonnet!" the OOD said, "Take over. Get us to depth and angle and then give it back to Moser."

"Yes, Sir!"

He stepped back. Bonnet moved in, "Now watch, Moser. You have to move this wheel not like you're driving a car. It's hydraulics. Every time you move the wheel it sends a message by oil back to the pistons that actually move the stern planes. Whatever you do up here is instantaneous back there, so you usually have to do it gently—"

"Ten rise," said the other planesman.

"OK, Moser, the other planesman is the bow planesman. He just said *'Ten rise.'* That means to us to go to five *dive*, meaning to compensate for what he's doing. He controls the depth. We control the angle. And the Officer of the Deck up there is the Diving Officer down here. So, you want to get back on here?"

"Yes, Sir." Bonnet stepped back. Moser again grasped the stern planes wheel.

A full half hour passed as the Diving Officer gave orders that pertained to getting their ship in trim, meaning fully balanced, as going into rough seas they better be balanced to face sometimes huge waves while surfacing.

From the Conning Tower and the captain of the ship, "Take us up!"

From the Diving Officer, "Full rise both planes!"

From the MC, "Surface! Surface! Surface!"

From Bonnet, "Wheel to the right, Moser!"

From...limbo, *ARRUUGA! ARRUUGA! ARRUUGA!*

From the Diving Officer, "Blow bow buoyancy!"

Came a distinct up-angle—

From the Diving Officer, "Blow main ballasts! Secure the planes!" The Diving Officer moved to the ladder leading to the Conning Tower.

Moser glanced at Bonnet and knew his eyes were wide.

"The starboard lookout will go up after the OOD," Bonnet said, "Then you, just get up there and start scanning the horizon, and report anything you see, including sea bats and whales." Bonnet smiled, "You did good, Moser."

He gave a half-smile back, "Thanks for your help, Bonnet."

"You're welcome. That's how you get qualified, man, so that you *won't* be a danger to every man on the ship. You get out there and learn!"

From the Chief of the Watch, "Red light on the Conning Tower hatch, sir."

"Very well." The lieutenant j.g. started up the ladder. The starboard lookout started up right behind him, then Moser.

Once back on the bridge he did as Bonnet had told him. He looked far and wide with the naked eye first then scanned with the binoculars, and saw nothing, "No contacts, sir."

"Very well, Moser."

So, it appeared Bonnet had a shred of decency inside him too, or was he just taking his job seriously and doing it? He didn't know. He guessed he would wait for the next confrontation—or meeting. He hoped it would be just a meeting, and not a confrontation. Time would tell. In the meantime he would begin his qualification process, but of course he had no idea where even to start. Certainly somebody knew of some kind of guidance of where to start, or at least a list of exactly what he had to know. He knew he didn't have to know everything...just *almost* everything. In the mean meantime he looked forward to getting to the Philippine Islands, and maybe some shore time.

# 35
## Richards, Second Class Petty Officer Part 2

Moser didn't know he had an overseer, that Second Class Richards had taken enough liking to him to take it upon himself to guide him and see to it that he started out and stayed on the right path toward qualification. Richards wasn't required to but a second class radioman had taken on the job of mentor for himself. The man had never said as much but every time Richards had needed direction Radioman Reeves seemed to have been there. A full year had gone by before Reeves admitted to it, just before the man transferred to the nuclear submarine fleet. The thing that stuck with Richards was not just that Reeves told him but *how* he told him, and, when, just before he left, "…yes, I tried to be there for you, kid, but not to get in your way. What I'm trying to say is, I did it for you, now you need to do it for someone else, but be sure you pick someone who will appreciate it and learn, and I don't mean take up with the next nonqual who comes aboard but pick the right one." Then Reeves shook his hand, said goodbye, hoisted his seabag, stepped onto the gangplank, and turned around, "Don't worry, Richards. When he gets here you'll know."

A little over a year had passed. Many nonquals had come aboard, some had qualified quickly with little help, others had needed a lot of help, others had gotten behind for one reason or another, were considered delinquent, and had to stay aboard with no liberty until they caught up, still others had given up completely and requested transfer back to the surface fleet or shore duty. With all those men Richards had just done his duty and helped where he could, but took none under his wing. With the arrival of Seaman Torpedoman Moser, Richards was pretty sure he had met his…what? Student? Not sure what to call him. He guessed in his mind he could say *apprentice*.

He knew Moser had gotten training on lookout, planes and the helm without him, which was fine. Without orders to do the training it would have been too obvious. No, his job as mentor would be for all the other times a nonqual would have needs, whatever they might be.

Their trip to P.I. was likely to be quiet, but there was bound to be shore time and liberty, and this likely would be the first time Moser had been anywhere but San Diego or Iowa farm country.

# 36
## Mercy

Next to Moser at the table sat Mercy, in his eyes, the most beautiful Philippine woman in the islands, "You want take me home, Moser?"

Arrival at Subic Bay had meant immediate liberty, and this time he did not have the duty. He would never forget leaving the choppy Pacific and entering the harbor of that huge naval base, as the water in the harbor got like plate glass, like they were in a swimming pool. Luckily he had lookout watch and had a front row seat.

Another thing he would never forget—just one day out of Japan—was coming to All Stop not too long after their first dive. Only then did he find out why they had stopped at that lonely Japanese harbor. Two new sailors with some kind of specialized ratings had met them there. And during that All Stop one had left by helicopter, and not to go to his next specialized and secret duty.  No, after his one and only dive aboard a submarine, he had decided he could not live aboard a submarine, not one moment longer. He guessed a huge and highly dangerous case of claustrophobia had come upon the young man, dangerous because if the man had lost total control of his emotions he could have caused damage that might have put the whole ship at risk, so the decision was made to airlift him off.

In the far distance he remembered seeing a really huge ship, and later learned from Second Class Richards, "Yep, that's the aircraft carrier, Yorktown, CV10. They sent that chopper over and plucked that guy up just like in the movies." And Richards seemed a bit perturbed about it, "But, I guess the poor guy didn't know he was claustrophobic. And, if he can't go…anywhere…well, that's going to affect his career, might even end it."

"What's his rating?" He remembered asking.

"Hell," was Richards' answer, "I don't know. Even my secret clearance didn't clear me to know that. But, if I had to guess, I'd say CIA, or even NSA, wearing a uniform."

"NSA…?"

"National Security Agency. They've only been around about ten years, or so."

"Wow, just like the movies."

"Right, Moser." Richards had given him the soberest look ever, "Just like the movies."

Just like the movies or not, Gunner's Mate Higgins had taken that young man out, both attached to the safety rail, about halfway between the bridge and bow, and there they waited while the chopper hovered over them, the blades whipping the waves like crazy and the hair on the two men's heads, then lowered a bucket, Higgins strapped the young man in. The men in the helicopter pulled the young man up and in. Then Higgins had to make a second trip with the guy's sea bag. Then that chopper lifted right away and zoomed back to the carrier. To Moser, riding in a helicopter above the waves of the Pacific looked a lot more dangerous than taking a dive in a submarine. But, to each his own, he guessed. Then he remembered that he had flown from the states in a jetliner, but the plane was so big as to seem unreal, not like they were actually flying over the Pacific.

At least during the trip from Japan he had been able to trace out all the hydraulics pipes, make a drawing, answer a few questions by the lead Machinist Mate, get it signed off, and then started on making a drawing of all the air lines and what they were for. Qualification seemed like quite a job, especially since he didn't go to sub school, and all this stuff was so new to him.

Then, a few days later, that ride into the beautiful harbor of Subic Bay. Then payday, then a jump into a dress white uniform, then a ride in an open-air taxi called a jeepney— reminding him of 50s American cars with their tops cut off— into Olongapo City and the famous street of bars catering to American service men.

Strange how he could think of so many other things with a beautiful Philippine girl sitting next to him, and she had just asked him a question. He hoped he had the right answer, "No, Mercy, I can't tonight." What was he doing? He had the best-looking woman in the bar sitting with him. She had just asked him to take her home, and he had just said *'no.'* But he knew why. Eighteen years old and he had not yet been with a woman. He wanted the first time to be special, and he knew it couldn't be special if he was drunk, and he was definitely drunk.

"I sorry," she said.

"Me too, Mercy, but I'm drunk."

"Drunk okay. I take good care of you."

He suspected that, *yes*, she would take good care of him, but just then Richards got up from the table where just men had been sitting and put his whitehat on, and started for the front door.

He jerked out a ten dollar bill and laid it on the table, then grasped both of Mercy's hands, "If we're still here tomorrow night, Mercy, I will come to see you."

She smiled.

He then jumped up and joined Richards at the door, "You heading back, Richards?"

"Yeah."

They both stepped out into the humid night, "Mind if I go back with you?"

"No problem." Richards stuck his hand up. A jeepney stopped almost immediately. "But I thought you had that dear heart goin' in there."

"I did, I guess." They climbed into the jeepney.

"You're gonna pay for this, you know...." Richards said.

"How so?"

"Well, there were about twenty or more of our guys in there that saw you leave with me when you had just sat with that pretty girl all night."

"So...?"

"So they're gonna wonder why you left with me and not with her, or did she shoot you down?"

"No! She asked me to take her home."

"And you didn't. How come? No money? Hell, you could've borrowed—"

"No! I...."

"Don't tell me you're cherry...?" Richards chuckled.

He hung his head and opened his hands, "Yeah, I am. Will that be a good enough answer for the guys?"

"Some of them, yeah." Richards shook his head and chuckled again, "But others of them will never let you forget it. Well, here's the base gate, better get your ID out."

"Right."

They both showed their IDs to the marine gate guard and jeepney moved on.

"Don't worry about it, Moser. The guys will kid you about it but it'll be in fun, and, what the hell? You'll get a better night's sleep, cause tomorrow we'll have our hands full."

"Oh?"

"Yep. Remember those seventy-five marines the XO told us about? Well, they're coming aboard late tomorrow and don't be surprised but what we get underway tomorrow night."

So he wouldn't see Mercy the next night. He hoped she would understand.

## 37
### Jungle Drum

They got underway the next night all right, at 1700 hours, and Moser found himself with twenty marines plus the dozen sailors that normally slept in the After Troop Space. He hoped none of the marines were claustrophobic, because an at-sea transfer at night maybe wouldn't go so well, but maybe they wouldn't be diving again, but likely they would, too, as they had to keep their trim right.

From his top bunk he watched the marines going about their business. Two groups were playing cards and smoking. Some were reading. Others were writing letters but not a lot of talk. Maybe that would change as they got closer to the Gulf of Siam and their Jungle Drum exercise.

Just an exercise but he had heard a lot more marines were going to participate. Maybe that guy sitting by himself would give out some info. About time to get up for his watch, anyway.

He swung down, got dressed, and looked over the marine sitting alone. Dark hair, shaved close on the sides, same as they all wore their hair, but this guy's might have been a bit longer. He then approached the one marine and stuck out his hand, "Howdy, my name's Moser and I'm just a farm boy from Iowa."

The marine, probably older than twenty and looked to be in excellent physical condition, looked him over good, then accepted the handshake, "Crosby. New York. What can I do for you?"

"Just wondering about your operation coming up. Can you tell me anything?"

"Sure, we are Raid Specialists of Company H of Battalion 2 slash 3."

He felt his eyes pop.

Crosby smiled, "That's Second Battalion, Third Marines. We're going ashore first to see what's cookin' before the main battalion arrives on the Lenawee, Washburn, and the Gunston Hall, regular troopships."

"Wow. So there'll be a lot of troops involved?"

"Not so many, a few companies, maybe a thousand men."

"Will there be any shooting?"

"Live-fire? I doubt it. Thailand is an ally, a friendly."

"Oh, well, thanks, Crosby. Ah, I've got the next lookout watch, so I gotta go eat. Maybe we can talk again." He gave a salute.

Crosby returned the salute, "Sure. Anytime."

\*\*\*\*

The cruise to the southeastern tip of Thailand's coast went quickly, to Sai Buri to be exact, just one of the many place-names that would burn into Moser's mind forever. A point of land where soon maybe a thousand marines would pour ashore, a safe place to practice their war game.

On lookout watch during the last inbound miles he saw in the distance other elements of the exercise including the attack transport—a civilian passenger ship re-outfitted before World War II for hauling marines and their landing craft—USS Lenawee, APA195, the attack cargo ship, USS Washburn, AKA108, also loaded with marines and their landing craft, and the dock landing ship, USS Gunston Hall LSD44. And where had he gotten all this information? From his main contact aboard the Hagfish, Second Class Electronics Technician, Richards, hailing from the great state of Texas, his good friend and—unknown to him—his mentor.

But something Richards did not know was how many marines would be going ashore and from which ships, "Our part of this operation is getting our seventy-five marine reconnaissance personnel ashore so they can recon the landing zone."

"Are we picking them up again?"

"No, in this exercise we're just delivering them. They'll go back to their unit on one of those other ships, but I do know that after this practice landing they're all heading for Danang, Vietnam, where a few thousand will go ashore to stay awhile."

"Awhile…?"

"That's something even I don't know, my friend. How long will we be here? That I don't know, either, but I guess these marines will be protecting the Danang Air Base. If we do stay in Vietnam for awhile…a long while, we will need air power.

"Yeah…." He hadn't really considered they would be in Vietnam that long, not personally, not himself, anyway. In fact in his long term plan he had figured to stay in the navy for his four-year hitch and then go back to his dad's farm in Iowa. He thought about his own Uncle Harold, an army veteran, who had stayed in Europe for the duration of World War II, which actually seemed like the right thing to do, yet, for himself…well, he didn't know. He guessed, for awhile, he would take things one day at a time. However, he suspected Richards was a true warrior, and would stay in Vietnam until things were decided one way or another.

"So where we going next?"

"I do know but I can't tell you, but when we're close the Captain or the XO will announce it."

****

In the distance land began to appear, just a darker line at first—

"Land ho, sir!" from the other lookout. In another second Moser would have thought about it and shouted it out himself. He felt he could use the positive press. But one thing positive: he had used the days from Subic to make a drawing of all the electronics on board, not the operations of those electronics, but the locations and main uses, then had gotten that drawing and answer session signed off by Richards' boss. Submarine qualification was going good, but he had a long way to go, and from the sounds of things they wouldn't be visiting any liberty ports for quite awhile.

As they approached land the ocean began to get smoother and marines and their equipment began to appear from the Forward Troop Space hatch, the part of the sub that sat highest in the water. Moser hoped he would be able to watch them launch. The land ahead appeared to be jungle, no buildings, just a lot of white sand. Maybe when marines hit the beach they required white sand. As he watched, the marine he had met the night before—now in full battle dress—appeared from the hatch.

He looked different. Last night he was just another relaxed young man sitting around in khakis and T-shirt, and not a threat to anything. Now he wore a helmet, bullet-resistant vest, suspenders with grenades hanging, a belt loaded with extra magazines for his M16. Moser grinned and waved. Crosby saw him but did not grin back and did not wave, likely had something on his mind other than being warm and friendly. Moser didn't blame him, and wondered if he, himself, too, would someday make that change.

Maybe a half mile from shore the Hagfish came to *'All Stop'* and began to partially submerge. As she began to sink away, the marines' rafts already inflated and loaded began to launch, and the marines began to paddle toward the beach.

# 38
## Underwater Demolition Team Launch

August and September saw Hagfish steaming in the combat zone of Vietnam conducting search and rescue operations. Then in November and December she would make two amphibious landings on the Vietnamese coast as part of the operation Dagger Thrust.

\*\*\*\*

The predawn recon mission would be launched from the afterdeck of the Hagfish as she lay on a fairly calm surface. Second Class Electronics Technician Richards would be part of the Hagfish deck crew. The frogmen of UDT 12 had become like a part of the submarine crew. Richards liked working with them and had made friends with First Class Boatswain's Mate, Pat Walsh. It didn't take long to inflate the rubber rafts and load equipment. While waiting for launch Walsh shared news with Richards of UDT's first Vietnam War casualty, "Yeah, we heard a few days ago. The guy—officer-in-charge, in fact—was just riding around in a jeep checking base security and the little mutherfuckers got lucky with a mortar round."

"Jesus!"

"Right, the shell must of had his name on it. Commander Robert J. Fay. Started as a frogman way back in 1951."

Then the word came up from below to commence the operation.

"Godspeed, my friend," Richards said, "And be careful."

"Will do." Walsh saluted and was reciprocated.

\*\*\*\*

Once below decks Richards was immediately pounced upon by Seaman Moser, "So what's goin' down?"

Richards grinned at his student and pointed toward the crew's mess hall, "Let's grab some coffee."

While getting their coffee and retiring into a corner they heard the diving alarm, "Now that the mission is underway I can tell you, Moser. The UDT boys are on the afterdeck with their rafts, and those rafts will be looped to our periscope. We're going to tow them in as close as we can get, and then they'll paddle in the rest of the way for their reconnaissance."

"Reconnaissance…," Moser asked, "What exactly happens?"

"They're going to check out the beach for underwater obstructions, and they'll patrol the whole area for enemy patrols and bunkers…and dispatch anything they deem necessary."

"Dispatch?"

"Destroy, Moser. Anything enemy they will destroy and/or kill to prepare the beach for the marine assault at dawn."

Wide-eyed, Moser shook his head.

Richards continued, "When they've finished their job they will radio to the troop ships offshore their hydrographic data and valuable intelligence. We'll stand by to assist in any way necessary, and later we'll just get out of the way."

Richards could see the question mark on Moser's face so he concluded. "The UDT boys will stay ashore to provide any last-minute security, and...the very last thing, they'll put up a sign for the marines."

"A sign...?"

Richards grinned, "Yep, a sign: *'Welcome, U.S. Marines— UDT 12—'*"

He then grinned too, "Kind of ironic huh, that the navy went ashore first...."

## 39
## Battle Stations!

An hour passed. The UDT personnel made their landing, the Hagfish backed out to sea and surfaced. Moser and Richards discussed mostly navy operations.

Finally Richards asked, "So how's qualifications coming along? I know you've been busy."

"Yeah, I'm almost ready to approach one of the officers for final—"

They felt the engines kick in and a tilt, as if they were making a quick turn.

Richards was up immediately and went to the nearby radio shack, followed by Moser.

"Corwin!" Richards shouted at the second class Sonarman, "What the hell's happening?

"Got an emergency!" The Sonarman held his hand over his earphones, and repeated quietly what was happening, "A South Vietnamese army group—about eighty men—is surrounded on a nearby beach, and some villagers…."

A sharp vibration was felt as the Hagfish poured amps to the screws.

"What about our UDT guys?" Moser asked.

Sonarman Corwin tightened his hand over his earphones, then answered, "Beach is secured and quiet. They'll just sit tight. The marines will soon be there."

Richards lifted his hand, "Thanks, Corwin," then headed back into the Control Room, where Gunnery Officer Williams was already giving orders to Moser's immediate boss, Master Chief Torpedoman Tetslow, "Gather your landing party, Chief. Two outboards, four men on each, fully armed. You will lead one, I'll lead the other. All sailors, as our UDT are all out on our earlier mission, and we are going in hot. Moser! Have you qualified on the 50 calibers yet?"

"No, Sir...."

"You stay below decks then." The lieutenant turned away and continued giving orders.

"Don't worry, Moser," Richards said, "Soon as we get a break I'll see to it you get qualified on the 50's"

He threw a salute, "Thanks, Richards."

"In the meantime you head for the After Troop Space. We'll likely be going to battle stations shortly."

He threw another salute, then turned and headed aft, just as the word came on the MC circuit, "Man battle stations! Man battle stations!"

\*\*\*\*

The Hagfish arrived a little before dark and received the request from the South Vietnamese Army unit plus some villagers to spend the night on board. A highly unlikely request as space on the submarine was limited, and they had no idea how many people were involved. So the captain radioed back, "Hunker down. We'll help provide protection for the night with flares and cover fire. We'll evacuate you in the morning and take you to your next position, and the civilians to swift boats for transfer."

Anchored offshore the Hagfish continued firing flares and intermittent 40 millimeters all night. At dawn the lookouts could see the Vietcong moving into position for a major attack. Laying broadside, the Hagfish crew opened fire with both 40's and the starboard 50 caliber. Meanwhile the landing party launched their outboards and jumped aboard on the port side.

Richards, holding an M16 at the ready, squatted behind Chief Tetslow as the two outboards and eight sailors headed in.

"Richards," Chief Tetslow said, "You get on the motor back there and you will stay with the boat. Looks like more than a hundred people we're going to have to haul out of here. So it'll take several trips. Bonnet will be the other coxswain. The lieutenant and I will take the rest of the men and help lay down covering fire."

"Roger, Chief." Richards had hoped to do some shooting himself, but, he would do as told.

They could hear the 40 millimeter shells exploding constantly, but just before they reached the beach they heard a terrific explosion.

"That was a secondary explosion," the chief said, "Must have hit an ammo dump. That should slow those little mutherfuckers down."

They reached the beach and loaded both outboards with villagers. Then Gunnery Officer Williams led the other five sailors to the front line of the pinned down South Vietnamese soldiers.  When the outboards returned, "The wounded go next!" Lieutenant Williams shouted, "They go topside too, aft of the sail." Then several trips of South Vietnamese soldiers and as much equipment as possible. Finally just one outboard returned.

"All right, boys," the lieutenant said, "Looks like the final call. The other outboard must be out of gas. We're all going to back out of here together."

Richards was the serving coxswain. He got the outboard as close as possible and sat broadside as the landing party waded into the surf and jumped aboard. Then he opened the throttle wide…*let's haul balls out'a here!*

## 40
### SEAL Team Lockout

During January 1965 Hagfish landed UDT personnel for beach survey work as part of Double Eagle. Just the day before, the XO had made the announcement to *'need-to-know'* personnel that they would be continuing operation *'Double Eagle'* and locking out six SEAL team members for their sabotage mission.

Richards would be the Escape Trunk Operator. Moser would be included in the group to watch and learn. They had been cruising just over the horizon. At commencement they dived and approached the coast on battery power at periscope depth at 1 knot. Up in the Forward Troop Space the six SEALs were preparing their equipment.

Moser was filled with awe. Here were guys not a lot older than himself yet had received ultimate and specialized training. He watched as they loaded up with their weapons and explosives and helped each other with their dual 90 tanks, and soon gave a *'thumbs up'* to Richards, who was already laying in one of the upper bunks where he would control the valves and pressurization.

From Richards, "Conn, Escape. Ready for lockout."

"Escape, Conn. Commence lockout."

"Conn, Escape. Commence lockout, aye."

Then two of the SEALs climbed the ladder into the Escape Trunk and closed the bottom hatch. A loud *'clack!'* followed. Moser watched the hatch wheel spin and felt a shiver go up his back. He knew what was coming. A lot of pressure on the ears. He had experienced that pressure at the fifty-foot level in the training tower at Pearl Harbor, and hadn't especially enjoyed it. These guys, according to Richards, would be at 36 feet.

He switched his main attention to Richards.

"Commence flooding," came a voice from the Escape Trunk.

Richards repeated the command on the 31MC circuit to the Conning Tower, "Conn, Escape, Commencing flooding."

"Commencing flooding. Escape, Conn, aye."

Richards cranked open the Flood Valve to let in sea water. He could hear the water cascading in, somewhat of a spooky sound, which sent another shiver up his back.

"Cease flooding," again from the Escape Trunk. From Richards explaining procedure to him earlier, he knew that meant sea water had reached above the top of the side door. Richards passed the word to the Conning Tower, while closing the valve, "Conn, Escape, ceasing flooding."

"Ceasing flooding. Escape, Conn, aye."

"Side Door undogged," came that voice from the Escape Trunk.

Richards responded, "Conn, Escape, side door undogged and pressurizing."

"Side door undogged and pressurizing. Escape, Conn, aye."

Richards then opened a valve that sent a blast of air into the Escape Trunk.

The sound of the blasting air again reminded Moser of his own experience at the tower at Pearl Harbor, which sent a third shiver up his back.

Richards intensely stared at the pressure gauge. Moser knew he was watching to see when the needle bounced, which would mean the Trunk had equalized with sea pressure and air was escaping out the side—

"Door's open!" came that voice from the trunk, and whoever said it had also closed the air pressure valve inside the trunk before Richards could do it.

Richards tightened his fist and gave a quick shake of his head, "They beat me," he said, then passed the word to the Conning Tower, "Conn, Escape. Door open."

"Door open. Escape, Conn, aye."

Again he knew what had just gone down thanks to Richards sharing information earlier. It was a game: One of the SEALs had pressed his foot against the door. The instant of equalization had allowed his foot to push the door open, which meant to Moser that the SEAL could usually win, as the door would have to actually open before any air bubble could get out. Likely only tenths of seconds would pass between a foot pushing the door open and bubbles actually escaping. So, who won maybe would depend on who was most focused.

He couldn't imagine either the SEALs or Richards being very un-focused due to the deadly game they were playing. But, he guessed, until the SEALs actually reached land and their sabotage target the game maybe wasn't so deadly, allowing those carefree moments of a racing game with the Escape Trunk Operator.

Richards kept his eyes on the pressure needle. Moser knew the moment the needle quit fluctuating, Richards could assume both men were out and the side door was again secured. Then he opened a drain valve which emptied the sea water into the bilges, turned the air pressure on again and soon had the Escape Trunk empty and ready for lockout of the next two SEALs. Richards spoke once more into the 31MC circuit mike, "Conn, Escape, door closed, Escape Trunk drained, ready for next lockout."

"Escape, Conn, commence next lockout."

"Conn, Escape, aye. Commencing second lockout."

The second and third lockouts went smoothly.

At the end: "Moser, and any of you other guys who want to know what just happened!" Richards gestured for the men to approach, then placed his hand again on each of the valves and went through the whole lockout procedure. "And I can give you a fairly good picture as to what's happening outside right now. The first guy out has the tanks on. He has to tread water till the mission is a go, so he needed the breathing apparatus. The next guy is getting a raft out of our open deck lockers. He'll pull the lanyard on the CO2 bottle, which will inflate the raft and it'll float to the surface. Another guy is getting oars, also from a deck locker…sometimes they use a small Evinrude motor. I guess this time it's oars because we are a little too close to some unfriendlies, so they'll have to paddle in quietly. Any questions?"

"Yeah," Moser raised his hand.

"Moser…?"

"How are they getting back?"

"Good question." Richards climbed down from the upper bunk, "The Conning Officer right now is turning us around. We'll go back out to sea twelve miles, just over the horizon, surface, and wait. And right now I'm heading for my sonar station." Richards headed aft.

The rest of the class stayed behind and busied themselves with other activities, but Moser tagged along, "Then what...?"

"You're good student, Moser. If I train anybody to do main lockouts it might just be you. As a torpedoman it should fit right in to your rating. How are you coming along with your qualification?"

"Hydraulics and electronics both signed off by NCOs."

"Good, and what are you working on now?"

"I'm making a drawing of the different tanks."

"OK, good. So you're confident that you have time now for this extra training?"

"Yes."

"Okay, I'm going to get some shut-eye and you should do the same, so put in a wakeup call for 0100. That's three hours, and then get back here to Sonar, where we will, again, wait."

"Gotcha."

\*\*\*\*

The three hours went by in a blink. Moser was pretty sure he had actually slept but when the After Troop Space watch woke him he felt wide awake, as if he had just downed the strongest of coffee. He then flew into his clothes and headed forward, through the Maneuvering Room—where submerged cruising power from the batteries were controlled by a whole bunch of mechanical linkages that he hadn't really studied yet—the Engine Room where two V-16 diesel engines provided their surface cruising power, the Mid-ship Troop Space that originally was the Forward Engine Room, then the After Battery berthing space and Mess Hall, finally the Control Room and the cordoned off Radio Shack that held all the electronics including Sonar.

Richards was already at his Sonar monitor with his headset on. At Moser's appearance Richards held up his hand and appeared to be listening intently…then he grasped his mouthpiece, "Conn, Sonar, two pingers bearing 269 degrees."

"Sonar, Conn, aye."

Only a moment passed before, *ORRUUUGA! ORRUUUGA!*

And two more seconds, "Dive! Dive!" from the 31 MC circuit.

He was close enough to the Control Room ladder to hear the lookouts and OOD come crashing down from the Bridge. That sound didn't produce a shiver but rather a thrill, as he had come to love lookout duty and operating the Bow and Stern Planes, and the helm.

Then came the *'Whooshing'* sound of the Main Ballast Tanks and Bow Buoyancy Tank filling with water and air escaping through the vents, again a sound that thrilled him.

"Green light on the Conning Tower hatch, sir," from the Chief of the Watch in the Control Room.

"Very well," from the Diving Officer, who kept giving orders but Moser was acquainted with the diving procedures, so again gave his full attention to Richards.

Soon came that distinct down angle. He braced on the Sonar Room door and saw an empty coffee cup first slide across a slick table, then get caught by a ready hand before it hit the floor. Seemed the up and down-angles always caused something to go sliding, somewhere. Whenever he felt the down-angle he always considered what actually was happening. They were diving, going under the waves in the deep, *deep*, water of the Pacific Ocean, miles deep in places. Of course, right then, they were close to shore and the ocean bottom probably wasn't too far away. They probably—

maybe—even were in salvageable water. And the chances of something going wrong and causing them to go to the bottom were so remote that he wondered why he would even think about it...yet he always did. After just a moment or two they leveled out. They always did.

He wondered if anybody else ever had those thoughts, but doubted he would ever actually ask anybody.

Richards moved one of his head piece receivers off his ear and looked up, "Now we're going back in for our boys and hoping they're all there and alive—" He had not considered the possibility that they wouldn't all be there and alive, so it finally occurred to him that, yes, what they were doing was kind of dangerous, more dangerous for the SEALs, of course, which sent the fourth shiver up his back. He hoped the shivers would eventually leave him, and considered asking his mentor about that...at some, more, appropriate, time. He also wondered if his good friend Richards realized that he thought of him as his mentor.

"Our usual way of Pickup is kind of neat," Richards was saying, "Sometimes, well, depending on the mission, we can pick them up the same way we locked them out—they just lock back in again—but normally we'll go in and get between them in their rafts—they went out in two rafts this time, as they might have prisoners—snag the line they have strung between their rafts with our periscope, and tow them back over the horizon, where we can surface, and take them in through the front door. We always do it that way with Special Forces...not always with SEALs and UDT. Anyway, both rafts have transducers hanging in the water, pinging at us, and that's how I was able to send their bearings to the Conning Tower."

"Wow," was all he could think to say.

"Wow is right, and, by the way, if I train you for this job it probably won't include Sonar…maybe, if you do it a lot, but mostly it would just be what happens in the Forward Troop Space."

He shook his head, and realized he suddenly had a lot to think about. Getting those men in and out seemed like a huge responsibility. But maybe he would get the training and then never have to actually do it. Time would tell.

# 41
## First Rumors

The 6-man SEAL team, having blown their bridge, came back fully intact with two Vietcong prisoners, and a rumor of American missionaries being harassed in the vicinity. A rescue attempt was considered but more intelligence was needed before considering interfering, plus a more urgent mission had come up. An air force pilot had been forced to bail out nearby and Hagfish was his nearest and best chance for recovery. Once the SEAL team and their prisoners were aboard the Hagfish steamed due north at full speed on their two engines.

The pilot was rescued and the word came down that they were to proceed to the same coordinates as the last mission for another similar one. That night a 4-man UDT team was launched. The Vietcong were waiting, yet their fire was ineffective because they could not pinpoint the frogmen's position because of darkness. A UDT search party was launched but more gunfire caused some confusion in the darkness. Hagfish, laying on the surface nearby, decided to launch their own search party, an outboard, with scout swimmers. For the last yards they would go in silently with paddles, launch the swimmers, and wait. The original recon team was soon located and recovered. But the original UDT search party had failed to return.

The UDT commander, with two men, launched yet another search party. Halfway to shore they launched a flare, which helped to orient the missing men. The Vietcong fired on the flare and the men manning the 40 millimeters and 50 caliber machine gun on the Hagfish opened fire on the gun bursts. Soon the Vietcong were quieted and all the UDT got safely aboard.

## 42
## Seaman Moser Gets the Upper Bunk

For the next six months Hagfish would continue to steam off the coast of Vietnam and remain available to help in search and rescue. She also would provide services at Legaspi, Philippine Islands, to train Filipino and American UDT personnel. Between local training operations in the Subic Bay area, she would work with Chinese Special Forces at Kaohsiung, Taiwan, and with Army Special Forces at Keelung, Taiwan. During many of these non-combat operations, several other men would receive training but Moser became the main Escape Trunk Operator trainee and having returned to the safety and glass-like waters of the Subic Bay area Second Class Richards began a crash course of Escape Trunk Training, and they had plenty of fresh Filipino and American UDT personnel to train. He held group classes nearly daily, on off-days he worked specifically with Seaman Moser, who liked the extra training but sometimes felt a little overwhelmed.

"OK, Moser," Richards said on one of the off-days, "You finally get your turn in the upper bunk."

That was different. Everybody else had been up in *'The Bunk,'* but he had not, so, he climbed up, slipped in, sort of like squeezing under a vehicle, and lay with his head close to the Escape Trunk valves, then looked back at Richards. "Ready."

"Use your right hand on the flood valve and air valve, and keep the MC in your left. You have to be ready to do whatever you need to do at a moment's notice—not even a moment! You plain have to be ready to *do* it, and it's just as important to stay in touch with the Conning Tower as it is to stay in touch with the guys in the trunk."

"Why…?" He didn't like questioning Richards, as if he thought Richards didn't know what he was doing, because that was not how he felt, but he did want the brass tacks facts of what he was doing.

"Mainly the Conn just needs to know, exactly, what's happening up here. We could use sound-powered phones but that would require four communicators instead of two. Time could be lost. No, there's lives at stake, Moser, the MC puts you in direct contact with the Conning Officer."

"Gotcha." Now he understood. Right, a sound-powered phone operator would take an extra few seconds—probably at both ends—to get the message through. And one or the other operators might even be dreaming about his last liberty. Richards was right. Communication between the Conning Tower and Escape Trunk operator needed to be immediate.

"We're going to go through the entire procedure, but of course you're not actually going to open any valves. Just put your hand on the valve and move your hand in the correct direction. Same with the MC. Talk into the mouthpiece but don't key it. OK, the guys in the trunk just told you to commence flooding."

Moser thought for a few seconds, then spoke into the unkeyed MC, "Conn, Escape. Commencing flooding."

Richards filled in for the Conning Tower, "Commencing flooding. Escape, Conn, aye."

He moved his right hand over the valve in a counter-clockwise direction.

Richards also filled in for the empty Escape Trunk, "Cease flooding."

He moved his hand in a clockwise direction, then spoke into the mouthpiece,

"Conn, Escape. Ceased flooding."

Richards again filled in, "Ceased flooding. Escape, Conn, aye. Good job, Moser, just keep going and I'll fill in for the Conn and the Trunk."

Two hours passed. They had gone over the entire procedure three times.

"That's enough, Moser. C'mon down. We'll be heading in to Olongapo this afternoon for our last liberty for awhile."

Close to inshore communication again, the men of the Hagfish again heard rumors of missionaries being harassed and some even possibly imprisoned near the southern Laotian town of Kengkock. But that was Laos. They weren't—officially—at war with Laos, course, they weren't—*officially*—at war with North Vietnam, either. The men on the hagfish discussed it but were certain the United States would never do anything about rescuing missionaries...officially, that was.

He could see the rumors really bothered Richards. He also suspected the man's reasoning was highly personal, so refrained from mentioning it. The rumors bothered *him* too: he couldn't help thinking of his little sister, Geri, growing up and, possibly, getting into harm's way, and favorite girl, Leah. Of course, both those girls were likely to stay at least in the U.S. Little Geri, though, he knew she had spunk, and she might just want to go out and try to help save the world, and if she ever did get into major harm's way, well, he would hope the U.S. government would try to help her. But little Geri was only eight, so he guessed he didn't have to worry about her, for awhile anyway.

So he understood his friend had some really personal feelings, and if he ever wanted to talk directly about it, he would.

# 43
## Pansy

While again sailing on that glasslike harbor entering Subic Bay, Moser had Mercy on his mind. They had been gone for a long time but he was pretty sure she would remember him. He felt she was that kind of woman, that she *would* remember him. Once tied up they got hooked to base water and all the showers were made available. At sea nobody took a shower unless they were willing to go in on the buddy system—two men under the same spray: *'Get wet' 'soap down' 'wash off'* and *'get out.'* Not exactly a pleasurable experience. But at sea once their fresh water from the last port was used up they had to run the stills, which required a lot of extra fuel. He did it once and decided *'never again'* unless he simply couldn't stand his own body odor.

So when the showers were opened he simply waited his turn, got in alone, got it done and got out, got dressed, picked up his pay, and headed for the gate. Usually plenty of jeepneys were waiting to take the sailors to town. That night he was one of the last to leave. No jeepneys. He started walking. Just as he got past the gate a jeepney arrived, made a U-turn and stopped beside him. He quickly crawled in, "Take me to Pennington's Bar."

"OK, sailor." And they sped off. Pennington's was a distance away, about in the middle of town. He used the time to observe His surroundings, sort of like a tourist, like he didn't the other time in port. Everybody seemed to be selling something. One man appeared to be cooking. He asked the jeepney driver.

"He sell monkey-meat-on-a-stick. Very good delicacy."

"Oh." He was pretty sure he wouldn't try any, as monkeys seemed a bit too much like people. Then he saw another person with bottles, "How about that guy...?"

"Brandy, maybe peach. Very good. You want girl...?" The driver pointed to an old man walking beside a very beautiful young girl, "She his daughter. He guarantee she be very good lover. He know for sure."

"No." He didn't know for sure what to say, and he wondered how the father would know *for sure* that his daughter was a good lover. The girl looked to be about twelve, if that, and it bothered him that, yes, girls that young, and probably even younger, were being pushed into prostitution. He hadn't thought about it before. Little Geri came into his mind. If some pervert male ever hurt her, like *that*, he would track the man down and kill him! He let out a breath at the strongest thought he had ever had, and now wondered about Mercy. He didn't know how old she was, had suspected at least eighteen or nineteen, and now he wondered if she, too, had been pushed into prostitution at a very young age. In fact, until that very moment, he had not thought of her as a prostitute...he had thought of her only as *his* girl, and that gave him a very strange feeling.

"Here bar."

He came out of his thoughts, pulled out the correct change for the jeepney, stepped out and handed over the money, "Thank you."

The jeepney driver waved and sped off.

He returned the wave and watched the jeepney disappear, then looked at the bar door. He hoped Mercy would be sitting and waiting for him at their table, but suddenly had the funny feeling that she would not.

The sound of gaiety reached him as he pushed the bar door open to near darkness. But he was expecting that. Bars were dark. Darkness added to the feeling of romance, and intrigue…and loneliness.

Out of the darkness came a hostess, "You want girl, sailor?"

"Yes. Mercy. Is she here?"

"You come with me." The girl slipped both her hands onto his left arm, "Mercy busy. My name Pansy, what yours?"

"My name is Moser. Would you please tell Mercy I'm here, please…?"

Pansy tightened her grip and steered him toward a booth in a darkened corner, "Mercy busy. You stay with me. I make you happy." She urged him to sit down, then slid in beside him and with her hips pushed him farther.

He slid into the darker darkness. He wanted Mercy but a sudden empty feeling in his stomach began to tell him he was definitely *not* going to get her.

"You want drink?" Pansy asked.

"Yes. Tom Collins." He handed over some money.

"May I have drink too?"

"Yes. Of course."

"More money, please."

He handed over more money, remembering that Mercy had asked for only one drink, and they had sat together for a half hour before she even asked for that. He suspected that Pansy would be quite different, and watched as she scurried off.

He didn't even know what kind of alcohol was used in Tom Collins. He knew it made him drunk. It had made him drunk last time he visited Pennington's, so it would again. He had turned eighteen years old while at GMU10 at Pearl Harbor, but still too young there to drink legally in Hawaii. So he had not tried entering many bars, just The Brightlight stateside, where he met Miss Crawford—for a few seconds an image flashed as he remembered Miss Crawford's body close to him, and her kiss, his *first* kiss—so he had not yet learned how to drink, or what was *in* drinks, had not even decided if he *wanted* to drink, to spend any time at *all* drinking. The other time he drank he had spent half the next day feeling not too good, a headache and upset stomach, and he wondered if drinking was worth it…

Pansy soon returned, set down the two drinks, then slid in beside him again, urging him to slide even further into the darkness. He obliged, took a sip, then, "Did you tell Mercy I was here?"

"I told you, Mercy *busy*." For just a second Pansy scowled, but no longer than a second, "You don't like *me*?"

"I…I, don't know. I don't know you."

"You cherry-boy…?"

He didn't know what to say, and felt very surprised she would ask such a thing, so quickly, but she was a prostitute. Maybe prostitutes were supposed to go straight for the jugular, "I…I—"

"You *cherry*-boy." The second time she said it not in the question-form, and he realized how much more experience this girl had than he, and wasn't sure if that was a good thing. "You want take me home, cherry-boy? I treat you good. I take good care of you."

Just then a splash of light came into the bar-darkness as the front door opened, and a sailor not from the Hagfish entered, arm-in-arm with Mercy.

"Mercy…." All he could think was getting back with the very first girl he had spent real good time with. Not even in high school had he spent such…quality time with a girl…just those very few moments with Leah, at her home in the dark yard. He remembered *that* kiss too.

Their eyes met for just one second, but Mercy looked away immediately. He pushed against Pansy, "Mercy…."

Pansy gripped the table, "Mercy still busy. You stay with *me*."

He released a breath and relaxed against the booth, and began trying to accept what he didn't yet understand, and took a long drink, and another. Pansy took his hand and squeezed it. "You love Mercy…?"

"I…?" He let go with another breath, then felt Pansy's hand on his cheek, pressing him to face her, so he did, and finally looked into her eyes. They were much like Mercy's, but Pansy was not Mercy, and he finally came to the conclusion that he could *not* have Mercy. At least he could not have her in the way that he had so naively *thought* he could have her, and right then he realized that he had even thought he could marry Mercy and take her back to the farm in Iowa, and suddenly that farm in Iowa seemed like forever ago, a place he might never return to…he was so far away—*I'm in the navy now*—and things would never again be as they were, "Yes, Pansy, I want to take you home."

"You pay money?"

"Yes."

"How much you have?"

"Well, how much do you want?"

"You want hour? Two hours?"

"All night."

Pansy's eyes opened wide, "I go see."

He watched her walk away, and realized his life would soon be changed forever. He could love Pansy just as easily as he could love Mercy, except there was a difference. He did *not* love Pansy, but he could easily make love *with* her, and he knew he would *never* get to love Mercy, and realized that was probably right. He was in the navy for another three and one half years, and maybe would enlist again. Yes, he was pretty sure he would. The war in Vietnam would not be over tomorrow, so it's not like he would be out of a job, so, yes, he probably would stay, and he could not afford to fall in love— for a few seconds Leila streaked across his mind. They had gotten to know each other so quickly and shared so many secrets…he shook his head and doubled his fists. No more love, thank you, not for a long while, anyway.

Pansy soon returned and told him how much *'all night'* would be, "Pansy, that's all I have. I won't even have jeepney fare to get back to the base."

"No worry, Moser." She gave him a warm smile, "I make sure you get back to base."

"Okay." He handed over the money.

She took the money and hurried off, and returned quickly, "We go now, Moser?"

"Yes."

She grasped his hand and started them toward the front door. He hung onto her hand and followed, but looked back. Several of his shipmates were looking his way and grinning. And Mercy was looking his way, and not grinning. On her face was…he did not know. For a huge second he felt his heart break and his stomach turned into a knot. Then he turned away and refused to allow himself to feel those feelings, to feel *any* feelings. Mercy was doing what she was required to do. He could *not* help her, so he would do…not what he was *required* to do but what he *wanted* to do.

Once outside Pansy released his hand and slipped her arm around his waist, and leaned into him, so he did the same. She felt good against him, and right to be there, and she felt like she *wanted* to be there…but she was a prostitute. She was doing what she was required to do, but she was acting like she *wanted* to do it, was even glad to do it.

"What your first name, Moser?"

"Brice."

"I call you *'Brice.'*" She leaned against him more closely, almost a *'snuggling'* feeling, not that Brice Wesley Moser had ever really experienced a *'snuggling'* feeling with a girl—well, except for Miss Crawford, and a very little with Leah, and quite a bit actually with Leila—but he suspected a *'snuggling'* feeling was what he was feeling, and it felt good, although *different* from how it felt with the other three girls. He pulled her closer too. She stopped and turned toward him, and, looked deeply into him—deeply, like a lover would, although, again, he didn't know what that would feel like, but he suspected it was how he was feeling…her eyes closed and her lips parted just slightly.

He wasn't sure if her eyes closed first or her lips parted first, and what the hell difference could it make? So when the kiss happened it was the most natural thing on earth. It was a good, nice, kiss, not earth-shattering like Miss Crawford's, and Leah's—and Leila's too, but just nice, gentle, and he felt his head take right off to the hereafter, and realized this was the reason he wanted his first love-making to be sober, maybe all his love-making would be—*should* be. If just a gentle kiss sent him into the sky, well, he was pretty sure the rest would be just as good.

"I like you, Brice."

"I like you too, Pansy."

So they walked on.

They soon crossed a bridge over…what? A river? He doubted it. There were no trees. It looked more like just a ditch, and even in the near-darkness he could see little pipes and troughs entering it, and discharges. What went through his mind was open sewer, but he dismissed such a thought. It was too disturbing, and there was nothing he could do about it. The Philippine Islands were not the same as Iowa farm country, and probably never would be, at least not for a very long time in the future.

\*\*\*\*

Returning to base the next morning, the jeepney Moser was riding in crossed that same waterway. He didn't mean to look, but did, and saw children wading in that brown-colored water. It occurred to him that those same children might never see clean and clear water, might never see the ocean just a few miles away, might never leave this area of town, this…no other word for it but slum. Seeing it in full daylight it looked…well, he was certain he would never want to live there.

## 44
### Ode to Mercy

The next morning after quarters, Moser, returning to the After Troop Space hatch, was joined by Richards, "So, how was it?"

"How was what…?" He had no idea.

"Well, for about a half hour the guys talked about nothing except you leaving the bar with that cute little girl and then not returning. The scuttlebutt was that you lost your cherry last night."

He felt himself turn ten shades of red, and had no idea how to answer.

Richards slapped his shoulder, "Don't worry about it. We all have to lose it eventually—so, did you?"

"Yes, but not with the girl I wanted."

"Well, that's something we all have to deal with too, Moser. We rarely get the girl we want, and I think I know who you wanted…that same one you sat with all night the last time we were in port. Right? And then didn't go home with her, right?"

"Right. Her name is Mercy."

Richards shook his head in a knowing manner, "I saw you leave last night, my friend, and I saw you look back at your

Mercy, but you had better decide to decide right now that that's how it's going to be. Those girls are prostitutes. That's how they make their living."

"But I saw a girl on the street last night—she couldn't have been more than twelve, man! And it looked like she was being sold by some old man—"

Richards stopped them back on the fantail and faced him, "Listen to me, Moser, that's how it works. We're not in America, okay? Although I'm sure it happens there too, just not probably so...openly. That old man you saw was probably her daddy. That little girl maybe is their only way of earning money, and he probably feels lucky that she is so pretty—she *was* pretty, right?"

"She was gorgeous. The cab driver pointed her out, like he even knew."

"If you had approached the old man the cabbie might even have gotten part of the money. You probably even thought about it, right?"

"I—"

"Don't even answer, Moser. I know you did. It would have been less than male if you hadn't, but most of us, I believe, stay away from the real young girls, but not all of us, and even if you didn't actually think about it, the thought absolutely *raged* through the back of your head."

He knew Richards was right. The thought had passed the back of his head, but so quickly as to be almost deniable. What passed the front of his head was his eight-year-old sister at home, but also just for a few seconds. The two girls were not comparable. His sister back in Iowa was safe, protected by her loving dad, her loving mother, her loving grandparents, her teachers and preachers, but this young Filipino girl evidently—*probably*—had nobody.

"But you didn't act on that thought, Moser! And that's what separates us—guys like you and me—from the barbarians."

He stared at his friend and nodded, "Yes, I guess so."

"To get back to your Mercy. You thought you were in love with her, didn't you?"

"Yes."

"And that happens to some of us again and again. This is my third Westpac cruise, and I have fallen in love at least thirty times, and that's not necessarily a bad thing. It means I cared for those girls. Not enough to marry any of them, no, but enough to treat them all like a lady, and they are all ladies, Moser." Richards stopped talking, evidently had reached the end of his lecture.

And he appreciated the lecture, "Yes, Sir." He hoped he could adopt at least some of Richards' philosophies.

"One more thing in closing, Moser. I found this out from the bar owner. That first night you were with Mercy, that also was her first night of working as a bar maid, and young girls are no different from young boys, you know, and first encounters are always the important ones. You gave her a good first encounter, my friend, and I'm sure she will never forget you."

## 45
### More Rumors & The Battle of Ia Drang

In July 65 the Hagfish joined operation Deckhouse II. In August, for Deckhouse IV, they landed UDT personnel on five successive nights for preinvasion beach reconnaissance.

Moser did become an Escape Trunk operator. Richards or another senior operator was always there too but not just for Moser, as a backup operator was always necessary. When UDT personnel returned there continued to be reports of missionaries being harassed, but also always not enough intelligence to back the reports up. And just harassment didn't necessitate a rescue. But both Richards and Moser stayed on top of any new information. Those missionaries were Americans, just like them, after all, and they were there not to kill people or do any harm; they were there to teach and to heal. Part of the problem for the communists likely was what they were teaching, and Christian missionaries taught only one thing. Also, no names of the missionaries had yet surfaced.

****

In November the new destination of Yokosuka, Japan, was announced for an extended Rest & Relaxation (R&R) period, to the men Intercourse & Intoxication (I&I.) During the trip up news of the battle of the Ia Drang Valley reached them. Moser was in the mess hall at the time, and heard all the varied comments, mostly from the youngest man on board and the very old and salty First Class Gunner's Mate, Higgins, "Over 200 American casualties,"

"Dead, or wounded?" From the young guy.

"Dead *and* wounded. Both, man. Casualties means both. If they're dead they'd say *'killed in action'* or *'KIA,'* and *'missing in action,'* or *'MIA.'"*

"Just one battle, Jesus."

"The first major battle, man. I'd say we're in it for the long haul now."

"How long?"

"Oh, a year or two for sure, I'd say."

"Were they ambushed?"

"Not according to the story. The official word for now is the Seventh Cavalry just had orders for *'Search and Destroy'* but were dropped by helicopter right into a nest of NVA. Both sides were surprised, and neither were prepared for such a battle."

"The Seventh Cavalry?" The young guy appeared impressed.

"Yep, ole Custer's outfit." Higgins appeared to be somewhat milking the situation. Moser wondered where the Gunner's Mate was getting his information. "Except Colonel Hal Moore didn't get massacred like Custer did."

"So how about the commies? How many casualties there?"

"Not known for sure," Higgins said, "Between fifteen hundred and two thousand."

"Wow—holy shit!"

Moser agreed. *'Wow'* and *'holy shit'* was correct. It looked like an American victory, yet over two hundred casualties was a lot. That meant over two hundred mothers and fathers, and wives, would get some very unhappy news. He thought of his own parents. They had not been happy to see him join the navy, but had accepted it, but he didn't like to think about the possibility of his parents getting that same news. So, they wouldn't. He would see to it. There was too much in life yet that he wanted to do, and places to go. He even thought he wanted to get married someday, so, he couldn't get killed in Vietnam. Though he kind of disagreed with Higgins about a *'year or two.'* If the North Vietnamese were willing to give up around two thousand men in just one battle, it seemed they were willing to go on for quite a while. The word during the Korean War, that other Asian war, *'They just kept coming....'* So, they likely would in Vietnam, too.

Later he would hear that the media was a bit mute about the battle of Ia Drang, as the American public would not like hearing about that many casualties. Word also was beginning to drift back that much of the public was definitely *not* in favor of the war

# 46
## Yokosuka

When they tied up at the navy base at Yokosuka, and while approaching, they were able to hear a regular radio station again, one of the first bits of news they heard was from Washington D.C., the march on the White House by 35,000 anti-war protestors, and the rally by the same protestors at the Washington Monument. It was starting to seem, somewhat strongly, that not all of America was behind this new Asian war, but then every American war had been like that. Even America's first war. A whole bunch of people wanted to continue living under the British crown, and strangely enough, even after losing two wars to the new United States, today the British were one of America's closest friends.

\*\*\*\*

For the time of year Yokosuka felt about the same to Moser as Iowa, mainly just chilly, but chilly enough for the pea coat. Not exactly meant for travel in the Arctic but he liked the pea coat. He felt it completed his uniform, and made him look…official, he guessed.

Another thing had happened during the trip to Yokosuka; it had taken a while, but he had gotten qualified and earned his dolphins. No ceremonies yet, but they would come. Even so, when he left on liberty that night, wearing a shiny new set of dolphins, he felt he stood a little taller, definitely prouder.

The world was already dark when he reached the main street hangout for sailors, the nearly endless colored neon lights advertising Girls, Dancing, and Liquor. At least there appeared to be few, or no, street vendors, like Olongapo. Course, Japan was a bit colder too. After getting his paycheck cashed at the Enlisted Men's Club he had walked out onto the street again, and decided there must be an aircraft carrier also in the harbor, because the streets were crawling with sailors.

So he kept walking, until there were fewer and fewer sailors, and then there were none.

One really bright neon sign soon appeared ahead. Such a distance from the main streets he figured the name of the bar would be in Japanese characters, but no, it was in huge English letters: Club Shangri La.

He stopped. There would be few sailors in such an out-of-the-way place, and he felt a bit leery of entering, but did.

"Good evening," an absolutely gorgeous Japanese woman said, "How are you, Sir?"

He didn't know what to say, so just answered her question, "I'm fine."

"Would you care for a drink, Sir?"

"Yes. Beer, please."

"Kirin?"

He guessed that would be the official Japanese beer, so, "Yes."

"Let me take you to a booth, Sir." She did, then left for the bar. In just a moment she returned. He had his money ready. "You may pay later, Sir. May I join you?"

"Yes, but may I buy you a drink also."

"Yes. Thank you very much."

He took his beer, poured his glass half full, took a sip, and watched the woman walk away. Yokosuka, at least the bar where he was, was not like Olongapo. He suspected Olongapo had nicer bars too, but he had visited just the one, and it certainly wasn't like this one. Rich-looking wood trimmed all doors, windows and mirrors, and there were plenty of mirrors. Even with the low light atmosphere the bar had several lush green foliage plants. Maybe they turned the lights on bright during the day, and were open to serve drinks only at night.

The woman soon reappeared carrying a tall glass of a light blue-colored liquid, a straw, and an umbrella. She slid into the booth beside him but did not push up against him as the Filipino woman, Pansy, had, "Thank you for the drink, Sir. What ship you on?"

"The Hagfish."

"Oh, a submarine."

"Yes. How did you know?"

"Other submarine sailors have come here, and their ships are all named after fish."

"That's good." He felt impressed that she had made such a deduction, "That's very good. So, do you go to school?"

"Yes. I go to college. English is my main course, and business."

Again he was impressed, "What is your goal?"

"Well, I would like to translate for Japanese and American companies someday."

"Wow...I'm glad for you."

"And I hope to someday travel to America."

He had found an educated woman, much more educated than himself, which he knew didn't take much. But he felt a little sad because he suspected she would not be the typical bar hostess, that she would not be for sale, or if she was it would again take all his pay. But to make love with such a gorgeous woman maybe *'all his pay'* would be worth it.

He gazed at her as she spoke about herself. She smiled often and touched his hand or arm often, just gentle, brushing, touches, the kind that left him wanting more, and he began to feel that the evening would end as he wanted, "What is your name?" he asked.

"I am Chloe-san. What is yours?"

For some reason he didn't really understand, he wanted this very pretty Japanese girl to know his first name, "Brice."

"Very happy to know you, Bri-san." She held out her hand.

H grasped it and held on, and turned it so the top of her hand faced up, then he leaned over and kissed it, "Very happy to know you, too, Chloe-san."

Her smile brightened even more as he raised up. It was the richest smile he had ever seen on a woman. She pulled slightly away, "I show you something."

He released her hand. She picked up her drink and slid a little closer to him, and nodded toward his drink. He picked it up, with his left hand.

"With your right hand, please," she said, then waited for him to change hands. He did. She reached toward him with her drink and nodded toward his.

He wasn't sure but thought she wanted a toast, so he touched her glass with his. She increased her smile and hooked into his arm, "We toast each other," then brought her drink to her lips.

Finally getting the idea, he did the same, and took just a small drink. Chloe-san kept their arms hooked. Her smile moderated. Her lips parted just a tiny bit; she tipped her head up also just a tiny bit. Again, this time without even thinking about it, he got the idea and leaned down to her and their lips came together.

It was one of the gentlest kisses he had ever experienced—for one solid second his kiss with Leah splashed, then the one with Leila, and the thought he was an asshole for kissing so many girls, all in the space of that one second. He dismissed those thoughts, and knew of course he had not experienced that many kisses, but he was pretty certain what he had just experienced was one of the very best ones. Their lips stayed just together for a full moment, just gently touching each other's psyche.

"You kiss very well, Bri-san. May I stay with you tonight?"

He wasn't entirely sure what she meant by that but answered, "Yes."

"All night?" She laid out a book of matches where a Japanese man and woman were facing each other, then she smiled and turned the book so that it showed the couple in the prone position, the man on top.

"Yes, very much so." Now he was pretty sure what she meant, and, again he was pretty sure it was going to take his whole pay check, but he didn't care. When one makes love with a woman there should be no time limit, and, with this woman he was pretty sure he would want to stay with her and hold her all night, as if they were married. Married. He hadn't meant for that word to cross his mind again. And of course he wasn't thinking he wanted marriage with Chloe-san, yet he wouldn't *not* want marriage with her either, but at least for the upcoming night they could act like they were married.

"I go talk to owner of bar."

"Okay." He watched her walk away and felt right about his decision. Strange, though, the talk he had heard so much on the boat was of guys just buying their love-time by the hour, or even just a half hour, rarely, usually never, for all night. Some of the guys had full time girls in Olongapo but most went by the hour in some hotel room, whereas Moser went to the girl's home, which, to him, made their love-making much more special. He couldn't help thinking yet again of Leah, his red-headed girlfriend back in Iowa—but she wasn't his girlfriend! Never had been, never would be!

Chloe-san returned and slid in beside him, and this time she slid in all the way and touched him, and a warmth came from her to him, making him doubly-feel that, yes, he was doing right. He suspected that Chloe-san, too, appreciated the idea of *'all night.'*

Many smiles and touches later they finished their drinks. Neither had hurried, nor rushed the other. They knew they had time and they both looked forward to that time, and would cherish all their time together. He felt love growing for this Japanese girl, and he remembered feeling love for Mercy at Olongapo, even, as the night had worn on, love for Pansy. He wondered if he even knew what real love felt like, because how could he feel love for three different girls, at three different times, and still think all three were true love? And Miss Crawford and Morgan Rhodes and Leila...and Leah, still his favorite...but...fading...?

He didn't know, and doubted he would ever know.

"Bri-san, shall we go home?"

"Yes, Chloe-san, let's go home." And, like before, what he paid for this gorgeous Japanese girl left him without even money for cab fare back to the base, but again his woman had said she would see to it that he got to his base, so he didn't care. He didn't want his love-making to be dictated to him by time constraints, nor, evidently, he felt, did Chloe-san.

## 47

### Love With Chloe-san

The ride to Chloe-san's home took ten minutes. Chloe-san paid the cabbie, then took Moser by the hand and led him into a narrow walkway lit by a dim lamp about every forty feet. It was dark, but appeared surreal, wet from the earlier rain. He dropped her hand and put his arm around her waist. She leaned against him, and again that warmth came from her to him, and again he knew he had been right in paying for *'all night.'* The buildings crowding their walkway on both sides looked…well, they didn't look like anything he had ever seen in America, and very different from those in Olongapo too. These buildings were small, yes, but elegant in comparison to Olongapo.

They reached Chloe-san's home. She unlocked the door and slid it open, then immediately removed her shoes. He took the cue and also removed his. The floor of her entryway was spotless, and chilly. He was not used to walking in his stocking feet. She again took him by the hand and led him to the door of the next room, slid the door open and they entered a warmer room. A kitchen maybe, he thought.

"Are you hungry, Bri-san?"

He hadn't thought about it, but at the mention of food, yes, he was, "Yes, thank you."

"Rice or noodles?"

"Noodles, please."

She led him to a chair by a table, "You may sit here, or wait by the television."

That would mean a different room. He wanted to stay with this very nice and pretty and kind Japanese woman, but wondered if he was getting goofy? He thought not, "I'll wait here, with you."

She smiled. Her smile looked sincere. He felt his love for her growing.

It took her only moments to prepare a pot of noodles. She also went to work cutting up something that looked like an onion, but he soon smelled something that did not smell like an onion, "Do you like garlic?" she asked.

He had never eaten garlic, "I don't know."

"It's for flavor, and is very good for you. Do you want to try?"

According to the smell he thought not, but wanted to please her, "Yes, I will try."

"Good, so when we kiss again you will not be offended by my breath. Garlic gives one very bad breath, but it is a Japanese staple."

Wow, not only a beautiful woman but also very caring and considerate.

Just a few more moments passed before she dished up two portions of noodles, "Saki?"

He knew his expression said he didn't know what Saki was.

"She smiled, "It is rice wine. A little will…help us to relax…but not so much that we won't appreciate each other."

"Sure. I'd like some Saki."

After the meal and a few sips of the wine, Chloe-san again offered the toast with their arms hooked. He was willing. The kiss happened again, too, and lasted a little longer but was no less gentle. He wanted the love with this wonderful Japanese woman to be that: wonderful, and slow, and gentle, and lasting. For the time he would be with this lovely Japanese girl he wanted to cherish her. And for that night he would.

In another five or six days they would return to the coastal waters of Vietnam, and do whatever their government required of them. Finally he realized Chloe-san had not asked the one question they had been warned about *not* answering, and remembered being told that the bar girls of Yokosuka usually ask two questions together. He remembered well when she asked, "What ship you on?" which he answered, but the second question, that he couldn't answer, "What ship numba?" did not come.

# 48
## Shore Patrol

The next morning Chloe-san gave Moser cab fare and directed him to where he could find a cab, one block straight down her street, turn right, then three more blocks. Feeling refreshed from a breakfast of rice and another kiss, he started walking. Ahead, about two blocks yet, he saw plenty of early morning traffic. The street where he walked was empty, and he saw no problem with that—

"Hey!" The voice, a bit unfriendly-sounding, came from an alley to his right. He glanced in and saw a sailor standing about twenty feet away, looking toward him as if…waiting? He had no idea.

"What's up, man?" he called, "You need to share cab fare, or something?"

"Yeah! Come on back." The other sailor did not smile, if anything even looked angry, but why?

He hesitated, weighing the situation. The guy was older, heavier, taller, and why should he enter the alley?

"Come on—what's the problem? I just figured you'd rather stand and wait in the alley here instead of out in the street."

"Why do I have to wait at all?"

"Because I need to say goodbye to my sweetie." He gestured backward with his thumb.

"All right." Still feeling uncomfortable he took two steps in.

Had he been a regular to Yokosuka's back streets he would have known there were countless alleys and pukas everywhere, and would have studied and weighed the situation much longer—

His arms were gripped in iron the moment he left the sidewalk. The guy he had been talking to became a slow-motion but instantaneous presence right in front of him, and his fist got there even sooner.

His hat went flying as he saw stars. The fist came again into his stomach. Finally a roundhouse that sent him flailing toward the side—where he hit a metal garbage can that went flying and making a terrible noise—as the guy holding him let loose, and the guy doing the damage kicked him in the middle before he even landed. He ended up flat on his back and still seeing mostly stars and a cloudy sky—

"That's my woman you spent the night with, buddy," the voice said, "She thought I was far out to sea, but I wasn't. Don't ever go near her again!" The voice was punctuated by Moser's hat landing on his face, then two sets of footsteps leaving the alley.

He got his head up in time to see both sailors disappear onto the street. Maybe two minutes later, as he started getting to his feet, he heard a siren—*the shore patrol?* He finished getting up, threw his white hat on, and glanced around quickly for an escape route…but there was none. Shortly, one of them sickly-gray painted navy pickups stopped right outside his alley, and two guys with shore patrol arm patches and batons already out and ready, left the pickup.

# 49
## Classified

Under new orders, the Hagfish cut its port call short and left Yokosuka after just thirty-six hours, then had again steamed quickly south and west. Moser stood his regular lookout/planesman/helmsman watches and kept mostly to himself, but when they arrived off Vietnam again, Richards finally approached him and asked, "Think you can see well enough to get me out? That shiner still looks kind of painful."

"Yeah, I can see fine."

"So the shore patrol just believed you and brought you back to the base, huh?"

"They did talk to the person who called."

"A witness…."

"I guess. I didn't get to see them, or my girl, either, not that it was necessary to involve her."

"I s'pose I should have warned you about going off alone like that. Most of us stay in the sailor part of town."

"Yeah, I reckon, but this girl was worth a little trouble— say, what'd you mean by asking if I can see well enough to get you out?"

"I'm going out this time, Moser."

"Going out…? I don't know what you mean…what do you mean…?"

"We've been hearing about those missionaries being harassed, well, now we're sure they're prisoners, and we don't expect the communists to treat them very well, so, we're going to attempt a rescue. We've talked about it before. There was a hospital in there that would help anybody, even wounded Viet Cong and NVA. It's run by American missionaries, and the Viet Cong kept attacking them and harassing them, and our intelligence says they were finally taken prisoner…awhile ago. We might already be too late. Anyway, I'm going out with the marines and UDT."

"But why are *you* going? Do you even have any combat training?"

Richards laughed about that, "I have as much training as anybody on board, my boy, maybe not as much or as detailed as the marines and UDT, but I have enough."

"But Laos? That's way inland."

"The new intel says they've been moved to a Vietnamese village not that far away."

He didn't doubt his friend had plenty of training. His problem was simply his shipmate, his mentor, his friend, putting himself in major harm's way. He didn't know what to say, and he couldn't say how he was feeling, he couldn't really let Richards know how much he worshiped the man, "But why do *you* have to go? Aren't the marines enough? Christ…."

Again Richards laughed, "Of course they are, but they don't have the intelligence that we do, that *I* do—"

"What intelligence? I haven't heard about any intelligence…." He was groping. He simply didn't want his friend to go. He did not want to, possibly, *lose* his friend—he had already lost so many, not to death he didn't think, but just plain had lost them!

"I don't tell you everything, Moser. This time I couldn't. We're going into some major hot ground. Not even the marines know what our mission tomorrow is, and they won't know until tomorrow night at 2200, just before they go out on deck with their rafts. Right this moment only the captain and myself know the details."

"Christ." He thought for a moment, then, "But you still haven't told me. Why *you*?"

"Somebody has to do it, Moser. Somebody who knows the details, knows the terrain, and…volunteers."

Again he thought for a moment, "But didn't they warn you in bootcamp about never volunteering?" He said it with half a grin, but knew it wouldn't matter, "If it's that classified why have you told me?"

"Because three UDT personnel, and I, are going first, tonight, for recon, and you, Moser, my friend, are going to lock us out."

If it was possible for a stomach to come unglued and leave one's body, that statement should have caused it. His heart stopped too, maybe for two or three seconds, then gave an extra loud bang when it started again. True, since his excellent training he had locked out six teams of UDT and one of SEALs, but none of them were his best friend, "Why me, Richards?"

"What do you mean? *'Why me?'* And think before you answer that. You're well-trained and you're well-qualified."

But, of course, he had no answer. There was no reason he could *not* do it, "Okay, I guess I can do it."

"Yes, you can." Richards patted his shoulder, "And don't worry. You'll do fine. We're going out at 2300, and that's in just an hour, so…see you up there?"

"Yes, Sir." Yes, he would be there, but for right then he needed to get out of his friend's sight. He needed to deep breathe for awhile, or shallow-breathe, he didn't know what he needed to do, but did know he needed to get his head wrapped around this concept of what he had to do in the next hour.

On his way to the After Troop Space, while passing through the Mid-ship Troop Space just aft of the After Battery he saw a familiar face, "Crosby."

The marine appeared to be inventorying his pack, and looked up, "Ah, Moser, one of the friendly swabbies."

He didn't know what that meant, "I don't know what you mean by *'friendly,'* Crosby, so, what do you mean? Are some of the guys *not* friendly?"

"Nobody is *not* friendly, Moser, I guess it's just that you are more so. Sometimes some of the crew mainly seem to want to just get past us."

He laughed, "Some of the guys are probably scared of you. You *are* marines, ya know."

Crosby shook his head, "And maybe some of *us* are not so friendly...."

Moser shook his head too, "Could be, my friend." He then approached and stuck out his hand, "How ya been, Crosby?"

"Fine, except that I got pulled from my command for this special mission. Not so bad though, there's eight of us, but, hell, we don't even know what's happening. But, hell, they never tell us jarheads anything anyway." Crosby gripped his hand.

*Not till you're ready to go on deck with your rafts.* He thought about telling him. After all, *they* were going into harm's way too and deserved to know, but that would betray his friend, Richards. What went though his mind was to ask Crosby to look out for Richards, to protect him, but he also knew that would be the total wrong thing to say, "They'll tell you, man. What the hell? They don't tell me anything either." *That's a lie.* "Half the time I don't even know where we are." *Another lie.* True in the beginning, yes, but since he had befriended Richards he probably found out about more stuff than most, "Well, I have some squaring away to do back in my compartment, then I have to get on watch." *Still another lie.* He had absolutely *nothing* to do back in his compartment. He simply needed to get alone with his thoughts, "So I'll see you later, Crosby."

"You betcha, Moser."

As he moved on toward the Maneuvering Room it occurred to him that even though he had only a confidential clearance—as all boat sailors required—he often, thanks to Richards, was privy to classified material. How classified he didn't know, and realized he had considered telling that marine classified material. It wouldn't likely have meant the end of the world, but still, he had to also get his head wrapped around the idea that classified material was just that: Classified. Need-to-know only. Richards had trusted him to know.

He reached the After Troop Space. A couple card games were going on, weapons inspections and cleaning, smoking groups…looked like a normal evening. He looked at his watch. Still forty minutes until lockout. A long time to wait. He sat down on the floor facing the door to the after head, drew his knees up to his chest, wrapped his arms around his legs, and stared straight ahead, at nothing. Plenty in his mind though, namely his past navy friends, Terry Hamm, Cordegan, Dokken, where were they? Had they gotten good navy commands? Did Dokken get his sub? Were they still in the navy? Were they even alive? Dead? In harm's way?

Shit! He shouldn't be thinking about guys, but girls, especially Leah, and now Leila, too, as Miss Crawford and Morgan Rhodes were fading a bit, plus he had Mercy and Pansy and Chloe-san—*what the fuck is wrong with me?* He should be thinking about the coming lockout!

## 50
## Lockout

Thirty minutes passed. Moser stood, and realized the shallow breathing was continuing, and knew it *would* continue, maybe until Richards was safely back aboard. Heading forward his mind went blank. Better that way. No more thinking about it or anything else. He knew his job and knew he would do it correctly, and let his feet find their own way.

Five minutes later he reached the Forward Troop Space and saw his friend suiting up. Richards looked no different from the other UDT personnel, just another warrior going out to do his job. He walked directly to the ladder leading up to the top bunk, and sent one look at his friend. Richards sent the look back. Basically, they had already said *'goodbye'* so no point repeating anything.

He grasped the ladder handrails and crawled up partway, then grabbed a couple solid pipes and swung into the bunk, then looked back at the Lockout team. The leader sent a *'thumbs up.'* He grasped the 31MC and spoke into it, "Conn, Escape. Ready for the first Lockout."

Immediately, "Escape, Conn. Commence the first lockout."

"Commence first lockout. Conn, Escape, aye."

The first two UDT personnel climbed into the Escape Trunk and closed the bottom hatch, causing that *'clacking'* sound that he had barely noticed before.

The first lockout went smoothly. With the Escape Trunk drained, he spoke into the 31MC, "Conn, Escape. Ready for second lockout."

"Escape, Conn. Commence second lockout."

"Commence second lockout. Conn, Escape, aye."

The third UDT member went up first, then Richards. He met his friend's eyes once more and received a *'thumbs up,'* which he returned, but in the far back of his mind he wished the *'thumbs up'* just meant one or the other was just going to take his turn at the pool table, or something else of a more benign activity.

Richards' feet disappeared and the hatch *'clacked'* closed, causing a sound that rang through his head. The shallow breaths finally stopped, then he took one deep one.

"Commence flooding," came from the trunk.

In the same movement he opened the flood valve and keyed the MC, "Conn, Escape. Commencing flooding." The sound of that water pouring into the Escape Trunk was louder than a waterfall. He felt he heard every drop.

"Commencing flooding. Escape, Conn, aye."

From the Escape Trunk, "Cease flooding."

He slammed the flood valve closed, and felt a breath leave him, and keyed the MC, "Conn, Escape. Ceased flooding." And another breath left him, but he wasn't nervous, not worried, so what then? He felt like he was somewhere else watching himself going through these motions; he felt totally out-of-body but also knew he was in full control.

"Ceased flooding. Escape, Conn, aye."

From the Escape Trunk, "Side door undogged."

Again in the same movement he opened the air valve and keyed the MC, "Conn, Escape. Side door undogged and pressurizing." The sound of that blasting air was like the thunder in an Iowa electric storm, but he wasn't in Iowa.

"Door open!"

Christ! He was staring at the pressure valve. He had even seen the needle fluctuate maybe one tenth of a second before hearing *'Door open!'* He could have *beat* them, and felt sure it was Richards' voice sending the commands. Richards must have held back that one tenth of a second to give him a chance to finally win at their game, and then he had to blow it anyway.

But, what the hell? He keyed the MC, "Conn, Escape. Side door open."

"Door open. Escape, Conn, aye."

He kept watching the pressure gauge. After only a few seconds the needle stabilized. *They're out.* Door closed. Automatically he spoke into the MC, opened the drain valve and the air pressure valve. Again he heard the sound of water, this time pouring into the bilges. The water sound stopped.

Then he opened the vent valve allowing a blast of air to come into the compartment. One more time he keyed the MC, "Conn, Escape. Team away and Escape Trunk secured."

"Escape, Conn, aye."

He placed the MC in its holder, relaxed against the bunk for a few seconds, and felt what actually sounded like a sob leaving him. He took another really deep breath and tightened his fists, then climbed down from the bunk and up the Escape Trunk lower hatch and opened it. A few drops of sea water hit his face and head. They felt good, and smelled good. For then his job was done. He headed aft. And for no real reason a memory nudged him.

## 51
### USS Thresher

It was early in 1963. He didn't remember the date, maybe March or April. But he did remember the sub's name and number: USS Thresher SSN 593, a nuclear submarine. He was in the barn with his dad milking the cows when the national news mentioned an atomic submarine lost. *Lost.* What exactly did that mean? Just can't find it? Mutinied? Sunk? The radio story was vague and gave no details, and nothing at all on their two television channels. A week went by before he stumbled on the story in a magazine, and, again, not a lot of details, except that, yes, it had sunk, in very deep water. So, not likely that it would ever be heard from again. He remembered hoping, for a long time, that it wasn't true, like the sub would somehow reappear out of the mist, like the happy ending of a fairy tale. But it never did.

He entered the Forward Battery Officer Quarters. He saw no officers. Likely they were sleeping, like most men on board. Even though they operated twenty-four hours a day, day was still treated as day, and night as night. So most men would be sleeping. He wondered how many men on board would know that this team of UDT, plus his friend, Richards, had gone out to recon the local vicinity for a possible prisoner-camp rescue.

Not many, probably.

He entered the Control Room. Not much activity there either. The Diving Officer, Lieutenant Williams, the Gunnery Officer, his boss, standing right behind the planesmen, ready for surfacing, which they likely would be doing in about a half hour or so. Another guy sitting beyond the planesmen on the tanks manifold, ready to flood Negative Tank if they needed to go deep in a hurry, or pump dry safety if they needed to slow or stop a descent.

Was that what happened to the Thresher? Did they get too heavy too quick and sink uncontrollably? He glanced at First Class Engineman Starsky on the air manifold, ready to blow all tanks if they needed a quick surfacing. *'Starsky,'* the name rang a bell, the same name as the engineman on the USS Charr, who gave him and Dokken the tour. Again, did the men in Thresher try to blow their tanks and surface, but for some reason couldn't?

Strange how he would think of those men now. He knew why. Those men all died with probably no chance. His friend Richards had gone out into harm's way…but at least with a chance. He had weapons and knew how to use them. Yes, Richards would have a chance. The men on Thresher had weapons too, but their most sophisticated weapons and equipment did not help them.

He passed the Radio Shack and glanced in. Second Class Sonarman Corwin sat on the Sonar station. Even though there would be no pingers from a rubber raft that night they still had to be there. There were Soviet ships always on patrol, although he hadn't heard of any very close. But they still had to keep the sonar and radar eyes and ears out there.

He thought of the sub movie he had seen not long after the Thresher went down. The Enemy Below, with Robert Mitchum on an American destroyer and Curt Jergens in a

German submarine. After seeing that movie on the big screen he had considered he, *maybe*, wanted to be a submariner, even though the German submarine was the so-called *'bad guy.'* That had changed now. The Germans were now allies, attested to by another sub movie he had seen recently right there on the Hagfish. The Bedford Incident, there again an American destroyer with Richard Widmark as captain, and they never got to see the Soviet sub commander because he never was allowed to surface. But another officer on board was German, and, through miscommunication causing an accidental firing of an ASROC missile, which in turn caused the sub to fire a torpedo, they all sank and died there in the cold frozen Arctic.

Again, he thought of the men in the sub, but at least on the Soviet sub they probably heard the ASROC missile explode, maybe a second or two before the sea water and pressure overwhelmed and killed them. Did the men on the Thresher hear anything? An explosion? Anything on the MC? Did the men know they were in trouble? Did the captain? Or did just the Diving Officer and the few men in the Control Room and Conning Tower know? Did the men feel their death? Or did it come so swiftly there was no time to feel anything? Maybe at least half the crew was asleep…and felt nothing.

He moved on into the chow hall. A few men were playing Acey-deucy. Two others studied their cards in a Cribbage game. Still another worked on building a sandwich of cheese, baloney, lettuce, tomato and mayonnaise. Everybody probably knew about the locking out that night. They locked-out enough that the crew had grown accustomed to it, he guessed, and realized that he, too, was accustomed to it and pretty much didn't think about it, until his best friend became a part of the team. He wondered if anyone else even knew that Richards was gone.

He hurried on, through the darkened After Battery sleeping compartment, then the Engineroom-converted sleeping compartment, also darkened, and didn't even slow down in Maneuvering. He just wanted to get up into his bunk with his thoughts and hope he could sleep. But with his friend out in harm's way he didn't expect a lot of sleep.

## 52
## Waiting

The next night arrived. At exactly 2200 the eight marines launched their two rafts and headed into the surf. Four would join Richards and the UDT, and four would remain at rendezvous. The Hagfish backed into deeper water, made a U-turn, then steamed back to the twelve-mile line just over the horizon, where they would, again, wait.

Moser, having stood his turn as After Troop Space watch, walked somewhat endlessly among the canyons and tunnels of the USS Hagfish, awaiting word of his friend Richards. At the Radio Shack he had asked several times if there was any word from the landing party. Depending on who was on watch his answers varied from *'no word'* to *'that's classified'* but he felt the Escape Trunk operator should have been allowed to know…whatever he wanted to know.

He even went to his boss, Gunnery Officer, Lieutenant Williams, "That's need-to-know, Moser."

"But *I* sent them out there, Sir." He felt lost, and probably showed it, for as he turned to leave.

"Wait, Moser." Lieutenant Williams gestured for him to enter the officers' wardroom, "I know Richards is a friend of yours—"

"A very close friend, Sir."

"A close friend, yes, I understand, but you need to get a grip. Richards volunteered for this mission. He spent his off hours for three days studying the terrain maps up in the Conning Tower. Why he wanted to go—I don't know. He didn't say and I didn't ask him, and he's our best Escape Trunk operator. I did mention that to him and do you want to know what he told me?"

He stared at his boss, "Yes…, what…?"

"He said *you* could handle the Escape Trunk as well as him. In fact, he said if he didn't come back that you should be put in charge, for any training necessary too."

"My god." He put his hand over his mouth. It almost seemed that Richards had a death wish, and he had to have had a reason for going out there, "Do you agree with him, Sir?"

"I've watched you work, Moser. You learn fast and you do a great job."

"I'm only a Seaman."

"Doesn't matter. Only your knowledge and skills matter, and there's something else you need to get a handle on…."

"Sir…?"

"This mission we're on *is* dangerous. Our intelligence says there not only is a prisoner camp out there—well-guarded I might add—there also are reports of a whole regiment of NVA close by…."

"Sir…what else?"

"Well, we've taken every precaution, but it's possible some of our guys could get killed, including your friend—"

Somebody finally said it. Somebody, maybe everybody, could get killed. Sure, he knew that. He even understood and accepted it. *No!* he *didn't* accept it, well, he did but…he suddenly couldn't think anymore. His stomach felt so empty, and so did his head, and his heart, he wasn't even sure if he would continue breathing.

"We're on radio-silence," Lieutenant Williams was continuing, "And if I hear something…bad, no, I won't tell you."

"Sir…?"

"Even bad news would be classified, Moser. The crew needs to stay together and stay focused and do their job, including you. We *are* at war, Moser. Period."

"Yes, Sir. I understand."

"I'm glad you do, because I don't always, but I do my job, same as I expect you to."

"Thank you, Sir." He stuck out his hand.

The lieutenant grasped his hand and for a moment a bonding occurred between the two young men, one an officer, one an enlisted man.

****

After that Moser quit bugging the people on watch in the Radio Shack. Lieutenant Williams had made it pretty plain that he wouldn't/couldn't get any information, and probably should quit trying. If somebody out on a mission got killed he would just have to wait for the announcement, like everybody else. They were batting a hundred percent so far: no casualties.

## 53
## No Rescue

Second Class Electronics Technician Richards, the three UDT personnel including the Boatswain's Mate, Pat Walsh, who Richards had met and befriended earlier, and four of the marines including Crosby, who Moser had befriended, stood behind a growth of jungle shrubbery. About two hundred feet inside the village was the smoking and charred hulk of what appeared to have been a wooden building. One post—or pedestal of some sort—was about the only thing still standing, obviously made of metal. At the bottom of the post appeared…impossible to tell from the distance, even with binoculars, what was there, but Richards had a very unpleasant feeling in his gut. Even in his subconscious mind he refused to consider what was there. It was too horrifying.

From nowhere appeared a peasant-looking man walking, carrying a basket, maybe of food. It appeared he would pass close by the eight watching men. Richards turned to the UDT leader, "Do we take him?"

"Yes. We'll wait till he's fully on the trail and out of sight from the village."

About one more minute passed. The peasant man and his basket was pulled into the jungle without a sound. The UDT leader put a knife to his throat, "Speak English?"

"Yes! The missionaries taught me."

"Where are the missionaries?"

"Some were taken away."

"Some...?"

"Yes, just some...." The peasant man glanced toward the still smoking ruins of the wooden building.

"What's there?" Richards asked.

"The missionaries they didn't take. Two women."

"Are there soldiers in the village now?" UDT Walsh asked, "NVA? Vietcong?"

"No. And most villagers have left."

"Take us to the two women," UDT said.

"You will not like what you see," the peasant man said, "But come. I show you."

Richards, Walsh, and Crosby, then accompanied the peasant man to the burned building, to the standing post. The man pointed, "They were tied back-to-back, with wire. I gave them water when I could, but they were never released for any reason. They were there for five days before...." He hesitated.

"Before *what*?" UDT asked.

"The soldiers were ordered to leave, and to execute the two missionaries because women were too much trouble on the trail...they simply set the house on fire. I hid...but I could hear the women screaming. The soldiers stayed until they stopped screaming. There was nothing I could do. This morning, after the building had cooled—"

"This morning? It only happened yesterday?"

"Yes. After the building had cooled I stepped as close as I could and said a prayer for those ladies, as they also introduced me to Christianity." The man pointed, "See the one's arm? It is almost severed at the wrist…that's how hard she struggled to get free. Those soldiers were monsters."

Richards turned away. He was afraid he would vomit.

"We'll bury them," Lead UDT said.

"No! There are more soldiers coming. There is a great amount of food here that the villagers left."

"How do you know?" Walsh asked.

The man pointed to a building that had an antenna, "A radio is there. I heard them speaking, and they mentioned this village. That is why I was leaving, and why you should too. They are coming from the north, not from the direction I was going when you caught me."

"Walsh," Richards said, "I think the man is telling the truth, but I don't know how we can leave without burying them…!"

Everyone's attention was taken by the sound of an engine approaching. They returned to the jungle and waited, and watched as a large force of NVA took up positions in the village.

Lead UDT Walsh said, "I think it's time to leave."

## 54
### The 50 Caliber

A full day had passed since the marines left Hagfish. There continued to be no word. Moser continued to stand his watches and passed by the Radio Shack and through the Forward Battery Officer's Space, whenever he had the chance, just in case, but he didn't bug anybody. Twice he made eye contact with the Gunnery Officer, but chose not to bug his boss, either.

Another day passed. Three days since Recon had gone out. Then four.

On the fifth day he was passing the Radio Shack when he heard a message coming in. He had no idea what the code names were but just the sound of the voice made him think *'landing party,'* then the few words he made out, "…one prisoner…" so he stopped at the Radio Shack door.

After a moment Second Class Sonarman Corwin approached with a slip of paper, and handed it over, "You've been dying to know, Moser, so get this message up to the Conn."

He grabbed the message. His feet flew him to the Control Room ladder, then up it. Communications Officer Lieutenant j.g. Bostwick had the Conn, was standing right by the ladder looking through the periscope.

Moser stopped at the head of the ladder, "Radio message, Sir."

Bostwick pulled away from the periscope, looked down, took the message and read it, then, "Quartermaster, check with sonar for contacts," then glanced back at Moser, "Thank you, Moser."

"You're welcome, Sir." He would have loved to stay right there at the head of the ladder, but knew they might be diving, or something, so climbed back down but heard the quartermaster.

"Two pingers bearing 265, sir, but sonar says they haven't moved."

And from the Conning Officer, "Helmsman, all ahead flank! Make your course 265."

*'All ahead flank?'* That seemed a bit strange.

From the helmsman, "All ahead flank! Course 265, aye, sir."

Then he was out of hearing and soon got back to the Radio Shack, and glanced in. Corwin sent him a thumbs-up. To Moser that meant everybody was coming back alive, and it looked like they would be picking them up on the surface. But it was daylight…. He headed for the Forward Troop Space, but met his boss, Lieutenant Williams, "Moser, get topside on the starboard 50 caliber!"

He stopped in his tracks, "Yes, Sir!" and spun, and headed for the control room ladder.

Just a few seconds later the word came over the MC circuit, "Man battle stations! Man battle stations!"

He flew up both ladders and got to the starboard 50 caliber. The starboard lookout already had the machine gun mounted and loaded with the belt. He got down behind it, cocked it and took a breath. He—thank God—had already fired it once, thanks to Richards showing him. One of the good things being at sea. They didn't have to worry about hitting anything but water.

Through peripheral vision he saw other sailors getting into position on the other guns, both 40 millimeters, and Bonnet got behind the second 50 caliber. If they got in facing the starboard side to shore they'd be able to fire everything but the port 50 caliber…and then he saw why they were up there at battle stations. He counted. Nine—*nine?*—men ran out of the jungle to shore where four other marines waited by the rafts.

Then he heard firing. Then he saw more men running out of the jungle.

"Forward 40!" the Officer of the deck shouted, "Commence firing! Moser and Bonnet, we're too far away for the 50, but stay focused and ready!"

"Yes, Sir! Ready to fire!" He could barely believe what had just happened. He had just been given an order to prepare to fire, to prepare to possibly kill people, and he had acknowledged the order. He was *ready* to maybe kill people, he *wanted* to, because those bad guys were chasing the good guys, and his friend Richards.

Moments went by. Even at flank speed it seemed to take forever to get there, to get close enough. He was so tense, his finger so tight on the trigger that he started to feel like it was going to sleep, that he wouldn't be able to fire when the time came, he even began to feel sleepy, and he really couldn't believe that but sleepy he felt—

"Fifties! Commence firing!"

His finger went to work, he held the trigger for three to four-second bursts, saw the empty shells ejecting from the left side of the gun, and the little canvass-cloths flying from the right side of the gun, and saw the bullets striking the water far short of their targets. He raised the barrel and continued with the bursts. Still short. He saw sand kicking up on the beach. He raised it a little further and pulled the trigger, and saw a man fall, then another, and another. He held his breath, and held the gun so steady at that elevation…he couldn't believe what he was doing. He was killing people, people he didn't even know, and the 40 millimeter was doing far worse damage, but it, too, had first undershot, then overshot, then began to nail those fuckers.

He kept pulling the trigger and began hearing somebody screaming, not really screaming, but roaring, just basically really making noise. It was a hideous sound. He thought it was human. But who could be making such a terrible sound? His trigger hit an empty chamber. He kept his finger tight on the trigger anyway. It took him several mind-numbing seconds to realize he was out of ammunition, and realized at the same time that it was himself making that screaming, terrible, hideous, sound. He stopped, and pulled his finger from the trigger. The starboard lookout was back with another canister of ammunition and threw the cover open. Moser lifted the slide and placed the belt as the lookout held it.

"Moser!" the OOD shouted, "Keep firing!" They were close now. The rafts were launched and coming. Motors running. Thank God they had taken the little Evinrude motors.

But the Viet Cong were close too. He could even make out faces. He cocked the gun, pulled the trigger, and must have had the gun at a perfect elevation for one of those faces he thought he saw disappeared. He didn't care. He was glad. He kept firing, and did not keep making that hideous, terrible, screaming, sound.

Suddenly from the hand of God they were there. The rafts had reached far enough into the surf. The Hagfish began making a wide U-turn.

"Aft 40!" the OOD yelled, "Commence firing! Commence firing!"

Sitting broadside with three guns blazing those little mutherfuckers started falling like crazy...until they were all gone, either all dead or had turned tail and ran, *Yeah, right, ya little mutherfuckers! Can't fight a submarine, can ya?*

"Cease firing!" the OOD yelled, "But stay on station and stay focused!"

You fuckin' right, Sir!

Brice Wesley Moser had just experienced several life-changing moments, and knew he would never be quite the same again, and also knew he had never used so much bad profanity before in his whole sheltered Iowa farmer life.

## 55
### Back on Board

"So that's where we found them," Crosby said, "Burned at the stake, basically. They were tied back-to-back against a column in the house, their wrists wired...to each other, I guess. One gal's wrist was even almost severed. I guess she really tried to get free."

"How do you know all this?" Moser asked.

"That prisoner we brought back. He said they got a radio message to kill the last two missionaries, because it would have been too much trouble to march'em to somewhere else, so they just took the two men missionaries and set fire to the house, and burned'em alive."

"My God. Those bastards."

"Yeah, that really got to Richards," Crosby said, "I thought he was going to break down, man."

And Moser hadn't even spoken with his friend yet. Richards had been one of the last to come down the ladder. He had even felt like hugging the man, but men didn't hug—well, except for his dad that one time. But other than that he had not seen any man hug another, not on television, the movies, and for sure not real life. But, strangely, he was so glad to see Richards that he had *wanted* to hug him. And something seriously had been on his friend's mind, for when they made first eye contact and that crazy thought of *'hugging'* had gone through his mind, he had seen in Richards' eyes something he had never seen there before, something like *'The Stare'* that he had heard described by soldiers who had seen men who had actually been in, or seen, real combat.

He guessed if Richards had seen the burnt bodies of those two lady missionaries that it would have been very similar to actual combat, and he wondered too if there had been something more personal involved. Maybe Richards knew one of the girls, maybe was his sister, maybe a friend of a sister, maybe someone he had loved but had rejected him. He knew by experience that rejection would not have changed the feeling of love for someone. He still remembered being a big second grader and the little girl in the first grade he had fallen in love with thirteen years earlier, and he didn't just remember her, he was still in love with Leah, and always would be. So all was not known about why Richards wanted to go on the mission, and he didn't know if he should ask, or should just wait till Richards offered. Time would tell.

"Even that Viet Cong prisoner we brought back," Crosby was continuing, "He couldn't believe the treatment of those missionaries, man. People who were there just to try helping people, no matter who they were. He said he still remembers that screaming constantly."

"Do you believe him?"

"Yeah, I do, and he speaks perfect English—not that '*perfect English*' should prove he's telling the truth."

"So what else? Any other actual combat?"

"No. We could have. We hid from that large patrol in the village, and two other patrols. We could have totally wasted them but there were so dang many patrols in the area, both Viet Cong and NVA, so even one unexplained gunshot probably would have brought hundreds down on us. I don't know how that last bunch got onto us, but we were lucky to get picked up when we did. That's how close those mutherfuckers were to us."

"What about your prisoner? Did you keep him tied and gagged?"

"No. We considered it at first, but the UDT guy decided he was trustworthy. Anyway, it turns out he's Laotian, not Vietnamese. He was brought out of Laos to help with the missionary prisoners"

"So he's not actually a prisoner?"

"Well, I guess he is, but truth be known I think he's as glad to get out of there as we were, and he had plenty of chances to give us away but didn't."

"Okay, my friend. Thank you, and you probably would like to get some rest. Yes?"

"Yes, and you are welcome, my friendly swabbie."

So he left Crosby in the berthing space and continued toward the After Troop Space. They were underway on the surface again at standard speed. He had to go on lookout at 1200 hours, which gave him three hours to sleep. He hoped he could, but his friend Richards, who had helped Brice Wesley

Moser in so many, many, ways, was troubled, and he wanted to help, at least be there for him when he was ready to talk. He would get off lookout at 1600, have some chow and maybe see his friend in the mess hall, if not, eventually, he would just approach him.

## 56
### Beth & Janelle

Two days went by.

Moser decided enough time had passed. It was time to approach his friend. He found him sitting alone in the Forward Troop Space, "How's my good friend and mentor?"

Richards looked up and nodded, "Beth and Janelle."

"The names of those two missionary girls…."

"Yes. You see, I thought of them as just young girls who had their whole lives ahead of them. Beth was twenty and Janelle was twenty-six, just young girls who chose to spend their lives helping others, and look what they got."

"I…heard what you found…."

"Yeah, I couldn't believe that a human being could do such a thing to another human being, and for sure not to a young woman. You see, Moser, my little sister, has chosen to be a missionary. Right after Christmas she's leaving for Africa. I don't even know what country she's going to—but you can be damn sure there's plenty danger in Africa too—and now, I'm not sure if I even *want* to know what country she's going to."

He was beginning to understand. *He* had a little sister, too, and felt the same way, and doubted he would want even one of his friends to go into a strange and maybe dangerous country.

He too had been shocked by hearing what they found, that men could do such a thing.

"But now we can at least inform the girls' parents," Richards was continuing, "It must have been hell for them not to know." Richards shook his head and looked down, and appeared to not want to talk further.

He reached out and put his hand on his friend's shoulder, squeezed and patted, "But you won't tell your little sister about this, will you? I mean, this has to be about the ultimate evil, which most people will never see."

Richards reached his hand to Moser's, stood up, then also squeezed and patted, "You're right, my friend, and, no, I won't tell her about this…I won't in a letter anyway, but if I go home for Christmas…anyway, but thanks for coming, my friend, and don't worry. Give me a couple more days, and I'll be okay again. But for awhile…I don't know, I guess I just need to be alone."

"Understood, and know that I'm available if you want to talk again."

*ARRUUGA! ARRUUGA!*

Seconds later from the MC, "Dive! Dive!"

"Hell," Moser said, "I didn't even know we were planning a dive."

The down-angle began.

"Yeah," Richards agreed, "Ya never know."

The two men, as usual, just bent their bodies enough to ride out the down-angle and didn't bother reaching for anything to help them stand. But the down-angle began increasing.

"Jesus…!" He turned toward the Forward Battery Compartment, and for just one second he saw and realized what a steep down-angle they were heading into, and had just enough time to grab a vertical hydraulic pipe on the bulkhead, and Richards reached out and grabbed Moser's arm, "Christ!"

Oil began pouring from a drip pan below a hydraulics manifold in the overhead as the down-angle continued increasing—

*ARRUUGA! ARRUUGA! ARRUUGA!*

"Surface! Surface! Surface!" came over the MC circuit.

"Full rise both planes! Blow bow buoyancy! Blow safety!"

*The farm…the cows…my old 1948 Chevie, Leah, the little first grader, my sister, Geri—Thresher!* He could not believe the thoughts he was having. He had heard of a person's whole life flashing by during the moment before death…but he couldn't be about to die! He had too many more things to do in life!

Even after the surface alarm the down-angle continued and for a few more terrifying seconds even got worse till the two men were totally hanging on. No way could they have stood without hanging on…the blast of air pouring into Bow Buoyancy Tank normally was not even noticed. This time it was.

"Starsky! Blow everything!"

But even with air blasting all tanks and pumps running the severe down-angle continued and continued. He stopped seeing his life flashing before his eyes. His mind settled out to no thoughts, no feelings at all, only his eyes kept working, seeing, comprehending the down-angle that seemed unable to change.

Suddenly they felt the whole submarine begin to shake, not a lot but they could feel it.

"Thank God," Richards said, "Somebody finally thought of reversing the screws."

And finally the down-angle stopped increasing and began settling out. Unbelievably-slowly they reached a level angle and then an up-angle, a severe up-angle, and suddenly they felt the sub pitching and rolling, meaning that, yes, they were back on the surface. *Holy cow!* A collective sigh passed through the aisles and was felt by all hands. They would live for another day.

The men of the USS Hagfish soon discovered what had happened. Normal operation of a Fuel Ballast Tank was to feed the engines as necessary and as the tank emptied the fuel would be replaced by the much heavier sea water, a process meant to go slowly and smoothly. What exactly happened would not be known until they reached port. What *was* known was that a whole tank had lost its fuel in basically a blink, and the sea water had came in and replaced it during that blink. That it happened during a normal trim dive would be considered by some as an act of God, and another act of God that they survived.

--0--

## Epilogue

When the Hagfish left to return to Pearl Harbor, Second Class Richards moved on to more schooling and eventual duty on the new Fleet Ballistic Missile submarines (FBMs.) Brice Moser transferred to another submarine that would stay in Southeast Asian waters and continue the same work; he wasn't as sure about his future as Richards. The following July, when he got the letter from his little sister, Geri, with the copy of Leah's wedding invitation for August, he became even less certain. Plus there was the short note saying she would visit Leah regularly, if she lived close by. A later letter from Geri told him that Leah and her new husband had moved to Des Moines, which was forty miles from the farm, but she would try to visit whenever she could.

Moser appreciated his little sister's enthusiasm but was pretty certain Leah was gone forever. How many *dear John* letters had been sent to soldiers and sailors over time anyway? Gazillions, for certain. This wasn't exactly a *'dear John'* letter though, for he, Brice Wesley Moser, had never really tried with Leah. However, he didn't try to discourage Geri, and if she ever sent a letter saying Leah was in trouble, or needed help, or anything, he would take leave and come home immediately. Time would tell. He didn't exactly like the idea of being married while in the navy, anyway, but, he guessed, for Leah, he would…saying she ever would be free again.

Not likely. It seemed he had set a course for a few years with no real planning at all.

In the meantime, he had Leila back in Hawaii to think about, though he probably wouldn't try to contact her—best if she moved on, and, hopefully, recovered from heroin addiction. Plus he had the war in Vietnam to keep him occupied.

With all that had happened during the past two years he just felt uncertain about nearly everything, and wondered if all boys joining the military so young at seventeen would reach this phase of doubt. He guessed he did not know, and the fact *was* he was *in* the navy; he had a job to do, and needed to focus mainly on that fact alone.

****

In 1965, the war in Vietnam (a Cold War era military conflict) had only begun to heat up. The war had actually begun November 1, 1955, (the first US military advisors arrived in 1950) but would not end until the fall of Saigon, April 30, 1975. The war would kill (minimum to maximum numbers, according to Wikipedia) 1 million to 3 million Vietnamese, 200,000 to 300,000 Cambodians (today called Kampuchea,) 20,000 to 200,000 Laotians.

And 58,152 Americans. (2255 unaccounted for)

# A sad, and true, Story

**Sorry, U.S. Government, this is buried deep in the internet but needs to be told.**

October 27, 1972, a small group of North Vietnamese soldiers invaded the southern Laotian town of Kengkock. They took prisoners, including Evelyn Anderson and Beatrice Kosin, young missionaries working for Christian Missions of Many Lands. Several other Americans managed to escape and radioed for help.

Following the capture, an American helicopter arrived and evacuated nine Filipinos, five Lao and the Americans who had radioed for help. Less than an hour later, Sgt. Gerry Wilson returned by helicopter to try and locate the two American women. Lt. Colonel Norman Vaught immediately set rescue plans into motion.

The American Embassy in Vientiane heard of the rescue plan and ordered from the highest level that no attempt be made to rescue the women. The peace negotiations were ongoing and it was feared that a rescue attempt would compromise the sustained level of progress at the talks.

On November 2, 1972, a radio message was intercepted which ordered that the two women be executed. A captured North Vietnamese soldier later told U.S. military intelligence that the women were captured, tied back to back and their wrists wired around a house pillar. The women remained in this position for five days.

After receiving orders to execute the two, the communists simply set fire to the house where they were being held and burned the women alive. A later search of the smoldering ruins revealed the corpse of Miss Anderson. Her wrist was severed, indicating the struggle she made to free herself.

A list of Characters & Places
(alphabetical by last names)

Part 1 In Training

Brice Wesley Moser, 17, TMSN Seaman Torpedoman (main character)
    Geri (8-year-old sister)
    Mom and Dad Moser (parents, from Ridge, Iowa, farming country)
    Leah (hometown girlfriend since the 2nd grade)
    USS Hagfish (fictional name representing the USS Perch APSS313)

    Master Chief Brecker (Company Commander, Bootcamp Company 321, (*Choker* Brecker)
    Master Chief Claremont (Company Commander, Company 299)
    Cordegan (best friend in Company 321, from Texas)
    Miss Crawford (dance partner at Brightlight Bar, and first kiss, San Diego)
    Dokken (best friend at Class A School)
    Durban (Company 299, marches behind Moser, steps on his heels)
    Terry Hamm (first buddy, met at induction center, Des Moines, Iowa)
    Hornstall (2nd Class Signalman, signs Moser in at Class A Weapons School, San Diego)
    Jessup (squad 4 leader, Company 299, first bootcamp company)
    Leila (girl from Idaho Moser meets on plane while returning from leave)

Mortensen (also met at induction, will become RCPO for Company 299)

(RCPO--Recruit Chief Petty Officer)

Elvin Nudell (Company 299, marches beside Moser in squad 5)

Morgan Rhodes (Pan American stewardess, met in plane ride to San Diego to bootcamp)

Starsky (1st Class Engineman, gives tour of mothballed submarine, USS Char, San Diego)

## Part 2 In Mission

Barnet (Fireman topside watch on Carbonero)

Beth and Janelle (fictional names for Evelyn and Beatrice, the murdered missionaries)

Bonnet (Moser's antagonist on Hagfish)

Bostwick, lieutenant junior grade [j.g.] (Communications Officer)

Chloe-san (Japanese bar girl)

Corwin (2nd Class Sonarman)

Crosby (Marine)

Higgins (1st Class Gunner's Mate)

Houst (1st Class Petty Officer)

Mercy (first Philippine bar girl)

Nagle (3rd Class Fire Control Technician)

Pansy (second Philippine bar girl)

Petecksky (chief engineman)

Reeves (mentor of Richards [from Richards' past; we never meet him])

Richards (2nd Class Electronics Technician, Moser's mentor)

Reinhold (Topside Watch, checks Moser in to Hagfish)

Starsky (1st Class Engineman [on the Hagfish])
Tetslow (Master Chief Torpedoman, Chief of the Boat and Moser's boss)
Uncle Harold (my late uncle, World War II)
Williams, lieutenant (Gunnery Officer)
Pat Walsh (1st Class Boatswain's Mate, UDT) (Underwater Demolition Team)


## Miscellaneous Names

Club Shangri La (Yokosuka)
Danang (the marines' first landing)
Kirin Beer (Japanese beer)
Kaohsiung, Taiwan
Keelung, Taiwan
Kengkock, Laos (first location of missionaries)
Legaspi, Philippine Islands
Olongapo (Subic Bay, Philippine Islands)
Pennington's Bar, Olongapo, Philippine Islands
Sai Buri (coast of Thailand where Jungle Drum III occurred)
Saki (rice wine)
SEAL (Sea, Land, Air Teams)
USS Gunston Hall LSD44 (dock landing ship)
USS Lanawee APA195 (re-outfitted passenger ship)
USS Washburn AKA108 (attack cargo ship)
USS Yorktown CV10 (aircraft carrier)
Yokosuka, Japan

## A More Personal Acknowledgment

I would be remiss if I didn't mention my own two commands also, although, while I was aboard, other than normal patrol, we "*mostly*" stayed away from Vietnam. They were the USS Carbonero SS337 and the USS Archerfish AGSS 311.

One of Carbonero's highlights was participating in the 1962 nuclear tests (Operation Dominic [before I got aboard]) off Christmas Island and Johnson Island in the central Pacific. Through her periscope, about 30 miles away, she witnessed an atomic blast from a Polaris Missile fired by the USS Ethan Allen SS-480. (Just 30 miles seems a bit...*close*, to me.) On April 27, 1975, Carbonero was taken to sea for the last time and sunk by a Mk48 torpedo fired by the USS Pogy SSN647. (Made me kind of sad to hear that.)

The Archerfish's highlight is the sinking of the Japanese aircraft carrier Shinano in November 1944, the largest warship ever sunk by a submarine, for which she received a Presidential Unit Citation after the war. And for all that, on October 19, 1968, she was sunk off San Diego by a torpedo from the USS Snook SSN592. (That sinking was sad for me to hear about too, but, maybe, for those old war-girls, sinking by torpedo is a *good* way to die.)

One more thing: Toward the end of her cruises, Archerfish's torpedo tubes were removed, a few civilian scientists came aboard, and AG was added to her name, which stood somehow for Oceanographic Survey, which for some reason required an all-bachelor crew (that's when I came aboard, just in time for a 6-month yard period.)

For my true navy adventures please see my autobiography *"Dying to Live."*

Some Navy Terms (slang and otherwise)

Deck                (floor)
Bulkhead            (wall)
Overhead            (ceiling)
Head                (restroom)
Flattop             (aircraft carrier)
Boat                (submarine)
Tin Can             (destroyer)
Surface Skimmer  (any sailor *not* a sub sailor)
Bubblehead          (a sub sailor)
Tube Sucker         (torpedoman [my rating])
Sonar Girl          (sonar operator [in San Diego we went
to the same base for sonar and weapons Class A School, so, of
course, we had to have nicknames for each other.])
Swabbie             (any sailor)
Line                (anything looking like a line, even rope)
Sweetie             (probably don't have to explain)

## Biography

James W. Nelson was born in a little farmhouse on the prairie in eastern North Dakota in 1944. Some doctors made house calls back in those days. He remembers kerosene lamps, bathing in a large galvanized tub, and their phone number was a long ring followed by four short ones, and everybody in the neighborhood could rubberneck. (Imagine that today!)

James has been telling stories most of his life. Some of his first memories happened during recess in a one-room country schoolhouse near Walcott, ND. His little friends, eyes wide, would gather round and listen to his every hastily-imagined word. It was a beginning. Fascinated by the world beginning to open, he remembers listening to the teacher read to all twelve kids in the eight grades.

He was living in that same house on the land originally homesteaded by his great grandfather, when a savage tornado hit in 1955 and destroyed everything. They rebuilt and his family remained until the early nineteen-seventies when diversified farming began changing to industrial agribusiness (not necessarily a *good* thing.) He spent four years in the US Navy during the Vietnam War (USS Carbonero and USS Archerfish.)

After the navy he worked many jobs and finally has settled on a few acres exactly two and one half miles straight west of the original farmstead, ironically likely the very spot where the 1955 tornado first struck, which sometimes gives him a spooky feeling.

Made in the USA
Las Vegas, NV
20 September 2021